SOMEWHERE ONLY WE KNOW

HEALING IN CINCY
BOOK 4

ELLEESE BLACK

SOMEWHERE ONLY WE KNOW

Healing in Cincy Book 4
A friends to lovers, second chance, and accidental marriage

AUTHOR'S NOTE

We've made it to the final book in my debut series. And possibly the most anticipated of the series. At least for me. Jax has been a prominent side character and being able to finally crack into who she is as a person, has been rewarding as a storyteller.

I would be remiss not to tell you this book contains on page spice, foul language, parental loss, and a verbally abusive side character. Jax and Nate are in college when this book starts and follows their journey throughout their twenties, so everything is consensual.

This story is told in the past and present. Each chapter is labeled so as not to confuse the reader. It was important for them as the main characters and me as the author to write their story in this style.

While you *can* read this book as a standalone, know that you will get spoilers involving couples and past storylines. So, if you want to avoid spoilers, start with The Night We Met which is available in Kindle Unlimited.

CONTENT WARNINGS

My books are not dark but do include some themes that could be triggering for some readers. The following are included and not limited to:

Foul language

On page spice

Parental loss

Manipulation

Body shaming (by neither of the main characters)

Pet loss (off page)

Mental health (suicide talk)

PLAYLIST

Poison & Wine by The Civil Wars
Cloudy Day by Tones And I
San Luis by Gregory Alan Isakov
The Smallest Man Who Ever Lived by Taylor Swift
Strange by Celeste
Dive by Ed Sheeran
Heartbeats by Jose Gonzalez
In The Air Tonight - 2015 Remastered by Phil Collins
Medicine by Daughters
In a Stranger's Arms by LEON
The Black and White by The Band CAMINO
Supercut by Lorde
The Last Time (feat. Gary Lightbody of Snow Patrol by
Taylor Swift, Gary Lightbody
Lovers by Anna of the North
everything by Kehlani
Gravity by Sara Bareilles
The Story Never Ends by Lauv
Falling by Harry Styles
Somewhere Only We Know by Keane

Crashing (feat. Bahari) by ILLENIUM, Bahari
Light Me Up by Ingrid Michaelson
Kiss It Better by Rihanna
Haunt Me by Yana
If the World Was Ending (feat. Julia Michaels) by JP Saxe,
Julia Michaels
World Spins Madly On by The Weepies, Deb Talan, Steve
Tannen
Could've Been (feat. Bryson Tiller) by H.E.R., Bryson Tiller
Hope Is a Heartache by LEON
I Think I'm In Love by Kat Dahlia
Saturn by SZA
Best Part (feat. H.E.R.) by Daniel Caesar, H.E.R.

somewhere only

WE KNOW

HEALING IN CINCY

ELLEESE BLACK

*To those of you who needed to heal and found that between the
pages of romance books.
This one's for you.
And for me.*

1

JAX

PRESENT DAY

"That should do it," I say, more to myself as I stand back and admire my handiwork—but also to Sully, my black lab who's laying on her dog bed with her head resting on her paws. Her dark brown eyes peer up at me in a look one can only describe as pathetic. But so cute that it makes me melt every time.

With my hands on my hips, I look around at the room that's in disarray with half-unpacked boxes and partially put-together furniture. But with that I also breathe a sigh of relief as my body finally unclenches.

I'm starting over.

And putting together my office is the second step.

After I ended what I'm now coming to realize was a toxic relationship, I needed to move to a place that was untouched by his presence. I got in so deep with that relationship that I made excuse after excuse for why he behaved and treated me the way he did. But the truth of the matter is that he was a waste of space and took out his shortcomings on me. I can finally see that now. I can see that he was never able to hold onto a job for more than six months before he would live off of me. I can also see that he purposefully isolated me from my friends and family. I could see that he was wasting talent that I knew he possessed if he only gave a little bit of effort. Now, that's I'm removed, I can see a lot of things clearly.

Could I see that clearly at the time? No.

But now I can see that my ex continued to take until I was left on empty. On days when I was feeling particularly low, I would look at older pictures of myself on my phone and I could barely recognize myself. I'd like to say that the sudden wakeup call to end it with him came after his outburst at my sister's wedding. That was a low point for me as I ended up crawling back to him. He had been let go from another job, thought everyone was out to get him, and he didn't like the way Mason's teammates were talking with me. Never mind that most of them were married and that I considered them family. It took two more instances for me to open my eyes that the relationship *I* nurtured, wasn't nurtured by him.

The second wakeup call eventually came from my manager and said that brands were looking to no longer work with me if I continued to deliver subpar videos. It's unfortunate that that was the moment that put everything into perspective. The moment that I could lose my financial stability. But then the third, and most important, kick in the ass was the small intervention my sister and friends organized for me. That was the lowest point for me. It was my rock bottom. It was when I admitted to myself that I didn't know how to get off a carousel that just kept spinning. The ride may be fun, but after a while it was the same thing over and over.

Sully huffing like her life is tough brings me back to the present and I look over at her with raised brows. Which, one could argue that her life was tough. I adopted her last month from the shelter. She was brought in as a stray puppy and had been there for a little over a year with no applications. It's a tough realization for black cats and black dogs, that nobody wants you. But when I saw her huddled in the corner of the kennel they had her in, eyes weepy, and body trembling, I knew I was taking her home.

I never pictured myself having another dog. After watching our family dog, Jersey, slow down and his face turn gray, I promised myself I couldn't handle watching another creature lose their life. But as fate would have it, when I was doing my nightly scroll through social media, the rescue's page popped up with the available animals and Sully's sad eyes spoke to me. I messaged the rescue that night to set up a meet and greet and the next morning I went to meet Sully. That was that. She came home with me that day and she's been my shadow since then.

I finish unpacking the necessities for my bookshelf in my studio and break down the empty box. After my breakup, I temporarily moved in with Kam and Mason while I looked for a new place. And I looked as fast and hard as the market allowed. I love my sister and Mason, but they're gross. In a cute way. Until it wasn't when turning every corner in their house started to scar me. When I was looking for a new place to live, I knew I wanted to dive in and get a house. Apartments and condos are easy, but having a house allotted me more freedom. And now having Sully, the empty lot next to my place has come in handy. So here I am at twenty-eight as an official homeowner.

I turn on some music and finish unpacking to get this room setup for getting back to work next week. With a packed filming and recording schedule, I need the place to be organized within an inch of its life or I can't work peacefully. Also, having the epiphany that my unpacking would be great for a new series, I pull out my smaller camera and get that setup. I don't utilize my vlog channel as much as I should because most of my work falls under the scope of my clients not wanting their work shown and I also stay home majority of the time. But having this footage will be good for me to have to look back on.

Two hours later I'm done. With my hair falling out of the messy bun and the sun reaching the highest point in the sky, it's time for a break. I snag my phone off the desk I set up and go to place an order for a pizza. My thumb hovers over the **Place Order** button all because of my ex's snide comment about my weight sliding back into my mind. I haven't heard his voice in a while—but it's times like this, when I'm enjoying where I'm at in my life, I'll hear him. Because at 5'2" I carry weight more noticeably than my sister who's a few inches taller. So I have cellulite on my thighs and I don't have a flat and firm midsection—we've gotta protect our organs somehow and my boobs range between a C and D cup. But with him no longer in my life, I say *fuck it* to the man I dropped and order the pizza for lunch.

"Wanna keep me company in the living room?" I ask Sully who's watching me from her dog bed. Her tail starts wagging as if I asked her if she wanted to go on a walk. That word, I know she understands.

One thing I didn't realize is that I would talk to my dog more than I would talk to people. But that's something I'm rather okay with. I don't have to rethink or carefully word what I'm going to say for fear of being berated. I don't have to walk on eggshells or make sure she's in a good mood before I start talking. Although, I do have to talk her down after the doorbell rings. That's one thing I didn't realize what happened in my relationship. My ability to speak freely was silenced.

My wings were clipped and I was placed in a cage. Even now that I'm free of him, I don't know if I'll ever fly again.

When I get to the kitchen, I decide I may as well start unpacking the dishes that I do have before my food comes. I've never been a cook, so what I do have to make meals is limited. I finish putting the last mug in the cabinet when I grab my phone to check on my order and the doorbell rings. Walking down the hallway and to the front door, I check the peephole just to make sure it's my food and open the door when I see it is.

"Thank you," I tell the delivery driver and tip him well.

Taking my food to my small dining room, I eat right out of the box. As I'm eating, I go through socials and respond to comments from viewers and comment on some other YouTubers posts. When I first started my channel, there was a collective group of us that were put in an unofficial class. Almost like a graduation class. We would constantly chat, send each other tips, and continue to show our support for each other to help grow our channels. We attended conventions and would travel to each other's houses for "creator weekends". But that stopped, at least for me, a few years ago and I hate that Trent caused me to lose those friendships.

Working from home is already isolating. But I was lucky to have that small community to talk with whenever I needed. Day or night. Well, mostly night as we all were night owls.

As my relationship with him furthered and then ended, the days passed and the messages I sent went unresponded to, I began to feel more isolated than ever. And I wondered daily if I would ever be able to get back to the career and friendships I had before.

I take a deep breath and send out a few messages to the creators I used to talk with the most and hope for the best. One creator, Ellie, started a sort of tutoring channel for kids and parents who needed extra help in school. It's extremely interactive and I sent the channel to Emily who now uses it in her classroom. Ellie was one of the creators I grew closest to. We had a bit of a similar background when it came to relationships, which helped us grow closer. But that relationship was cut just as quickly as it began. I have no idea how she is, but I send a longer message just to check in and apologize.

PODCAST

"You know, I was just thinking this the other day. About how difficult it is to break the toxic patterns that you find yourself in. I spent so long doing and feeling the same thing, day in and day out with the same person—who at the time, I had no idea was draining me. That when I was finally able to break that pattern, I realized how absolutely unprepared I was for a new normal. No one talks about that. How you need to find yourself without the crutch of toxicity. For the longest time, I've always been of the mindset that I can handle everything on my own. Give me my planner, a pen, my dog, and I will create and shift my focus. But that shifting of my mindset only works when I allow it to. And I could not allow it to. I spent so long with someone who put me in a pattern of needing him, comforting him, and staying with him. That when I decided to break that pattern, I realized I didn't know how to create a new pattern that only involved me. So, today on this podcast, to those of you who tune in every week, I'm making a promise to add something new and something good to my pattern. Let's say I'll do this —for six months. And I'll will check back in with you all in the new year. I guarantee you it won't be life changing at first, but I am hoping that this trying a new pattern leads me to something incredible."

"I would go on, but my dog is nudging my leg. She's part of my new pattern and that seems to be all that I have for you on this episode of *Life Not Simplified*. I'll see you all next week."

2

JAX

I untuck myself from my chair and work to get everything sent to my editor. My episodes are generally thirty minutes long. Sometimes, when things happen in my life, the episodes can stretch to an hour. Sully gets up from her spot when I turn off the studio lights and looks at me like I can read her mind. Our routine has gotten easier. Between the first week filming, recording, and her restlessness I think we were both on edge. She was scared of the lights and I was just a scared dog mom.

Wordlessly, I grab my phone and shut the overhead light off as Sully trots behind me as I head up to my room to change. Who needs a man when you have your faithful, loyal sidekick?

～

"Go get it." I tell her as I lob a tennis ball across the field for the fifth time. Bringing Sully to the park reminds me how energetic labs are. We're out here for about an hour before another dog eventually joins and I smile as I watch Sully play.

"I'm sorry. He's been cooped in the house all day," a petite brunette, with a full colored tattoo sleeve down her left arm, says next to me.

I look over at her from behind my sunglasses. *Break the pattern, Jax.* "That's okay. I work from home so this is her first time out as well."

"I'm Sophie," she introduces herself to me, "and that's Hank."

"Jax and that's Sully." We watch them play together for the next ten minutes. I'm not great at making conversation with strangers so we stand in awkward silence, but maybe it wouldn't hurt to try. "Are you new to the area?"

"Is it that obvious? I scream transplant," she jokes and it lightens the mood. I shake my head as she turns to look at me. "Me and my fiancée just moved here last month. He actually got traded so this really is my first opportunity to get out of the house."

"Traded?" I ask, my nosiness coming out to play.

Her eyes widen. "Oh, yes. He plays shortstop for Cincinnati."

"That's so fun." I tell her.

She smiles and sighs. "It is. But it's also exhausting. Him having such a heavy schedule has forced us to work our wedding around his season. We were in Atlanta for the last few years. So this is a bit of a change in pace for both of us."

"My brother-in-law would flip if he knew I was standing by an Atlanta adjacent member." I'm already planning ways to rub it in his face.

"He's a big fan?"

"You could say that." I say and toss the ball when Sully brings it back with Hank on her heels. "Although now that he retired from Cincinnati, he has more time to stalk the stats."

Sophie quirks her head. "Retired?"

"He was Cincinnati's starting QB."

She coughs and hits her chest. "Mason Brooks?"

"Mm hmm."

"My fiancée is going to be so mad that he had to miss this outing for practice." She jumps up and down like she can't believe her luck.

I pull my phone out of the side pocket of my leggings and unlock it. "How about you put your number in and we can do a group thing."

Sophie and I chat for a little while longer while our dogs play. And as more dogs join the park, I whistle for Sully while Sophie does the same for Hank.

"Well, it was great meeting you." I tell her as I hook Sully's leash.

"Likewise," she says.

We part ways with a wave and happy, but tired dogs.

Despite the park being right down the street, I take the long way home. In my single-dom, I'm realizing how much I missed and how much I'm rediscovering in terms of Cincinnati. I look down at Sully who has her tongue lolling out of her mouth and a slow walk, I realize how much she needed this time at the park. Luckily, an ice cream shop is on the way home, so I stop in for a treat which immediately perks her up.

I guess you could say this is also part of my new pattern. Ice cream and my dog. This is the after me. The me after the toxic ex. The me who learns to love herself. The me that wants to create a new pattern. The me that finally wants to live a happy life.

THE SOUND of the ice clinking against the sides of my glass fills the quiet in my house as I look out the windows in the back of the house. It's just after ten in the morning and I've finished recording next week's podcast and took a break before uploading my next YouTube video. I'm hoping this second iced coffee will keep me energized through the editing process.

Since my breakup, I've buried myself in work. When Kam and Mason went on their honeymoon, I buried myself even further in work. Anything to keep me occupied.

Having a house to furnish has helped me the most and kept my mind busy. But now that I've finished decorating my new space, I'm finally able to call this place home. Will it be my forever home? It could be. I lucked out finding a four-bedroom home. With the way I've changed throughout the years, I was able to curate the space and the rooms just the way I like them.

I walk down the short hallway and up the stairs into my office. The shining sun and distant sounds of birds chirping is a sound I used to take for granted in dark years of my life. My office overlooks the city which is a bonus because I love seeing the hustle and bustle. When my realtor sent me homes to look at, I could not stop thinking about this place. So now I work from home with an insane view. I connect my camera to export the video to my computer and while that's transferring, I open up the door to the balcony to let the fresh air in.

Nails tapping on the floor alerts me that Sully has wandered up from the living room and straight to the open balcony to find her spot on the dog bed. Bending down to kiss her on the top of her head, I head back over to my desk and log into my dashboard to reply to any comments left on my videos. This is one thing I stopped doing while with my ex. I stopped connecting with those who supported me in the early days of my career and for that my work suffered drastically. But now, my work has improved to where it was before he and I started dating. I took no time to mourn that relationship to reset my life before diving back into my blog and channel, eventually working hard to gain 5,000 new subscribers on each platform.

My computer pops with a notification that the export is done. So I slide my blue light glass on my face and get to editing with hope that I can finish this in a couple of hours for tomorrow's upload.

"JJ?!" A voice shouts an hour later as I'm deep in the editing cave.

"In my office," I shout before attempting to zone back in on my edits but it's no use.

"You really did a great job decorating this place," Kamryn says from the hallway.

"Thank you."

My sister in all her natural beauty finally breezes into my office and dramatically falls onto the couch I have in here. Sully gets up from her bed and greets my sister, covering her face in kisses. "What are you doing this weekend?" She asks and sits back up to halt Sully's love.

"Um, other than my usual work and taking Sully to the park, nothing. Why, what's up?" I ask and turn to face her.

"Well, Mason got us tickets to go to the Cincy game. How great is he?"

"Good for Mason?" I deadpan.

She throws a pillow at me but it falls short of reaching me. "No, good for us, silly goose. You and I!"

"Who are they playing?"

"Philly. Say yes, please!" She holds her hands in front of her in a prayer pose and sticks her bottom lip out.

We may have been living in Cincinnati for the last five years but we're still Philly girls through and through.

"Okay, I'm in. Plus, I can see if my friend is going to be there." I say thinking of Sophie.

My sister sits up straight. "A friend?"

"Easy. I met her at the dog park. Her fiancée just got traded."

"Look at you, making friends."

I throw a pen at her which actually reaches her and she swats it away effortlessly. "But, yes. I'm in."

"Yay!" she exclaims and pops up with the energy of a toddler. "I'll come over around twelve and then we can just walk to the field."

"Sounds good," I tell her.

"Later tater. Bye, Sully girl."

And with that she's gone. I love my brother-in-law, but I love baseball more than football. It's a good thing he's retired and doesn't have to hear me complaining. My relationship with my sister is also on the mend. Whether she knows it or not, the closer she got to her wedding with Mason, the closer I got to Trent and that pulled me away from her. Kamryn and I have always had an easygoing relationship. There was never any competition and it helped that we're two years apart in age. But with her years away at college and me still in high school, she was out of sight out of mind. I mean, she still came home for breaks. But it was never the same as when we were kids.

While sometimes I resented my sister for hogging the spotlight, that just meant I was free to do what I wanted. And now that the spotlight is mostly off of her, I feel like there's an unspoken rule that I have to follow her path to success.

3

JAX

"Jax?!" I hear called out when my sister enters my house. Sully's nails echo as she rushes down the stairs and to the door to greet Kamryn.

"In my room!" I call out to her.

The adjustment period when you move somewhere new takes getting used to. Somedays it's still weird being in a new space to call my own. It took some work to train myself not to head to my old apartment as that was where my career launched and where I lived for five years. But then all I have to do is remember the bad and that helps me to redirect to my new safe place.

"Are you ready?" She asks, calling up from the living room. A squeaky toy is squeaked in quick succession as Sully asks for her to play.

"Just about. Will you let Sully out and then we can walk over?"

"Yep. Let's go silly girl," I hear Kamryn coo.

As soon as I finish up in the bathroom, I look in the mirror at my outfit. I decided to not rock the boat with what I wear, so I have on a black mini cotton skort that hits mid-

16

thigh, a red bodysuit, white hightop Converse, and a black baseball hat with a dainty baseball embroidered on the front. The red thankfully goes with both teams. Unlike my sister, I never ruined my curl pattern. But for the sake of the summer, I've pulled my hair into two dutch braids that lay over my shoulders. Knowing the stadium's stance on bags, I transfer the essentials to a phone sling and pop my phone in the holder last. The gold chains of the sling are cool in my hands, but when I loop it over my body the pieces instantly warm up on contact.

I walk out of my room and head down the stairs right as Kam comes back in with a happy Sully. Remembering my patterns, I pull up my phone to text Sophie.

Me: Hey, it's Jax.

Me: From the dog park.

Why I am so awkward?

Me: Are you going to the game today?

Sophie: I am!

Sophie: Please tell me you're coming too.

Me: My sister got us tickets.

Sophie: Perfect.

Sophie: Let me know when you're here and we can hang for a bit.

Me: Sounds good.

"Ready?" I ask my sister although I can clearly see that she is if her tapping her foot is any indication.

My sister has mastered the art of sporty attire. It helps

that she's a fashion designer and a former WAG. While we've been in Cincinnati for the last few years, that's not stopped her from wearing the opposing teams merch on the rare occasion that they're in town. Her black distressed shorts, Philadelphia jersey, and Air Force Ones is what she went with today.

"So ready to crush them!"

I snort and fill up Sully's water bowl then grab the house key. "Easy, tiger. How'd Mason feel seeing you wear another team?" I ask as I lock up the front door and hop down the front steps.

She lets out a wistful sigh. One full of love for her husband and I'd be grossed out if I wasn't beyond happy that my sister got her happily ever after. "My husband doesn't get jealous often. But him seeing another team on my chest really–"

Scratch that. I'm still grossed out. I hold my hand up to stop her. "Okay, I get the picture. I mean, I don't but...can you not?"

Kamryn cackles as we jump onto the sidewalk towards the stadium. Silver Lining to moving is that my house is close to the baseball stadium. Well, if you count crossing the street a few times and walking under freeway underpasses close, then sure. But even when I'm not headed to a game that Cincy is playing at home, I can now pour myself a glass of wine and sit on my back patio and listen to the faint sounds of the crowd cheering. So, yes. The roundabout way to the stadium makes heading to the games a breeze.

"How are you holding up?" Kam asks and loops her arm through mine.

I let out a breath and look forward. We're getting closer to the ballpark and fans pour in and out of the bars or out of friends' apartments, laughing and talking animatedly.

"I'm...adjusting," I say the word slowly. "Yeah, that's the word. I'm still adjusting. Having Sully helps too."

"Has he texted you?"

I sigh. The *he* my sister is referring to is my ex. "He did at first. But after the first week of constant texts, I blocked him."

"Good." Kamryn says and gives my arm a squeeze. "I've missed you."

I look over at my sister. "I never left."

"You know what I mean," she tells me.

Yeah. I do know what she means. While Kamryn and I were never best friends, not only because of the two year gap between us and her going states away for school, we always had each other to count on. But because my sister didn't know what she wanted to do until later on in college, while I *always* knew what I wanted to do. Then the divide between us grew with her losing Liam and my tumultuous relationship with Trent—Kamryn and I were so disconnected from each other. We tolerated each other as siblings and eventually with me working with her. But in the last year, we've built up a true sister-bond.

"Well, now we have the chance to get back what we had. But, way better."

"You bet your ass we do." Kamryn says and wraps her arms around me.

We chat and laugh the rest of the way to the stadium. She bounces off ideas for game attire for women since most of it is catered to men. If it's one thing, my sister is always going to find a way to work even when she shouldn't. Fans flood the entrance and our pace slows as we join the lines.

Kamryn grabs my hand and takes me off to the booths. "So I know we're early, but we also have field passes."

"Have I ever said you're the best sister ever?" I ask her rhetorically when we're at Will Call.

"You know I haven't heard that in a very long time," she teases.

"Well I'm only telling you once."

She rolls her eyes and I take a moment to take in the joy on this sunny and cloudless day. I hear the distant sound of the crack of a wooden bat hitting baseballs, the music from the stadium as a warmup song pumps up those of us waiting to get inside, and the beeping sound of tickets being scanned. This is what I've missed. This is what I didn't realize I missed.

My ex really wasn't big on sports which was crushing to me because growing up in Philadelphia I was surrounded by sports. I can't remember a time in my childhood where we weren't at a football, baseball, basketball, hockey, or soccer game. We breathed sports in Philly. But I pushed my obsession for the game as a fan to the side to appease him.

When I came to the first home opener, I felt like I had a sign on my head that read "newbie to the game" and everyone was watching me. That clearly was all in my head though. Now I'm able to enjoy the game like every other seasoned fan.

My excitement reaches new levels when we get our passes from Will Call and my steps are light in a way that almost has me bouncing.

"Are you excited for the game or something?"

"Don't ask dumb questions," I tell her. "I am more excited to see them warmup."

"That was always your favorite part." Kamryn holds her hands out like she's squeezing their butts.

"And you're the older one," I sarcastically say.

Her laughter echoes off the tunnel's walls as a security

guard leads us through the dugout and to the field. Now that we're closer to the field, I can feel the vibrations of the ball being hit off the bat reverberating through my chest. The smack of the pitcher's ball hitting the catcher's glove with a solid thwack. It's a feeling and sound I've loved since I was a kid. The sun beats down on us again when we step out of the tunnel from the dugout and onto the field.

"This look on you is incredible," Kamryn boasts as she takes a picture of me.

"You're one to talk. You haven't stopped smiling in the year since your wedding. It's weird."

"It is a weird feeling for me, I won't lie. I didn't know if I'd have that."

"I always knew you would. Despite my original reservation." I tell her with a hip check and look back out over the field to pay attention so we don't accidentally get smacked by a wayward ball. When Mason reappeared, I was skeptical to say the least. My sister was coming off a successful Fashion Week run and I was worried how his reappearance would affect her. But it turns out my worries were for nothing and Mason turned out to be her number on champion. "So do you know anyone who's playing?"

"Actually, I do. I found out that Chance got traded here a few weeks ago, so it'll be good to see him today."

I turn and look at Kamryn. "Weird. The girl I met at the park is engaged to someone who got traded here a few weeks ago.."

"Really?" My sister asks and turns to meet my gaze.

"Yeah. Small world if it's actually him. But you must be excited to see him, right?"

Before Mason—and after, there was Liam and his college team. While I now know Liam was broken, it wasn't until after he passed that Kamryn realized he hid the darkest parts of himself from her. My sister lost her ex-boyfriend almost six years ago in a car accident. His former teammates came to the funeral and lashed out at her claiming she should've been the one to fix him. They blamed her for something beyond her control. Chance was among those who blamed her. And that was when I truly lost my sister. She shut down and shut me out and on one of the few days after the funeral, his parents stopped by her place to drop some things off for her. Apart from the ring she wore, she never spoke of what else was in the box. But whatever it was caused her to retreat further into herself.

Has she forgiven them? Has she even talked to any of them?

"Wait, have you talked to him since, you know...the funeral?" I don't know why I whisper that last part. But it almost feels like talking about that time is a guaranteed mood-killer.

"Chance reached out a couple of years ago. Even though I put that day behind me I think he had been hanging onto that guilt for the way he treated me."

"Guilt and grief make people react differently," I say from personal experience and look around the field.

"That it does," Kamryn says with a sigh and looks out onto the field. "Oh! There he is."

"Kamryn Rawlins." Chance says as he picks her up in a hug. "How've you been girl? It's been a long time."

"Way too long, in fact. And it's Kamryn Brooks now." She holds up her left hand for him to see her engagement ring and wedding band.

His eyes bug out, as does everyone else's when they see the size of her ring. "What? You and Mason?"

"Mm hmm. For a year now." I can see it's taking everything in my sister to not jump up and down. Watching my sister as a fashion mogul is different from watching her interact with friends and talk about her husband is a different character. She's looser with how she holds herself. But not too loose as she knows eyes are on her.

"Wow congrats! You deserve it," he tells her earnestly.

"Thank you. And what about you? You're playing for the Major League now. I always knew you had it in you."

"Thank you. It's still a pinch-me moment. Oh, and I'm engaged now." He tells her with the biggest smile on his face.

"Jax was just telling me about a girl she met at the dog park and we connected the dots assuming it was her. Is she here?"

He looks around the empty seats and then towards the outfield where fans try to get a free ball from the outfielders. "You must have met my Sophie. She should be here soon. It's good to see you, Jax."

"You too."

"I do remember her telling me about meeting you." He looks over his shoulder and we see his Coach waving him back in. "Well, I gotta get back. We should get drinks after the game. Bring Mason." He points this request at Kamryn.

"He's at the office, but I'll text him."

"You still have the same number?" He asks as he walks backward.

"Yeah. And bring your fiancé. I'd love to meet her." My sister replies.

"Will do. I'll shoot you a text."

"Cool. Bye Chance," she says and we watch him return to his warmups.

I shake my head bemused and we turn to head back to the dugout. "How is it that you don't get flustered around athletes?"

"Really? Do you not know who my husband is?"

"Tru–" I start to say, but the word trails off as I feel my body burning from the heat of someone's stare and I look up to see familiar eyes on me. It's like seeing a ghost. Someone I never expected to see after he up and left our final year of college with only a semester left.

"Jax? What's wrong?"

My voice gets stuck in my throat the longer he and I continue to stare at one another from across the field. He still looks the same. Although, that could be my imagination playing tricks on me.

"Nothing," I finally tell her and look away from him. "Let's go get food and watch the rest of the warmups from our seats."

My body continues to burn as we leave the field. And it's not from the sun. No, that burn is reserved for the boy I knew at eighteen, who I fell in love with at twenty-one, the boy I almost gave my virginity to, and the boy who texted me over winter break and never came back to college.

4

NATE

COLLEGE, SPRING SEMESTER - MARCH,
JUNIOR YEAR

My vision goes dark and for a second I panic until the scent of jasmine and vanilla surrounds me and I know exactly who it is.

"Guess who?" The intruder with a voice as sweet as honey asks.

"Well, you're definitely not my advisor," I tell her to throw her off.

"I am most definitely not a sixty-year-old woman," she agrees with disgust dripping off her words.

She's right. My heart doesn't skip a beat when I'm in a meeting with my advisor like it does when she's around. My heart most definitely does not ache for her when she's not around. Did you catch that sarcasm?

"I'm gonna guess, my best friend?"

My vision is restored and the light causes me to blink to clear the haze. "Lucky guess," she huffs out as she pulls out the chair next to me and takes a seat.

Jax Rawlins sat next to me the first day in Biology 101 our freshman year and claimed the spot as my best friend.

Never mind the fact that we were strangers and I rarely spoke more than five words a day to her. Jax talked enough for the both of us and she staked her claim that no one has dared to challenge her. It's been three years and we've been thick as thieves. Jax, much like our freshman year, still does most of the talking. But that's okay. I like hearing her voice.

Coming to a university out-of-state, worried me in the friendship department. I mean, I'd have my team, but I can't hang out with them all of the time. And the guys I grew up with back home went local or stayed in-state, so we're not as close as high school made us out to be. When she found out I'm not a local, Jax took it upon herself to make me come home with her on the days the campus shuts down. And in that time, I've inadvertently become one of the family.

Although, I definitely don't have familial thoughts when it comes to her.

Somewhere between the Biology 101 class to now, in our third year of college, my feelings have morphed from a spark of a crush to something uncontrollable when it comes to Jax that goes beyond friendship. Every smile, every laugh, every teasing jab has made my crush for her simmer like a boiling tea kettle waiting to release. But I can't risk losing her or the comfort I feel when it comes to being her friend. I can't lose her. So I bury it. I let her rattle on and on about some guy in her marketing class that flirts with her and pray that she can't tell how irrationally jealous I get that he's even an option. *Hi, I'm here!*

"You're done with class already?" I ask and tap my pen on top of my textbook. Anything to mask the sound of my thumping heart and ragged breathing. Jax makes me breathless in a way I've never been before. I also have no idea how she sneaks into the athletes only section of buildings and I'm not sure I want to know.

She nods and pulls her phone out of her back pocket and sets it on the table with a thud. "I had a marketing test that I completely breezed through. So that probably means I failed it."

"Oh, hush. I'm sure you passed."

That's an understatement. Jax is a genius. Where it takes most people continuous repetition to grasp something, she gets it on the first go. Being around her genius mind is terrifying some days. Other days, I wish I had unfettered access to how she does it.

"You have too much faith in me, Nathan," she says and her honey brown eyes clash with mine before darting away. In times like this, when our eyes meet and nothing is said, I wish nothing more than to know what she's thinking.

"Someone has to."

Jax quickly looks at me again and turns away. I watch as her cheek lifts in a small, almost dismissive, smile in the reassurance that someone cares about her. I think Jax is starved for attention. Not that she's been neglected, but she's mentioned her family-dynamic a handful of times. And the times I spent with her and her family, I've never noticed any tension. Her parents dote on her, so maybe it's something she's held onto since childhood? Maybe repressed resentment? I do know she has a sister that I've yet to meet even though she now lives close by to Jax's family's house with her boyfriend. Maybe they're not close anymore? But maybe Jax has hidden what she's felt for longer than anyone knew. Fortunately for her, I'm a patient man and I can't wait to uncover the rest of her.

She sits up and flips her curly hair to the other side of her head. I shift in my chair as a whiff of the fragrance from her hair products floats my way and I wish I could bottle that scent up and save it for only me. It makes me wonder what she would do if I buried my nose in her hair like a drug addict getting their next fix or twisted a spiral around my finger like kids do with the string from balloons.

"So are you done for the day? No practice later?"

It takes a second for me to respond but I shake my head, ridding myself of those thoughts because at this rate Jax and I will never happen. "I had my individual practice this morning so I'm free for the rest of the day."

My time during the spring is exceptionally limited when the baseball season really gets going. But we have a couple more days before our next home game series and the coaching staff agreed that tiring us out beforehand would be unwise. We'll have a full team practice tomorrow, but today I'm all done.

"Perfect. Let's go get food." She exclaims and pops up from her chair, grabbing her phone on the way.

I pack up my things and follow her out of the athletic wing like a man on a leash.

I'm not sure when my one-sided crush started. Do people really write that down? Because if you asked me, I would tell you there was never a time that I don't remember feeling something for Jax. My crush for her wasn't instant and I never went into our friendship with the intention of more. But Jax—something about her pulls me to her. The way she laughs, her horrible dance moves, how she doesn't care to carry a tune when a song that she likes plays...my crush for her rolled over me like the gentlest wave. Sometimes I feel like I'm drowning in my feelings for her. But then she'll so something that pulls me above the surface to where I'm finally able to breathe around her again.

It's weird. Being friends with a girl and never acting on those feelings to want more. I'm sure people have things to say about the two of us. And I mean, I won't lie and say that I've not thought about when the right time would be to tell her. But I'm also fearful that if I do say something about my crush and she doesn't feel the same way, could our friendship recover? My feelings for her have always been strictly platonic. Until they weren't.

I hold the door open to the union and follow her inside and together we hop in line, moving forward inch by inch. When Jax puts our food on her tray, I go to grab my card to swipe for our food, but she beats me to it.

"Stop doing that," I growl in her ear. Is it my imagination or was that a hitch in her breath?

She turns her head which puts her lips dangerously close to mine. "Be faster." Jax says and pauses when she notices our position. I don't miss the way her eyes flicker to my lips and a flush covers her cheeks before she's turning around and stepping forward. My heart continues to thump heavy in my chest. Like that moment before a kiss where the nerves are so apparent, but it's clear that you're both on the same page.

We're quiet as we finish going through the line. That loaded moment sits heavy in the front of my mind. If she would have made the move first, I would have followed. Is she thinking the same thing? Can other people tell we just had a moment? Or is it that my imagination keeps playing tricks on me? I keep thinking I have a neon sign flashing "I have a crush on my best friend!". But maybe that's just my imagination.

Jax and I have never once crossed that friendship line. Sure, we've teased each other. But we've never had a moment like the one minutes ago.

Once our food is paid for, we bag it and head to the spot

that only we know. Maybe it's not actually a secret spot. But it's become, what I like to call, mine and Jax's spot. Really, it's just an abandoned picnic table behind the football stadium with zero shade. It's a bitch to sit at in the late summer when the semester is just beginning. But when it's spring in Philadelphia, like now, it's nice to have the sun warm our bodies after days of snow and windchill.

We eat our food in silence. Silence that I usually love, only now it makes me want to pluck each piece of hair out of my head. The sound of cars driving and honking on the other side of the tree barrier is a low hum and that's the one thing that I can hold onto as I try to find a way back to normal. At least a normal where I stop thinking about our almost moment. When I'm done, I crumble up my trash and put it in the paper bag. That minimal noise is comforting as I let out a heavy sigh.

Noise. Noise. Noise. That's all I need because this silence is suffocating.

I clear my throat and break the silence. "So, that was—"

"Different?" Jax finishes for me.

I lean forward and rest my elbows on my knees. I turn my head to look at Jax who's currently mastering the art of avoidance and gathering up her own trash.

"Weird different? Or a good different?" I fish for more from her. I keep my face blank as I ask her this because I've been known to have a terrible poker face.

"Nate, we can't," she says, almost defeated and still avoiding eye contact.

"Why not?" I ask through what feels like glass in my throat.

"Because you're my best friend and I would be destroyed if I lost that."

I rear back. "Who said anything about losing something?"

Jax finally turns to look at me and it's like the hopeful feeling I felt before has been snuffed out by the mournful look on her face.

"I saw firsthand what happened with my sister when friendship lines were crossed and I don't want that for me. For us."

I turn away from her and look towards the breezeway under the stadium. The pathway is dirty from decades of shoes traipsing along, squished gum, and a few pieces of trash littering the area.

"So it was a good different?" I ask again.

"I won't answer that. I won't ruin a friendship like my sister did."

"You know, I hear a lot about her and you. But what about you and me?" I've never once gotten angry or been angry with Jax. There was never any need to. She makes it too easy to be happy around her. But now?

"There is no you and me, Nate. There can't be."

Jax refusing us is something I should just accept. My parents have told me that when a girl refuses you, you don't push. But that look we shared earlier was not one-sided. It's clear Jax is scared. But I can't hold her hand through the fear. I grind my back teeth together in an effort to keep from blowing up at her. With a short nod, I gather my things and hear her gasp. "Okay, then. I have to go. I forgot I have a study group session to get to. I'll see you around, Jax."

"That's it?" she shouts at my back. "You're just gonna walk away?"

I turn around and look at her. The furrow in her brow and her arms crossed over her chest in a defensive pose is what I'm committing to memory. But I also clock the tremble in her jaw and the watering of her eyes like she's afraid to lose me. Like what she voiced is already happening.

"What do you want me to say, Jax? Do you want me to just forget that the crush I've had on you since I was eighteen means nothing?" I stalk back to her until I'm in her space. "Do you want me to forget that every time I'm around you, all I think about is kissing you and never coming up for air?" My hands come up and I gently cradle her face and tip her head back so I can look into her eyes. My thumbs lightly rest on her throat and I watch the movement as she swallows. I feel the quickening of her pulse under my other fingers and it sickeningly soothes me that this riles her up. That the possibility of losing me over this terrifies her. "I dream of the day when I can finally call you mine. I've tried to squash my crush for you. I've tried for the last three years. But day after day you have wormed yourself so deep inside of me that I have been waiting for you to notice. But you're so sure that if we cross the line you'll lose me and instead you don't want to try at all. So you lose me instead."

"Was that all our friendship was to you?" She asks and I don't miss the tears threatening to spill over. Or her hidden question.

"No, J. It has never been about that and deep down you know it."

I wait for the words to click. For her to say something. But she doesn't. We just stand there. Toe to toe. Brown eyes to brown eyes. And still, she says nothing.

I swallow through her rejection and lean forward, pressing a kiss on her forehead. I linger there and feel her hands encircle my forearms of the hands that are still cradling her face, hoping this kiss kicks some sense into her. That she can get on the same page as me. But all too soon her hands drop and I rip myself away from her, walking quickly back to my dorm. Away from the girl who's had my heart for the last three years.

Unknowingly, Jax has had the power to undo me all along.

And today she did just that.

5

NATE

PRESENT DAY

It's like seeing a ghost. Our eyes locked from across the field and what felt like hours is really only a minute. When she leaves, my gaze stays glued to the spot where Jax was standing with her sister and Chance.

I haven't talked to her since I left the semester before we were set to graduate. I didn't plan to leave. But when my dad got sick, being states away and baseball were two things that no longer mattered. And as I think that to myself, I realize that in leaving school and baseball, I also left Jax behind. That was always a fear of hers and I unfortunately made that fear come to fruition.

A baseball hitting me in the chest brings me back to the present. To what I'm supposed to do. To my job. I look over at Bryce who threw the ball and give him my best glare.

"Girls later. Baseball first," he tells me. And he's right. This game is one of many that will help us when we're in the playoff hunt.

I pick the ball up off the ground and throw it back to him. I try to put all thoughts of Jax out of my mind. But it's hard when I know that she'll be in the crowd watching us play. That little piece of knowledge feels like college all over again. And it's clear, after years apart, that she's still a base-ball fan. So, at least that's one thing that stayed the same.

I go through the motions of our warmup and stand by my teammates as the National Anthem is played. I've never once regretted being drafted to Cincinnati all those years ago. But now after seeing Jax, who's gotten even more beau-tiful as the years have passed, it's throwing me for more than a curveball. It's making me wonder how we've been in the same city and have never crossed paths.

We take the field and I jog out to the sideline to take a couple of warm up throws. When the umpire signals, the guys and I take our respective spots in the field. I love playing in the outfield. Most people look at outfield posi-tions as a last resort. And for a defensive position, it is. We're the three spots keeping the infielders from running to the fence to get a ball. We're the ones who keep a long single from turning into a double. We make the diving catches and climb the wall to save a fly ball from becoming a home run. It's my favorite thing about this position. But as I try to keep focusing on why I love this position and my mind from looping back to seeing Jax, it's the one time I wish I played an infield position. At least that would give me a reason to focus. Because being in the outfield is a surefire way for my mind to wander when I should be focusing on my job.

I adjust my hat as the count is up in our favor and chew my gum harder in an attempt to focus. But it doesn't work. I keep thinking about her. The girl I left behind. The last text I sent.

More often than not, I always wondered what Jax was up to. I assume she got her degree. Does she use it? I would hope so. All she talked about was marketing. The small things she would do to help companies reach their tended audiences. Did she meet someone after I left? Are they still dating? Or worse, is she married?

The crack of the ball against the bat jolts me back to the game. It sails into left field and I move into position before it's caught.

Three up, three down.

We jog off the field and into the dugout. I'm not up to bat until later on, so I take a spot at the fence with some of the guys.

"What's up with you?" Chance asks. "You've been off since warmups."

"Girl problems?" Bryce chimes in with a question.

We watch as our guy hits the ball between shortstop and third. Cheers from the crowd and dugout are rampant.

"I just saw someone that I hadn't seen since college and it threw me off," I tell my two gossiping friends.

Chance and Bryce are the two I'm closest to on the team despite Chance just getting traded here a few weeks ago. That's normal for baseball as it's a business first and foremost. It also took nothing for Bryce to add him to our twosome.

"Unrequited love. My favorite," Bryce says.

Chance laughs and I glare at him. But it's not a far off assumption for him as Bryce is more of a romantic than most of the married guys on the team.

"It definitely wasn't unrequited," I tell them both.

"Oh, shit. This is grounds for drinks after the game." Chance declares before getting his helmet and batting gloves on then leaving us to go stand in the on deck circle.

I groan but don't argue. They'd drag me out after the game regardless if we won or lost.

～

AND THAT'S where I find myself hours later. I take a large pull of the beer Bryce set in front of me. I don't usually drink during a series, but if I'm spilling my guts to him and Chance, I need something. Because if I'm going back into the recesses of my mind during that time, alcohol will certainly help dull that ache.

"Did he say anything?" Chance asks when he barrels into the bar and clambers onto the empty bench. He's very reminiscent of my mom when she goes to meet up with her girlfriends for their monthly lunch dates. Those women can gossip like no other. And so can baseball players.

I give him a look and he blows me a kiss.

"So...who was it that you saw?"

"My–" *soulmate, love of my life, the only one I've wanted to be with*...what do I call Jax? Because calling her my friend would seem so little of a word than what she was to me. "We went to college together, met at eighteen, boy falls hard..."

"Did she reject you?" Bryce asks with panic in his voice.

I look down into my beer, hoping it will give them the answers that I have yet to still get from that day. "Not at first."

"So what happened?"

"My dad got sick my final year and I transferred closer to home with a semester left."

The text that I sent to Jax over winter break still haunts me. I never saw myself to be one of those guys who ends a relationship over text. Because that's the coward's way out. You can't say you love someone, tell them they're your future, and then end it through a text. That means you didn't love them enough to face them head-on. But I had no choice. My dad was too sick by the time I returned home that I was terrified to even go to the bathroom for fear of what I might find when I came back.

But I did what I did with Jax and that's the biggest regret of my life.

"You transferred with a semester left of school?" Bryce and Chance shout at the same time. Thank goodness we're the only ones on the patio. This tavern is a staple in Cincinnati and one we don't tell people about because we choose to keep this hidden gem to ourselves. So them freaking out like this keeps my face off of social media with possible rumors flying.

"Yes. And it was the right thing to do," I tell them.

Well, maybe not the right thing considering going from a top tier Division 1 school to a barely known Division 1 school made getting drafted that much harder. But I made it after busting my ass that semester so that scouts would take notice. They did and I've been in Cincinnati for the last six years.

"I mean, you did right by your family. But was leaving that easy?" Bryce asks and in our years of friendship, this is the most serious I've heard from him.

No. "Next to my dad getting sick, leaving was the hardest thing I ever did."

This is much too heavy talk for drinks after a game. So I finish off the rest of my beer and look to them for another round. Standing up from my seat, I head to the bar and when I get the bartender's attention, I ask for another beer and a refill on our pitcher.

I doubt that Jax would ever want to speak to me. After all, I did leave her when I promised that we would graduate together. I promised a lot of things to her, and to myself.

I'm looking at the alcohol on the shelf when the door to the bar opens and my mind goes back to that day.

6

JAX

COLLEGE, SPRING SEMESTER - MARCH,
JUNIOR YEAR

I find the room I'm looking for and bang my fist against Nate's door five times until the side of my hand automatically aches from the force. The sound echoes down the empty dorm hall and I'm hoping he's in here because I've been all over this godforsaken campus looking for him after he left me at the picnic table behind the football stadium. As soon as I pulled myself together, meaning I dried my tears and made sure I didn't resemble a panda, I threw our trash out and began my search for him. He wasn't in his usual places he hangs out at so with one last hail mary I came here.

It's just after four in the afternoon and I know I'm not disturbing anyone. With a huff, I start to bang on his door again when it flies open. My fist hangs suspended in the air as I take in his ruffled and annoyed state. Clad in only grey sweatpants, my mouth goes dry but then I remember my anger.

"You just leave and that's that?" I screech. "You tell me you have a crush on me and then leave? Nate!"

He rests his hands on his hips. "What else do you want

me to say, Jax? Do you want me to take it back? Trust me, I weighed the consequences for a long time, but it's out there." Defeat weighs him down and it's my fault. "Is that all?"

"I–" no other words come out. Because what else can really be said? He said he has a crush on me and I'd be lying if I said I didn't feel the same way. But, he's my Nate. And he has been for the last three years.

"Nothing else to say?" It's a rhetorical question Nate asks when he steps closer to me. "You always regale me of your day and talk about guys in your classes that flirt with you and suddenly you're speechless. Tell me what you want me to say, Jaclyn."

I wince because the only time someone calls me by my first name is when I'm in trouble or when I've hurt them. And it's clear I've hurt Nate. My eyes burn into his. With him this close, his body heat reaching out to mine, I can't think straight. "I–I don't know, okay? It's always been easy with us. I don't—how am I supposed to handle this? You're my Nate and..."

"Stop talking." Nate demands roughly before he snakes his arm around my waist and slams his lips to mine. He takes advantage of my gasp and slides his tongue against mine. We back into his dorm and the door slams shut. My body is pressed up against the wall and my hands claw at his waist, wanting to get closer than I already am.

With this position, I can feel how hard he is through his sweats and a whimper travels up my throat. He hooks his arm under my leg and wraps it around his waist.

"Nate," I gasp out when his lips travel down my neck. My eyes close of their own volition as I feel everything down to my toes.

His hands traveling over my body leaves fire in its wake.

All of the simple kisses with boys in high school have nothing compared to this with Nate.

"Jax," he sings back.

Nate doesn't wait for a response before he's bending down and picking me up by the back of my thighs, moving us to his bed and laying me down. His body follows until he's nestled in the cradle of my thighs. In this position, the feel of him pressed against me is unlike anything I've ever felt. Which I have nothing to compare it to and it feels better than I ever could have imagined.

My arms wrap around his neck and our lips move in sync. Nate runs his hand through my wild curls and tugs on the strands, sending lightning bolts of arousal down my spine. His hands roam down my body and travel back up, his hands cage my ribs and I revel in the feel of his thumb rubbing the underside of my breast. My nipples harden and I wonder why I've starved myself of his touch.

"Wait, wait." I say, breaking the kiss. My chest caves with my deep breathing and I lightly run my thumb over his kiss-swollen bottom lip.

He pulls back an inch with confusion written over his face. "What's wrong?"

"I um...I've never," I try telling him that I've never gone further than kissing and elementary over-the-clothes groping. But I think he catches on when his features soften.

"Are you–Jax, are you a virgin?" Nate asks softly.

I bite my bottom lip and play with the gold chain hanging around his neck that he never takes off. "Yes?" I don't know why I phrased that as a question. It's not like I'm waiting for anyone special. I could've lost my virginity in high school like my friends. But it felt more like marking an item off a checklist. And I didn't want that for my first time. But coming to college–I don't broadcast that I'm still a virgin at twenty-one. Nobody does because there's this urban legend that by eighteen you're supposed to have lost your virginity, like it's a pair of keys that you're destined to never find again. And once the horny college guys hear a girl is still a virgin, they'll jump at the chance to befriend her and then leave her once they take what she willingly gave them. I mean, I'm sure I would like sex, love it even, when I get the hang of it. It's like riding a bike. Or so I've been told by my countless *Sex and the City* marathons.

"Hey." He starts and gently lifts my chin up to meet his eyes. "If you think I'm about to blow past every stop sign to be with you, then you haven't been paying attention. I want this–us, as more than friends and more than I've wanted anything."

"Oh," I say. I feel like an idiot and don't know why I lumped Nate into that category. But after years of our friendship and him never making a move on me, I just assumed he wasn't into me. Joke's on me though. Because it's clear he's wanted us to be an *us* for longer than I suspected.

"Yeah, *oh*. I won't rush you, okay? We can take this as slow as you need to. But just so you know, as soon as my lips touched yours, I became yours. And I hope you became mine?"

I nod my head as best as I can while on his pillow and meet his eyes. "Yes. Slow. And you're mine."

Up close I can see each perfectly curled eyelash that guys are blessed with and the amber flecks splattered in his brown eyes.

"There she is," Nate says and that gets me smiling. "Now, can we go back to kissing? Because that's all I've thought about for the last three years."

"You have?" I ask, thinking he's joking. Although he's said something along those lines but in my confusion and hurt, I refused to believe him. I thought he said that in a moment of anger. But now laying under him, with his still hard erection pressing into my center, it's clear that he wasn't lying.

"Yes." He tells me and dips his head to lay a kiss on my neck. Tingles spark all over my body when he kisses me there and the necklace he's wearing dances along my chest. "I've wondered what sounds you would make if I kissed you here." A breathy moan escapes as he kisses and suckles on my neck. "And here." A whimper travels up my throat when he nibbles on my earlobe. Nate hikes my leg up high around his waist and rolls his hips into my clothed center. His eyes flare with renowned heat when I moan and grip his arms. "And that. I won't rush this with you, Jax. I promise to go as slow as you want."

"Okay," I exhale shakily.

Nate dots kisses over my face. Relaxing me. Getting me comfortable with him before he's kissing me like he's been walking through the desert for days with no water. He kisses me like I'm the only person alive. And maybe now I finally do feel alive.

I never thought kissing was a big deal. I always thought it was a means to an end.

Turns out I haven't been kissed by Nate Holloway.

7

JAX

PRESENT DAY

"Jax!" I hear my name yelled as we're following the crowd to leave the stadium. Kamryn and I look at each other before we both stop and turn around.

"Sophie! Hey," I greet when she walks over to us. She's donned in Cincinnati memorabilia with what looks like Chance's number on the breast pocket. "Kamryn, this is Sophie. Sophie, my sister Kamryn."

"Hi. Big fan of your clothes," she gushes. Sophie is clearly sunshine personified.

"Hey, thanks. Jax says you just moved here with Chance?"

"You know him?" she asks Kamryn and not in a mean girl way.

"Yeah. I went to college with him and his brother Brandon. Small world." Kam says and pops her sunglasses on her face.

"Really small," she notes and then gasps. "So you're the sisters we're supposed to meet for drinks?"

"Guilty."

Our laughter echoes and blends in with the sounds of

others still leaving the stadium. Still high with excitement off of the win.

"Chance said we're all meeting at the Tipsy Tavern for drinks?" Sophie questions after she looks up from her phone.

"That's right down the street from my place," I chime in.

"Perfect! You can just ride with me if you didn't drive here."

"We actually walked. But a ride would be great and I'll give you directions. It's kind of confusing to get to." I tell her as we set off to the parking lot.

But as we set off towards her car, all I can focus on is the *we're all meeting* part of what Sophie said. I won't be the girl who asks who all she means because I'm a twenty-eight year old woman, dammit! I can conquer whoever's going to be at the bar. *Right?* My self-conscious questions a little nervously. *Right!* I tell myself.

I put on a brave face and wordlessly, we follow along with Sophie. She's definitely a bubbly person and I can see how Chance became enamored with her. You can't help but want to smile and be happy around her.

"So what do you do for work, Jax? Not to sound like a creep, but I know what your sister does," Sophie says casually as we climb into her car.

"I help Kamryn out on the marketing side for her brand, I have a podcast and vlog channel, and then I have some other brands that I work with when needed."

"You're like a marketing genius, then."

"I guess I do okay," I say, not the biggest fan of being praised for my work.

"Don't let her fool you, Sophie. I can't do half of the stuff she does. So all of the social media stuff and the website for my company is all her doing."

Absentmindedly I fiddle with the ring on the middle finger of my left hand that has bees printed on it. I don't know what encouraged me to wear it today after all these years. Maybe I'm trying to embrace summer with open arms and bees signify that. But now after seeing Nate, I'm kind of regretting it. Sophie and Kamryn chat like they've been friends forever and I occasionally interrupt to direct her where to go but their chatting gives me time to think. Think about who I saw. Think about what this means that I saw him. Think about how the ring on my finger feels tighter than ever and I spin it to hopefully loosen it up.

The downside to living near the stadium is that the ride to the bar takes no time at all. Sophie finds a spot to park and I purposefully take my time getting out. I trail behind them as we walk down the sidewalk to the bar.

You can do this, I tell myself over and over again as the bar gets closer. After all, we're adding new patterns to our life and this seemingly small deviation from our routine is a new pattern. Crap, I'm regretting telling the world that.

The door to the bar sticks and weighs a ton, as shown by Sophie struggling to open it. But once we're through the scene that greets us is one brought to you by the old school looking taverns. The well-worn bar is shoe-scuffed with metal hooks under the countertop for purses and bags. A shelf of liquors, with a mirror, lines part of the back wall to get you to look at yourself as you choose your next drink. A digital jukebox sits on the opposite wall and the black low back stools line the entirety of the bar.

"Hey, Sophie," a voice I would know like my own greets as we walk further inside. I have to swallow down my wince when he speaks.

"Nate. Great game." Sophie greets the man who was once mine with a hug.

"Thanks. Chance and Bryce are outside," he tells her.

"Cool. Nate, these are my friends, Kamryn and Jax." Sophie holds her hand out to point us to him.

"Nice to meet you," he says and his voice has the audacity to hit me where it hurts and simultaneously make me swoon.

"You as well," Kamryn greets.

I, however, avoid eye contact although I can feel his eyes burning a hole in my face, and I loop my arm around my sisters and we follow Sophie outside to the covered patio. My sister isn't the only good secret keeper. But I do admit that keeping this from her for years has eaten me alive. She doesn't know Nate—well, she knows of the guy who was my best friend before he became something more. So it was easy to ignore that part of my life when she was dealing with settling into adulthood and then losing Liam. And then again when everything with Trent happened. But now that he's here I know I can no longer ignore that I'll have to tell Kamryn about the history she's blind to. I also know that if my friendship with Sophie continues, I'll have to talk with Nate. There is no avoiding it anymore.

"Baby!" Sophie squeals when we walk out to the patio.

Seeing them together is comical. Where she's around my height at 5'2" with tattoos that I can now see, covering every available inch of her body, Chance towers over her with naked skin. But they work and seeing how they light up around each other brings that green monster around.

"Hi, Baby Belle," he coos.

Kam snorts. "Care to enlighten us on that nickname?"

"If you insist," Chance chides. "Oh, this is Bryce and Nate should have been at the bar getting another beer."

"He was." Sophie answers for us and moves to sit on the bench that lines the back wall of the space.

"Nice to meet you both," Bryce tells us.

"Likewise," I say with a smile. "So back to this nickname."

Kamryn and I take our seats and I realize too late that an empty one is next to me. Asking my sister to trade spots would look juvenile, so I stay where I'm at while every muscle in my body tenses with his impending arrival.

"He came into the bookstore I was working at in Tampa," Sophie starts.

"Don't forget to mention you were wearing a yellow dress." Chance interrupts and pops a kiss on her cheek.

"I was getting there, ya goof." Sophie says with an eye roll but looks less than annoyed and if the smile on her face is any indication I doubt we'll get the full story of how they met. "Anyways, I was stocking the shelves with new releases when he came into the store looking for one of the newest fantasy books for his sister. I thought it was sweet. Until he came in the next week and the week after that and so on," Sophie says with laughter in her voice.

My body coils like a snake ready to strike when the chair next to me now holds a body I know quite intimately. And that familiar cologne mixed with his natural body scent wafts towards me. I do my best to ignore him and focus on my new friend's love story.

"Did he keep using his sister as an excuse?" Kamryn asks.

"Nope. His mom, then his aunt, then his grandma, and then his other aunt."

"What? The women in my family are readers," he claims and we all laugh at that. "Soph made me nervous."

"You? Nervous?" Kam asks, baffled. Which is understandable because on the rare time I visited her, Chance was the class clown of their group.

He shakes his head and they share a look that can only be had from years of knowing one another. "I was never nervous because Liam always made the jokes to ease the tension."

"That he did."

Despite Kamryn being best friends with Liam, he and I never had that brother-sister relationship that some might think. Liam was practically a stranger to me. And I'm sure it wasn't on purpose. But once him and Kamryn got together, they couldn't keep their hands off each other. Plus, they had James and Emily to do couple things with. So I never truly experienced his fun personality like Chance and Kamryn reminisce about. Mainly because I was locked in Nate-land. It was the safest place for me to be. So I kept to myself the majority of the time. And I liked my life like that.

I look over at Nate from the corner of my eye and see him with his elbows on his knees, looking into his glass of beer. His corded forearms are a beautiful brown ochre decorated with floral prints and an older looking digital camera captured. His wrist is decorated with an expensive looking watch and a gold bracelet. Simple and understated. He shifts my way and I look back towards the group.

"But anyways, after the fifth trip to the bookstore I finally asked her out." Chance says and looks at Sophie with the gentlest of eyes.

"Fifth?" Bryce asks with humor.

"Yep." Chance follows that up with wrapping his arms around Sophie. "She was wearing this light yellow dress that dipped low in the front. And when I finally got the courage to speak to her, I called her Belle."

"So, the nickname makes sense," Bryce says as he watches them with fascination.

"Exactly. And then I promised to follow him anywhere," Sophie finishes.

"When's the wedding?" I ask and don't miss Nate turning his face in my direction. Does my voice affect him as much as his affects me?

Sophie leans into Chance's side and they share a look. "We just got engaged a few months ago but were thinking next November with a joint bachelor and bachelorette party after the season ends."

"Well, if you need a wedding dress, I've always wanted to make one," Kamryn offers.

Sophie's squeal is piercing enough that I plug my ears and I don't miss anyone else's covering of their ears.

"Damn, Sophie." Chance mutters and wraps his arm around her shoulders, pulling her back into his side.

"Sorry," she announces. "But a dress designed by THE Kamryn Brooks is every girl's dream."

She's not wrong. It took considerable effort to keep my sister from making her own wedding dress and it's something she recently dipped her toes into to offer to other brides. While wedding dresses aren't her brand's main focus, I can see the wheels turning in her fashion designer brain just ready to tackle something else.

"I'd be happy to do it."

Bryce sighs. "Since we're on the topic of love, you all can help us out with Nate and his love dilemma."

I chose the wrong moment to take a sip as I choke on my beer and continue to cough to clear my throat.

"Are you okay?" Kam asks.

"Yeah," I wheeze out and grab a napkin from the table to wipe my chin. "It just went down the wrong tube."

Kamryn rubs my back and looks around me to look at Nate. "Love dilemma?"

"It's nothing I can't handle," he says and tries to dismiss her. But I don't miss how the grip on his glass has gotten tighter or the clench in his jaw.

"Oh, come on," Bryce starts.

I for one want to sink through the floor if I know where this is going to go.

"Your not so unrequited love from college that you had to leave because your dad was sick who you magically see today? If that's not the making for a second chance, I don't know what is."

I see my sister look at me from the corner of my eye, but I avoid her. The noise around me fades as I think back to that winter break. We made plans. So many plans. And they were gone quicker than the first snowfall in Pennsylvania.

8

NATE

COLLEGE, SPRING SEMESTER - MAY, JUNIOR YEAR

Thank goodness we're local for regionals and super-regionals. I don't think the team would survive a road trip for these games. This is the best we've played all season, but it would only take one blow on our house of cards to ruin the mojo we've got going on. But now since campus is closed, those of us not local have had to find other places to stay. Luckily, or unluckily, for me Jax urged me to stay at her family's house. I felt like I was living in a museum for those few days when she went out of town for her sister's graduation. Thankfully with baseball, I've been out more than in, but when I'm there all I do is make up reasons to kiss her. And that's bad for someone whose focus needs to be on baseball. *Okay, maybe a little temptation is fine.*

> Me: Headed to the bus and then I'll be at your place.

> Jax: Are you finally going to tell me where we're going?

> Me: Nope. See you soon girlfriend.

You would think that with us testing the boundaries of our new relationship it would be awkward. But, no. I just have the added bonus of knowing more intimate details of my best friend. We're in the winner's bracket of the tournament. Otherwise, I wouldn't have planned a date with Jax for today. Her parents mentioned how much she loves greenhouses, butterflies, and learning about all different types of plants. That gave me an idea.

The seat next to me fills with one of my coaches. I take off my headphones and give him my attention.

"What's up coach?"

"Have you given any thought to what's after college?"

"Look for internships or maybe enter the draft," I say with less confidence than I've ever felt.

"You should. Enter the draft that is. Nate, you're one of the best outfielders I've had the pleasure of working with. You do solid work at the plate, you see the outfield better than some of the professional players I've watched, and you're an excellent teammate. Any team would be lucky to have you."

I look at him like he's sprouted two heads. I like baseball, but enough to have it as my career? Five year old me would be jumping in his seat. But twenty-one year old me? Not so much.

"Thanks, coach. That means a lot."

He pats me on the shoulder before going back to his seat. As we travel down the highway and back to campus, I try to picture myself as a professional baseball player. It's not that I think being an athlete is a bogus job. It's that I've never been able to picture myself as a professional athlete. Well, that's a lie because every kid has dreamed of playing professionally. But the realistic side of me always thought I would use my architecture degree.

I've loved how buildings were made since I was little. And I'm not talking about the actual building of them, but the blueprints. We all have to start somewhere and that's what architecture is. Starting from scratch and becoming something worth something. Same with photography. While I knew I would never pursue a simple hobby and attempt to turn it into a career, finding a subject and turning it into art means something. But baseball? That's all talent and despite what my coach says, there are more talented baseball players than me.

We round into the school and start gathering our things. Once parked, we all hurry off with instructions to be back here at seven in the morning. Groans chime in, but it's lighthearted. We have one more game until the next round and while I'm excited, I'm also nervous. These could very well be my final games here if I decide to enter the draft. This could mean leaving Jax and I'm not ready for that. She's been by my side for the last three years and to think our time together is limited scares the shit out of me.

Throwing my bag in the trunk, I round to the front of my car and start up, heading to Jax's house like I've done dozens of times. A few minutes later I pull up to her family's house and park on the street. I walk up the long driveway and give a courtesy knock before walking through the front door. The house is quiet with her parents at work and her sister living with her boyfriend.

Sliding off my shoes and lining them up next to the others by the front door, I take the stairs two at a time and turn right when I get to the top. When I first came over to Jax's house freshman year, I was floored by how big her house was. My parents house in Virginia is nothing to scoff at, but this house is huge. Naturally, I was intrigued by the angles and lines of her house and how this place is an actual home instead of just a blueprint.

The low hum of music comes from Jax's room whose door is wide open. I find her on the balcony that looks over the backyard with her iPad in her lap and doodling away. Quietly, I place my bag in the hallway and creep into her room. When she gets her iPad out, sirens could be going off and she wouldn't hear them. Is it dangerous? Yes. But she also gets this cute look on her face and her tongue peaks out from the corner of her mouth.

I step up behind her and cover her eyes the same way she usually does to me.

"Holy shit," she gasps.

"Guess who?"

"The plumber?"

"Nope," I tell her feeding into this.

"Hmm. If not the plumber then maybe my boyf–" Jax cuts herself off. While I've been shouting from the rooftop that Jax is my girlfriend, she's still shy when it comes to labels. That hasn't bothered me because I know where I stand with her. But to hear her getting close to finally uttering that word is a feeling unlike any other.

I move my hands from her eyes and come around to sit on the matching footstool and move it closer to her. My legs cage her in but Jax avoids my gaze and looks back down at her iPad. Wanting her to talk to and look at me, I carefully take the device from her hands and place it on the other chair.

"What was that you called me?" It's a rhetorical question but one I need her to say out loud. I bring my hand up to her face and gently pull her bottom lip out from between her teeth and angle her face up to meet my eyes. "Talk to me, J."

The yellow of her shirt brings out the flecks of gold in her honey brown eyes. There are days when I feel I could get lost in them and never find my way out.

"You've been calling me your girlfriend for the last month and I'd get all flustered when you would call me that. I tend to do that when you're around." I listen intently and smile as she rambles. One thing I've learned about Jax is that she needs to get her words out to get to the point. "You should hear the thoughts running through my head. The things I want to say to you, but don't because I'm me and you're well, *you*. And I shouldn't be nervous around you because you're my Nate and maybe officially putting a label on us like that is juvenile..."

Jax trails off and I let her words soak in. I do wish that I could hear her thoughts. It would make it so much easier to finally know what she's thinking. Jax is an enigma. I've been trying to figure her out for years, but in doing that I've fallen so hard for her.

"It's not." I tell her when she sits there awkwardly waiting for me to say something. "And you're my Jax. But yes, you are also my girlfriend which by default makes me your boyfriend."

Boyfriend, I watch her mouth the word and the smile that spreads across her face melts every bit of tension I felt from a few seconds ago. "Doesn't that mean this should be sealed with a kiss? You know—just to make it official," she says through a smile.

"I have heard that's what you do when you come to an agreement," I play into it. "Come here."

Jax leans forward and our lips meet. Soft at first. Just a light touching of our lips before she's leaning closer to me. My hand dives into the hair at the nape of her neck and hold her still, not wanting to go further than this. But her hands and fingers claw at any piece of fabric she can grip onto. Realizing this is a battle I'll lose, I lean back and haul her into my lap. Jax's legs on either side of my hips are like a weighted blanket when you need something to ground you.

I may have been waiting years to kiss her. But Jax seems to have been waiting her whole life to kiss me. She's as starved for my touch as I am for hers. Roaming my hands along her body, I wrap an arm around her waist and the other around her thigh and walk into her bedroom. Not breaking the kiss, I crawl onto her bed and rest myself in the cradle of her thighs. Even though I still haven't showered from my game and we have places to be, I can't find any reason to stop kissing her.

Jax's hands slide under my shirt and grip at my skin. Our tongues dance together like they've done this a hundred times before. I hike her leg high around my waist, opening her up and rolling my hips into her center. Her sigh-moan lets me know she likes this. That she wants more. And with the sounds she's making, her hips moving and searching for something—Jax makes me want to forget all about us taking this slow.

Breaking the kiss, I trail kisses down her neck. Licking and suckling at the skin. Reveling in the sounds traveling up her throat. Jax tries to slide my shirt up my body but I pull away from her and try not to smile at the pout on her plump lips.

"No." I tell her with lightness in my voice. While I'm certainly not a virgin, I haven't been with anyone since coming to college and I'm definitely not as experienced as other guys my age claim to be. And with Jax, I'd want our first time together to be special.

"Why not?" She asks and plays with the drawstring on my shorts. The tugging of the strings sends little shockwaves through my body and I have to focus on tomorrow's game to get through this. *Temptation.*

"Because I haven't showered and we have some place to be." I emphasize my point by placing a quick kiss on her lips and rolling off her bed. "I'll be ready in fifteen minutes."

Jax leans up on her elbows. "We could've been done in five."

"No we couldn't have." I tell her and pull her to the edge of the bed by her ankles.

Her chest heaves and she looks up at me with eyes so full of hope, wonder, and desire. "Why not?"

"Because I need at least five, maybe ten, minutes to make you come with my fingers," I explain. My hands trail soft paths over her exposed thighs and goosebumps pop up in response. "Then I need another ten, maybe fifteen, or even twenty minutes eating your pussy." The room has gone deathly still. Not even the sound of our ragged breathing is audible over the lust covering us. "And then, only then, when you're ready and begging for my cock," I map out what I plan and my hands spread the width of her thighs, my thumbs coming dangerously high to her center, "will I give you what we both want."

I back away as quickly as I can and beeline towards the room I'm staying in. I turn the water in the shower to ice cold and hop in, hoping it will calm me down. It slightly does the job, but my blood is still simmering under the surface. Getting out of the shower, clean and cold, I hurriedly dress and walk back out to a waiting Jax. She's changed into a dress with thin straps and sandals that show off her hot pink toenails. I smile because it's so her and wrap my arm around her shoulder as we walk back out to my car and to the place I know she'll love.

9

NATE

PRESENT DAY

"So, what was it?" Bryce pushes and I kind of want to throttle him for not being able to read the room. "Or *who* was it is what I should be asking."

"She was my best friend in college," I tell the group. And I don't miss Jax chugging down the last of her beer.

Bryce slaps his hand on his chest. "Friends to lovers. A true classic. My sister is going to love this."

"Are you a romantic, Bryce?" Kamryn asks in a teasing way. Maybe not really searching for an answer, but she's about to get one regardless.

"Are you kidding? The trust that's already built up. The comfortability between two beings. You can't get that anywhere else."

"But that's unrealistic," Jax pipes up and her words just shoved a dagger in my chest. "It doesn't matter how much trust is between two people. All it takes is one moment or one *text* to destroy it all."

Bryce looks on the verge of tears and despite all of the teasing he's going to make someone very happy. "But what about the second chance?"

59

She leans forward and sets her empty glass on the table. "I don't think it's realistic for everyone. Sorry, Kam."

Her sister nods and eyes her sister like she's a stranger.

"Damn, girl. You've been burned," Sophie chimes in.

"Two times, too many," Jax admits and I want someone to hand *me* a shovel so I can start digging my own grave. She clears her throat with a cough mixed with a laugh. "You know, I forgot I have a meeting with my manager. Good game today, guys."

"Do you want me to come with you?" Kamryn asks as Jax abruptly stands. She's so close to me, but so completely out of reach.

She shakes her head. "No, you stay," she urges and hesitates with her next move, but pushes on. "Bye, guys."

Jax leaving abruptly sends weirdness through the group. And once she's out the door, it takes everything in me to not run after her. But I'm not that person for her anymore. Maybe she has a new person she leans on. Someone who stays, someone who is willing to meet her halfway, and that someone is not me. It hasn't been since I sent that damn text message.

"What don't we know about your sister?" Chance asks after no one has said anything for an awkward few minutes.

Kamryn crosses her leg over the other and swings her foot. "My sister is as complicated as a Rubik's Cube. You may think you're given the right moves, but unfortunately she's something that you can never solve. Trust me, I've been trying to figure her out for the last few years."

That's an understatement, I say to myself.

"I don't know much about what happened in her college years, as I was mixed up with my own stuff, but her last relationship was not good."

Chance sits up. "Who do we need to straighten up?"

I look at Chance and then over at Kamryn hoping she gives a name. I don't resort to violence, but anyone who hurts Jax deserves to be taught a lesson.

"He's a nobody. Just a waste of space who used my sister's connections to get seen."

"How long were they together?" Sophie asks.

Kamryn draws a design in the condensation on her glass. Possibly stalling telling us her sister's business. "Three years too long. But they were more off than on. It was toxic."

I bite my tongue and silently do the math. What happened in the three years after college? Surely I could look everything up, thanks to modern technology, but that seems way too intrusive for a guy like me. No, I want to know about Jax the woman. Not what a generic internet search will tell me.

"Huh," Bryce chimes in. "Can we loop back to Natey?"

"Please, no." I groan and sit back in my chair.

"How long had you known her?" Bryce asks, ignoring me.

I look over at him and he cheeses in return. I lift my hat off my head to stall and resituate it. "We met on the first day of college."

"Babies," Sophie coos.

"That is cute," Bryce agrees with an exaggerated nod of his head. "When did you tell her you had feelings for her?"

I sit back in my chair and look around at the group waiting for my answer. "Towards the end of our third year."

Thinking back to that time, had I just buried my feelings for her, leaving wouldn't have been as hard as it was. I mean, it still would have been hard. But then I wouldn't have had the bonus hardship of a relationship. I never went into our friendship with less than honorable intentions and if all we got to be were friends, I would have gladly accepted it for what it was. But even when Jax finally reciprocated my feelings, I still never rushed her.

"Why so long?" This question comes from Kamryn.

One thing my parents taught me was to always look someone in the eye. Not only as a form of respect but so that they knew you were speaking directly to them. So I turn my head to look at Kamryn and answer her question. "Because she saw what happened with her sister and best friend at the time. How confessing feelings at the wrong time can ruin any solid friendship."

I don't mean to spell out that the girl I'm talking about is Jax, but I can see when it clicks for her. Kamryn's entire demeanor changes. And it's as if she's gone into mama-bear mode to protect Jax, but also wanting to push her sister to happiness. I'm not sure which one I would prefer.

"Okay..." Bryce starts and then looks at the time. "It's getting late so I think it's time we wrap this up."

Wordlessly, I nod and am the first to get up from my chair to head inside to pay my tab. The only thing I'm looking forward to is heading home and getting ready for tomorrow's game.

"Good luck tomorrow," the owner says as I cash out.

I drop a $20 in the tip jar. "Thank you."

I don't bother saying goodbye to anyone else. So I push out the door onto the street hoping I can leave before I'm stopped.

"Hey!" A voice yells out to me moments later.

Fuck! Stopping, I turn and see Kamryn stomping her way over here.

"Nice try. We're not done talking. So you're going to take me to my car," she orders in the way Jax used to.

We hold our stare and it's clear she's not going to let up. "Fine. Where to?"

"My car is at Jax's place."

Because of course it is. I drop my head back and decide now is a good time to curse that we're in the same city. Cincinnati of all places.

Stepping back a few paces, I motion Kamryn to follow me. Silently, we walk up the short hill to my truck. And because I'm not a total douche, I open the door for her. Rounding the back, I exhale roughly before hopping in the driver's seat.

"You're her Nate," Kamryn says when I start up and give a swift nod. "I may not have been as attentive when I graduated college, but I still listened when my sister told me about this guy friend of hers. Which was not a lot, might I add. My sister is not as open as I am."

We hold eye contact until I force myself to look away. "Which way?" I finally ask before I pull into the street.

"She's at the other end. So take a right at the third street," she says and sits back in the passenger seat. "Wow. You really did a number on my sister."

I swallow through the lump in my throat. "I didn't mean to leave the way I did."

"You said your dad was sick?"

"Yeah."

"And how is he?"

I know Kamryn doesn't mean it in a rude way. "He passed away before I graduated."

The doctors could never figure out how or why a seemingly healthy, middle-aged man could pass away so fast. One minute he was going to his weekly appointments and the next he passed away in his sleep.

"I'm sorry. I can't imagine what that's like."

"Thank you." I say and flip the turn signal on and slow to turn. "You may think I left Jax and never thought of her.

But you'd be wrong. She's all I've thought about since I left. But I don't regret going home and spending those unknown final moments with my dad."

Kamryn is silent but instructs me to take another right. "I want to be mad at you. My sister–she helped me through my grief of losing Liam while still trying to get over you. But I also want to commend you for putting your family first. I guess that's one thing you and my sister have in common."

I glance over at Kamryn and see she's blinking away tears for what her sister went through. I never so much as looked at another girl my final semester. And when I got drafted, I focused on baseball. Meanwhile, Jax never left my mind.

"Turn right at the next street and then she's at the new builds." Kamryn instructs.

I do what she says and tighten my grip on my steering wheel. "I never got over her." I confess.

"Had your dad not gotten sick, do you think you two would be together?"

"Yes." I answer with zero hesitation and slow down once I get to the new townhomes and whistle. Jax is a complete stranger to me so I have no clue what she does for a job.

Had my dad not gotten sick, we would have graduated together. Those plans we made would have come true. I mean, who knows if Jax would have followed me to wherever I was drafted but I know we would have stayed together. She loves being around her family so she may have stayed home and just traveled to meet me where my games were being played. But I do know, in the depths of my soul, that she and I would be married by now. Maybe with a kid or two. The thing about futures is that to operate, they need wrenches. That's what happened with us. A wrench was thrown and I have no idea how to fix the damage.

Kamryn points to the last unit and I roll to a stop when I pullover. "My sister settled with her ex."

I look around her toward the front door and then at Kamryn. "What do you mean she settled?"

"Jax loves love. She always has. You probably know this. And I think she was constantly searching for what she had with you in other people. That led her to someone who was the complete opposite of you in every aspect."

"I didn't want that for her," I say and I realize my voice has come out tight.

"I can see that," she says and looks at me before looking out the front windshield. "In a perfect world–one where you and Jax can live in peace, would you be with her?"

I nod my head.

"Then fight for her. My sister is so used to being the one to fight for everybody else and for what she wants that now it's time for the roles to reverse. She needs someone to fight for her. And I think, just from being around you, that you're the person who's going to fight for her."

"How do I do that? She wouldn't even look at me," I speak and don't know if I accurately masked the hurt. While I know I hurt Jax. Her looking through me hurt even worse.

Kamryn unbuckles her seatbelt, lost in thought. "I was the same way when I got back together with my husband. Must be a familial trait because we wear our hurt like they're masks. Okay, she's going to hate me for telling you this, but she has a podcast, *Life Not Simplified*. You should give it a listen and see if you can reach her that way."

"Okay. Thank you," I tell her as she opens the door. Movement from behind the curtain in the front room shocks me.

"No. Thank you. Now I finally know a little more about

my sister." Kamryn hops down from the truck. "Hopefully, I'll see you around."

I lift my hand in goodbye and wait for her to walk inside. Before I pull off, I pull up the podcast app and type in Jax's channel. With over fifty episodes to choose from, I scroll to the bottom and press play. With one last glance at Jax's house, burning it into my memory where she lives, I look behind me and pull off to head home.

10

JAX

COLLEGE, SPRING SEMESTER-MAY,
JUNIOR YEAR

I hit the beat to the Phil Collins song with air drums as Nate lip syncs next to me in the driver's seat while we're at a stoplight. After I mauled him at the house, he dragged me away from the confines of the four walls I'd rather keep us in. Anywhere with him is a place I wanna be. Although, the place I would rather be is rolling around on my bed; I still don't understand his need for us to get out of the house.

When the song ends and the light turns green, Nate places a possessive hand on my exposed thigh. I curl my hand around his bicep and look at him unabashedly. He really is handsome so it's plagued me why he would want me. His rich brown skin is warmer from playing baseball and if I lift up his shirtsleeve I'll see a very defined tan line. Nate's jawline is peppered with the beginnings of a beard that he shaves off whenever possible and his nose has a little bit of a curve from a baseball that hit him when he was younger. But his eyes, which are framed with envious curled lashes, are my favorite part of him. They're a mix of my favorite shades of brown, but when he's in the outfield the grass pulls out the green that likes to stay hidden.

For so long I would only be able to get glimpses of him without making it obvious that I just wanted to stare at him. I'd get a flashes of his perfectly straight teeth that would show when his mouth would pull into a teasing grin on the off-chance that I wasn't quick enough to look away. But now I get the opportunity to look at him and not have to look away.

He was my Nate before. But now he's my Nate in every way that counts.

"What's got you smiling, Bee?" he asks, interrupting my thoughts about him.

"You."

When Nate first called me Bee, I was stumped. First of all, bees terrify me so I give them a wide berth when I'm outside. Secondly, nowhere in my name is there a 'B'. He told me that bees are all about the sweetness of the world and that as cheesy as it is, I bring that into his life.

"Prepare to have your cheeks hurtin', baby," Nate exclaims with glee and then swears under his breath. "I didn't mean it like that."

I can't stop the laugh from spilling out. The giggles overtake me until I'm huddled over trying to catch my breath. I feel the car sway as we turn and I will myself to sit back up and my laughter dies off when I see where we're at.

"How did you–"

"Your parents let me know how much you love it here and I thought we could spend the day and get lost," Nate says and pulls into a parking spot.

I undo my seatbelt and lean over the console once the car is in park. Nate stays perfectly still and I place my fingers under his chin, gently pulling him forward and flipping his hat off until we're a breath apart.

"This may be the sexiest thing you've ever done." My lips

brush against his as I speak and I don't miss the way his eyes heat or his breathing has changed. All traces of earlier humor have completely evaporated.

Nate licks his lips and I swallow roughly at the brief contact. "You've been keeping track?"

"Yes," I breathe.

"What else has caught your eyes?"

At this point I'm so close to him, only our noses are touching. But I inhale every breath he exhales and vice versa. No part of me wants out of this moment.

"Well for one, when you're studying," I begin and his eyes bore into mine, "you get this furrow in your brow and I just want to smooth it out."

"You can touch me whenever you want," Nate's voice takes on a desperate pull.

My other hand comes up and slides around his neck. It's one of the only other ways I can touch him in this cramped space. I'm about to close the last breath of space when a car honking scares us both and we fly back in our seats. I look over at Nate who's running his hands over his head and then putting his discarded hat back on.

"To be continued?" I ask to lighten the mood.

Nate takes my hand in his and kisses the back of it, making my heart flutter and soar. "You will be the death of me."

I smile obnoxiously as we climb out of the car. Nate rounds the back and waits for me with his hand outstretched and his camera around his neck. Linking our fingers together, we head off to the entrance.

"Tomorrow's the Championship game, right?"

"Supers and then the championship," he breathes out.

"You don't sound excited," I say with a hint of curiosity in my voice.

He unwinds our hands to pay for the tickets and then we're off through the turnstile. I can't wait to get lost in this place with Nate. But first I need to find out why he doesn't seem as excited.

"I am. But it could be my last game."

"What do you mean?" I ask and hold my hand out for him. My smile takes over my whole face when he holds the camera up and snaps a photo.

He takes my still out-stretched hand and then we're off. "On the way back, Coach asked about my plans for the future."

"I thought you were looking at internships?"

Nate has had his sights set on some of the top architecture firms in the country. While I know he would love to own his own company, he would need some serious financial backing and a fleshed out business plan for that to come true.

We stroll through the entrance of the gardens to the first exhibit. The flowers are in full bloom. Bees, butterflies, and birds flit around the flowers and through the sky. It's magnificent.

"I was—am. But Coach said it wouldn't be a bad idea if I looked into putting my name in for the draft."

I look at him with so much awe. I know how much he likes sticking to the plan of a job after college, but this is the professional league we're talking about.

"Bub, why do you seem so hesitant? This is great news, right?"

He drops my hand and pulls the camera up to his face again. I see him do some movements on the lens and adjust some settings before I hear the click of the shutter. I look and see his focal point is of a bee buzzing around some flowers.

"If I enter, with the possibility of getting drafted, I would miss our final year." Nate says it as if him being drafted is a done deal. But if I know him like I think I do, he's already in shutdown mode.

I give him a chance to find his words and take us into the butterfly house. Nate is in heaven as he snaps pictures of every available surface. I take the camera from his hands and ask a woman to take a picture of us. *Thank you*, I mouth to her and then hand the camera back to Nate who looks more comfortable behind a lens than in front of it.

I hold my hand out for him to grab once we leave the small area. "Come on."

His brow furrows but he does so without protest. I lead us over to a bench that's off to the side of the water show. Nate takes dozens of pictures from our spot and I know it's his way of avoiding talking. He's never been a big talker. I've always been the chatty one in our friendship and I've never minded it. But now I need his words more than anything.

"Hey." I start and stretch up to kiss him on the cheek. "Talk to me, bub. Where's your head at?"

"I have given it a quick thought. I mean what kid doesn't dream of playing professionally?" He grabs my legs and rests them over his lap. We're as close as we can get without me sitting on his lap. My hand falls on his that are on my legs and I rest the other one along his shoulders. "Say I enter and I get drafted. I leave you and my family."

"Is that why you're so unenthused? You're worried about me and your family?" I look at him with serious eyes and his slight nod is enough for me to continue. "I adore you more than you know for thinking about me. But your family would call you an idiot if you passed this chance up. And I would have to agree with them."

"I could always enter the draft next year. Fine tune my skills, condition more..."

I shake my head as firmly as possible. "Your skills don't need any fine tuning. If anything you have the best technique and natural ability of any baseball player I've seen in years."

"You're just saying that to get in my pants," he jokes.

"Nathan, this isn't funny."

He sobers quickly at my use of his full name and leans over to kiss my temple. "I know. Honestly, I would rather get my degree and then enter the draft."

"Then that's what you'll do. And when you sign your big contract you'll then draft up plans for the house we're gonna live in."

"Planning our future already, Bee?" He teases and holds the camera out selfie style, pulling me closer until we're smooshed together, he takes the picture.

"Yes. Because I am so certain that you are my future."

Since Nate and I said to hell with being just friends, my imagination ran wild and now I see him in every aspect of my future. I see more than just where we're at next year. I see us in ten years, married, maybe living in a city, with two kids and them running on the field after a game. Whether he sees a future in baseball or not, my future has him in it.

"Ditto, baby," he says and leans in, connecting our lips.

11

JAX
PRESENT DAY

The rumble of his truck fading in the distance as he drives down the street infuriates me. If I were a lesser person, I would make the same sound as his truck. But I don't. Okay, maybe my huffing in frustration is enough because it veers more to a growl than a huff. And when Kamryn shuts the door behind her, I pounce.

"Why didn't Sophie give you a ride home?" I ask harsher than intended. But I'm angry. And mad. And hurt at seeing him for the first time in almost eight years. He doesn't deserve to know where I live and my sister just gave him the roadmap.

My sister's eyebrows raise for battle and she crosses her arms over her chest. And I know, from the stance she's taken, that whatever it is he told her, she's about to turn right around and question me. "Why did it take him telling a story about the girl he had to leave in college for me to connect the dots that it was you?"

Fuck. "He told you?" I ask like a scared child.

"No. I mean, not outright. But I put the pieces together before we left the bar." She says softly and toes her shoes off before walking forward and sitting on my couch, patting the spot next to her. "J, how come you never told me about him? And I don't mean him as the guy you were dating. But why didn't you tell me about him as your friend?"

I shrug and begrudgingly move from my peeping Tom spot at the window and drop next to her. The cushions envelope me in a soft embrace and I run my fingers over the soft material. I use the material to bring me calm because if anything, speaking about my past with Nate will be anything but calm for me.

"I didn't know how to bring any of it up. Nate being my best friend and then my boyfriend." I start with a shrug. "You were states away for college. We weren't as close as you like to think, so to tell you about this friend of mine who's important to me, didn't seem necessary. And then you and Liam were finally happy which then turned into fighting all the time and coming to my big sister with boy troubles just seemed insignificant then."

"Hey." She scolds and grabs my hand. "Nothing about what is going on in your life is insignificant. Do you understand me? God, I kick myself for how far apart we were back then and I wish you would have come to me during that time."

How can she say that? From my end, the amount of tearful phone calls I got from her was enough to make me keep my issues to myself. So no. I couldn't have come to her when she was already drowning.

"You don't get it, Kam."

"Then explain it to me," she pleads desperately.

I stand up from the couch and pace. I pace and pace until Sully walks up to me, sensing my distress, and rests her head on my stomach, looking up at me. How do I explain that the nine months Nate and I spent together changed me? We had already mastered the friends part of our relationship. It was just a matter of mastering the love part and we did that with our whole hearts. Nine months is nothing to most people. But nine months was plenty of time for us to fall head over heels in love with each other and move the pieces for our future.

"When he told me he had feelings for me, I shut him down," I tell her and look at Kamryn who drops her chin in her hands. She scrutinizes me thoroughly and usually I don't mind her stare on me. But this time it's unnerving. It's like she's using the small amount of psych techniques she picked up on and is now using that on me. And I hate it.

"He said the girl he liked didn't want to be like her sister and ruin a friendship with feelings," Kamryn mumbles and looks up at me with mournful eyes.

"I didn't," I choke out. "Kam, seeing the way you were after Mason—especially, and Liam, that was the last thing I wanted for myself. Instead of embracing love, I was terrified of it after watching you sulk around the house heartbroken. And I always made sure to hold him at arm's length. I was a master at doing that. But no matter what, I could be having the best day or the worst day—he was always my Nate and that was the most consistent thing I could rely on."

One of the hardest things about having to forge your own path, is figuring out who to dig that path out with. When Kamryn went to college, I had to learn to stand on my own. Sure, I had Emily, but James went to college locally so she was as disconnected from high school as one could get. Slowly, I began to find me as Jax. And not me as Kamryn's sister. And then I met Nate. Well, more like I bulldozed my way into his life and he didn't push me away. But soon I began to find my way into adulthood with him by my side. We took turns digging out a path that was wide enough for us to walk side-by-side. I never would've guessed or planned for him or I to develop feelings for each other. Of course, my feelings were slower to form because I'm terrible at reading romantic signs. But Nate, his patience with me and how much he understood me, made his leaving that much harder to handle.

"Until he left," Kam finishes.

"Yeah. And I know you're probably kicking yourself for not stepping in, because that's what older siblings do when they realize their younger sibling was hurting. But I needed to crawl out of the hole on my own."

For the most part I'm as independent as one can be. But there are times when I need someone else to depend on. There are times when the loneliness is *too much* loneliness and I need someone by my side. Someone else to carry the weight of the heaviness and loneliness of living in a world where you were completely lost. I always thought Nate was that person until I became too dependent on him. And I was right back to being lonely.

"And then Trent entered the picture," Kam surmises.

I groan and drop onto the floor with Sully moving to lay her head in my lap. "It's weird that as soon as I buffed and shined myself after the dirt of that hole I was in and the loneliness was a thing of the past, he came along and slowly scuffed me back up. But, hey. At least I was no longer lonely."

"So why did you–" Kamryn looks like she struggles to find the word when that's never been her issue before.

"Stay?" I ask and my voice cracks on that small, yet impactful, word. There are several reasons why some choose to stay in, unbeknownst to them, toxic or abusive relationships. For me, it was comfort and maybe I was a little terrified of what would happen if I broke up with him.

I was terrified for myself because I was once again dependent on someone to help make me whole. So yes, I was comfortable with Trent. But I was also fearful of what he would do if one more person crossed him and I didn't want to be in that destructive path.

"Yeah," my sister whispers.

"I was just clinging to anyone who helped keep me out of that hole I found myself in. And if I got scuffed along the way I could deal with it. Now, I realize how unhealthy that was."

Sully nuzzles my hand for more pets and I give her just that.

"And where do you stand now?"

"On what?"

"Love," Kam starts, "you used to be the biggest believer. But, I'm scared that both men have tainted your idea of it."

I look at my sister and roll my head to the side. I smile a smile that doesn't reach my eyes as I feel the familiar burn of tears stinging in my eyes. "I still believe in love. That moment when it all clicks into place. But I think my heart is just too bruised to even think about letting someone in."

Valentine's Day...as cheesy as the Hallmark Holiday is, is one of my favorite days. It's the one day where love is the main focus. Sure, telling your partner you love them every day should be the norm. You don't need an excuse to bring them flowers or take them out for a fancy dinner. But for some inexplicable reason, Valentine's Day ensures that those you love know that you love them.

"Hold on the fact that you're still willing to let someone in despite being burned." Kam says and stands up from the couch, heading back to her shoes.

I give her a puzzled look. "What do you mean?"

"He didn't want to leave college–you."

With those words she shakes the foundation that I believed in. From my point of view he made it seem like leaving was the easiest thing he could have done. Just one text and that was that. But with Kamryn saying this, I no longer know what I'm supposed to believe.

"What are you saying?"

Kamryn stands back up after tying her last shoe and gives me her undivided attention. "I can't tell you anymore than that. But I remember you during that time, J. I may have shut everyone out, but I remember. And I think you should hear him out. Because I like who you are now. I like getting to know my sister again. And I think Nate can make that permanent."

I stay seated with my dog softly snoring in my lap as my sister heads home to her husband. I want that. Not my sister's husband. But someone to go and come home to. I see what Kamryn, Emily, and Sarah have and I wonder if I'll have that. I know that I *can* have that. But has my time run out to get my happily ever after? Has my luck on love run out?

I have so much to be grateful for. I have a job. A place to live. A place to sleep. But in dropping Trent and seeing Nate again, my heart is at war. Do I run back into the arms of someone that made me dependent on their company? Or do I do everything in my power to continue building a life that I can be proud of, alone?

The black and white of the two choices: dependent or independent, sound loud in my ears.

Which one do I choose? Is there a way to have them both?

I bury my face in Sully's fur and cry because for the first time in my life, I have no clue the direction my personal life will go. And Nate reappearing threatens the uncertainty.

12

NATE

COLLEGE, SPRING SEMESTER - MAY,
JUNIOR YEAR

"Win this on three, boys!" Mike, our captain chants. "One, two, three...win this!"

One of the things I love most about baseball is the routine of it. I know my role and play it well. When the umpire calls for play, we run out to our positions to the roar of the crowd. In right field, I have an incredible vantage point. My focus is on the pitcher's mound, but on occasion my eyes will sweep over the stands and land on the girl who's holding a poster that says "Score for me number 21" with baseballs dotted around the empty space.

"Is this supposed to have a double-meaning?" I ask Jax when I come up behind her at the kitchen table.

It's long after her parents retired to bed for the night, so it's been us living in temporary domestic bliss.

She stands up from her bent over position and I wrap my arms around her waist. "If I say yes will you?"

Since we got home from the garden, Jax has made it known that she doesn't want me to wait for the perfect time despite me never having told her that's what I was doing. When thinking about taking our relationship to the next level, it makes me nervous. I want to cross that line with Jax, but I also want to make her first time good and memorable. I want our first time as a couple to be memorable.

"If I don't score, then what happens?"

"I guess I'd be okay with waiting," she relents with an over-dramatic sigh.

"Don't sound so sad, Bee." I tell her and kiss the side of her head. I look at the time on the stove and back at her poster. "Are you about done? I have to head to bed."

"Yeah. I'm just gonna soak these in water and I'll head up with you."

Not even two minutes later we're headed up the stairs on the opposite end of where her parent's bedroom is. It's a big house and I don't know why Jax insisted on staying in the dorms. The carpet in the hallway mutes our steps and her dog pops his head up from the window seat he made himself comfortable at.

"Are you nervous about tomorrow?" Jax asks and wrings her hands in front of her.

"Don't do that." I say and move into her space.

Her chest heaves as she tips her head back to meet my eyes. "Do what?"

"Make small talk when you want something else." The hem of her shirt brushes against the waistband of my shorts as I move an inch closer. This might be for both of us, but it's also for her. We can't go any further unless she tells me what she wants. "What. Do. You. Want?"

"Kiss me," she says so quietly. I raise a brow and silently push her for more. "On the mouth. And with tongue."

My cheeks twitch with a smile as I cup my hand around the back of her neck and tip her head back. Jax's eyes move like a pinball machine as she looks over every detail of my face as I do for her. From the freckles that have started to pop out on the bridge of her nose and cheeks, to the fluttering of her lashes, and to the small opening between her lips. I duck down and kiss one closed eyelid and then the other. Moving over her face like I'm outlining a constellation of stars. A breathy moan leaves her when I kiss the corner of her mouth and then the other. Her mouth opens in protest when I seal my lips to hers. Our tongues instantly tangle and I lift her into my arms and carry her into her room.

I sit on the cushioned bench she has at the foot of her bed and groan into the kiss when the feel of her hot center rolls over my erection. My hands roam over her body and under her shirt. Sliding into her hair and tugging on the strands. Pulling her closer as this kiss goes further than a quick goodnight kiss. Jax's hips roll over my erection and I know if I don't stop, then I'll say to hell with prepping her and take this all the way.

Breaking the kiss, I move to her jaw and pepper kisses there before trailing to her neck. My tongue flicks out and licks at her rapid heartbeat. It's as wild as mine and the signal I need to stop. I stop her hips from moving and take a deep breath.

"Nate," Jax groans.

"You're a minx, you know that?" It's rhetorical, but she smiles. I push back wayward curls and stand up, making sure her feet around solid footing. "Goodnight, Jaclyn."

"Goodnight, Nathan."

I shake my head and close her door before heading to mine and debate taking care of the situation before I go to bed. But I don't. With as much strength as I can muster, I pace in the guest room until my erection is no more and go about getting ready for bed.

. . .

I STIFLE a yawn and pound my glove as Felix, our pitcher, strikes out a batter. Two more and then the win is ours. I stay loose as he winds up for the next pitch, continuing to stay present in the game for the last couple of plays. The ball is hit to third, I move into position towards first for the backup and hear the thwack of the ball landing in the mitt. Brian, the centerfielder, and I do our two up signals to each other as I'm walking back into position. One more and then my girl and I can lay out by her pool for the rest of the day.

Making the decision to not enter the draft until next year wasn't a hard choice. In fact, it was the easiest choice I ever made. I get to finish school, be with my team for one more year, and build my relationship with Jax. I pop back into the game as the ball is sailed to home and I wait with bated breath to see if the ball is hit or missed.

It's hit to third on a rocket of a ground ball, fielding clean, and thrown to first for the final out. We did it. We rush the pitcher's mound as the umpire signals the game and dogpile in the middle of the field.

I black out during the trophy ceremony and from the noise of the crowd. This series was almost unwinnable at times. Our opponents were just as hungry for this win as we were. But we rallied every inning to stay on top. Once our last teammate gets his shirt on, the captains hold the trophy up and we move to the fence by the dugout and sing the school's fight song with those in the stands. I spot Jax singing and jumping with some of my teammates girl-friend's and seeing her joy sparks my joy.

I motion for Jax to join me at the gate and soon other family members and friends are joining in.

The security guard holds open the gate and then she's flying in my arms.

"That was insane!"

"Were you locked in the whole game?" I ask, even though I know the answer. Jax is probably a bigger fan of baseball than I am.

She jumps and pats my stomach as a way to get out her excitement. "Are you kidding? I went through two bags of sunflower seeds. I'm going to need to drink a gallon of water just to get the taste out of my mouth."

I laugh and pull her into my arms and kiss her on top of the head. "Thank you for being here."

"I love supporting you in anything you do." She says as she looks up at me. The sun has pinkened the top of her cheekbones making her look younger than her twenty-one years. And the light dusting of freckles that cover the bridge of her nose are no longer hard to ignore; it makes me want to just stare at her so I can count them all.

My name is called out and we look over at where the guys are huddled. I love my team, but I only want to celebrate with her. "I won't be long."

"Hey, I'm not going anywhere." Jax tells me and leans up to kiss me on the cheek before going to stand in the minimal shade by the dugout.

Her being here and today's game, makes me feel like a winner in more than one way. When I get back to my team they all dogpile on me for being whipped for the only girl I will ever love.

Woah. *Love*? I mean, I'm getting to that point. Or I've gotten to that point but haven't put a name to the feeling. Jax has always said it before we went from friends to more. But feeling love for someone in a non-friend way is big. It's huge. And not something that I'm taking lightly if what I feel for Jax goes beyond the casual like.

13

NATE

PRESENT DAY

I round the corner and huff as I push my body up the hill in the loop I've mapped out. It's a cloudless day in the city with smells from nearby grills firing up for dinner and cars traveling down the one way street to head home. I've passed the street to Jax's street four times in the last hour. And every time I tell myself to turn and just go to her house. When Kamryn directed me to her place, it hit me just how close we live to each other. We're close but also so far from the people we used to be.

As I was getting caught up on her recent episodes, it dawned on me how far she's come in her personal journey. Her voice went from unsure, like she was scared to say the words aloud, to confident, her voice steady and strong, and I'm wondering just how much damage her ex inflicted. And how much was it because of me? Deciding to end my run early, I finally turn down her street with hopes of catching her. All I want is to talk. To hear her voice in real time. If she yells at me I'll even take that. Because that last text I sent her plays on a constant loop and has sat heavy in the front of my mind for eight years. If I know Jax like I think I do, then it's sat in her mind too.

It seems luck is on my side as I'm running down the hill when I see Jax, with what looks like her dog, about to set out on a walk. *Thanks, Dad.* I pause her episode and slip my earbuds out and slow to a jog. I wipe off my brow with my shirt and tuck it back into the back of my shorts. I'm vain enough to hope that my shirtless torso gets her to listen to me. After all, she did love it when I took my shirt off.

I take advantage of the distance and trail my eyes over her. Jax was always who I thought I could never have. But now she's an irresistible type of woman that I want, but still think I can never have. Her legs are toned and kissed by the sun turning her skin a deep terracotta color, the top she's wearing shows slivers of her midriff all the way around, and the hat she's wearing keeps the sun out of her eyes while keeping her curls out of her face. My eighteen year old self would punch the air if he could see who I'm looking at now.

I pick up my speed and make my footfalls known as I smack them on the pavement. Jax moves to the side and looks over her shoulder, but does a double-take when she sees me. The scowl settling on her smooth face would make me laugh if we were on better terms. I keep a good distance between us as I slow down to walk beside her.

"Hey," I say as one of my first words to her that aren't around other people. *Hey?* I say to myself, horrified that I led with those three letters.

Jax ignores me, as to be expected and picks up her pace. But it's no match for me and I easily catch up to her with my long strides. I always imagined what the first words I said to her would be. I don't count the bar as me speaking to her as she ignored me like I was nothing more than last week's news. And despite me running through different scenarios through my head, I'm clearly failing if I can only manage one word. Maybe I underestimated just how angry she would be. During our time as friends, I can't recall a single time when Jax got angry at someone and maybe that's why I'm already striking out. Jax disarms me at every turn.

"Can we talk?" I ask and try reaching her that way. Jax was always a talker. It was one of the things I came to love about her. But with me abruptly leaving school, we never got to fully embrace that love the way we were supposed to. Jax's voice had the innate ability to soothe me when I didn't even know I needed it. So now I need to be the one to talk. And I'm terrible with words despite my years of media training. But Jax isn't the media. She's my Jax and she always has been. "I'm sorry, Jax. I am so fucking sorry for leaving you, us, the way that I did."

We stop at the crosswalk and I look over at her. Her jaw is clenched and she's blinking fast as if she's willing the angry tears away. That's what I never understood. Why do we cry when we're angry? Is it an alternative to keep from yelling when that's one of the more effective ways of getting your point across? Or is crying when angry a defense mechanism?

When the light flashes for us to cross, she does so without saying a word to me and I follow along like her second dog. If she needs me to get on my knees, I'll do so. Gladly. Bark? Sure. But I don't do any of that. I need her to hear me out. I want her to hear me out. Jax's steps are sure as we walk past a smaller park and to one of the larger ones with views of the water. Whether intentional or not, Jax leads us to where there are no other people and unhooks her dog from her leash and tosses a ball.

Small steps.

"You stayed for your Dad," are the first words she speaks directly to me and not around me. And her voice. God, I have missed the sound of her voice like I miss the sun and heat after days of snow and gray weather.

"I did," I tell her.

"And how is he?"

It's like a knife to the gut. When I left she really pushed me out of her mind. I can't blame her because if I were on the other end I would have too. But her not knowing, stings more than I want it to. "He passed away before I graduated."

I notice her head turn towards me and then she's looking up at me with eyes so full of pain for me, and maybe for herself.

"I'm sorry, Nate."

Those three words are enough to undo me. "Thank you."

Jax turns and takes the ball from her dog when she trots back over. Her jaw is still clenched and her breath is coming in pants through her nose. It seems to me like Jax hasn't been able to break and I don't want to be the cause of her pain.

"Can we start over?" I ask because if anything that's what I want us to do.

"I–" she clears her throat and tries again. "I don't know, Nate."

Her black lab trots back over and plops a foot away from us panting. I never thought of Jax getting a dog. I mean her family had a dog when she was growing up. But pets mean roots and Jax has always talked about wanting her life to be on the go. Helping companies in different cities and maybe other countries. Getting a pet means settling down in one space. Is that what she's done? Settled?

"I need you back in my life, Bee," I start and see her

flinch at the nickname I gave her and if I'm honest, it hurts saying it. Jax's chin trembles as she continues to avoid looking at me. And maybe it's for the best. Because if she were to look at me, I'd either crumble on the spot or skip the talk and kiss her like I used to. Like the way I've missed for the last eight years. It's all consuming. This need to have her back in my world. "There is no way we can forget the past. That's shaped us to who we are today. But if I'm in your life, even as a friend, then I will hold onto that. I can't make a promise that I'll always be here because, as you know, my promises break. What we had was..." I wrack my brain to find a word to describe what we were. The problem being that finding one word to describe us is far from simple. But Jax beats me to it.

"Everything. What we had was everything," Jax finishes and I see a tear trail down her cheek before she has the chance to swipe it away.

Everything.

Every fiber of my being wants to take her in my arms and let her fall apart. To let me be the one to catch her as she breaks. But Jax is tense. She doesn't trust me. She's like a Jenga tower one move away from crumbling. We barely know each other anymore. So despite my need to comfort her, I make the choice to stay still until I can no longer hold myself back and need to leave.

"Do you still have the same number?" I ask and hope she does because I've had it memorized for ten years.

She gives a nod of her head and I think that's all I'm going to get from her. I should be lucky to get anything.

"Okay." I say and put an earbud back in and start walking backwards. The bill of the hat she has on shades her teary eyes so I can't tell if she's looking at me or to the side of me. When I get a good enough distance from her, I turn and run back home.

Kamryn said to fight for Jax. But she never warned me that this fight could be unwinnable.

14

JAX

COLLEGE, SUMMER BEFORE SENIOR YEAR

"Come on, Jax baby. You're not gonna win this," Nate taunts as we play best out of five games of pool.

I chalk up my pool stick and round the table, finding the best spot to sink another striped ball. When I find the best spot to go, I get into position and line my stick up. My eyes flicker up to Nate and his eyes darken as my tank top gapes in the front revealing the skimpy lace bralette I'm wearing. Smiling to myself I rear the stick back a couple of times and hit the cue ball, watching as it hits the striped ball with a small tap and sinking it into the side pocket.

"Woo hoo!" I stand up and cheer with a dance as I round to the other side of the table. "What was that you were saying, Natey baby?"

Since baseball ended, we've been spending our time doing what most college students do when they don't have jobs: hanging around my parents house, playing pool, and letting the sun crisp us up. Nate is headed home for a couple of weeks and I'm dreading the silence around here. Kamryn's living with Liam so she's barely around and I don't have many friends from college that I can call up. Those that

I do hang out with are girlfriends of Nate's teammates, but those are proximity friendships and nothing substantial. Having no friends never bothered me until the possibility that Nate won't be here forever started to haunt me.

He sighs heavily and tilts his head down at me. "Don't be a sore winner, Bee."

"I haven't won yet," I gloat and find the spot where the eight ball is at. Determining my next move, I call it. "Eight ball, corner pocket." When the eight ball sinks in the pocket, I don't gloat, I don't cheer. I simply set my stick on the table and bit my lip on the inside as I watch Nate. His furrowed brow and narrowed gaze is on the pocket where the ball disappeared to. And when he realizes he can't will it back out so that I miss and he gets a chance, he sets his stick on the table with a sigh.

"This is what I get for challenging you."

"I'm so glad you're admitting defeat," I say with a smile.

"It's not my fault you have a whole arcade in your basement," Nate whines.

I smile and shrug. My parents had the basement finished a few years ago and throughout that time added all their favorite arcade games along with the pool table. It's one of the things that I'm hoping will keep me occupied until Nate comes back up here for school. On the other half of the room is a small theater that's slowly getting broken in with the movies we've been watching this past week.

Nate walks over to the small couch and pats the spot next to him. Gladly, I walk over to him and drape my legs over his when I drop on the cushion next to him.

"Are you ready to see your family?" I ask and gently squeeze around his neck, massaging the area until he relaxes.

"Yeah. Plus, my sister is begging for me to take her to the water park."

I smile just imagining them there and her dragging him all over the place. "Is it weird having a sibling so much younger than you?"

"It was at first. But now Kayla is like my small, broke bestie that tags along when I have errands to run," Nate says with a warm smile. "When we graduate next year, you're coming with me for a visit."

I nod fast. "Yes. And then you'll have two girls teaming up on you."

He drops his head back on the coach with a groan and a laugh mixed. "I take it back. You can't visit."

"No way!" I start and move my fingers to tickle his sides.

He squirms and holds my hands in place. "Mercy."

"I'll accept it," I relent. "So we're for sure planning for the future?" I ask, rounding back to that.

"Yes. And I hope that doesn't freak you out."

I bite my bottom lip and shake my head. "What about the draft?"

"That doesn't happen until mid-July. But I texted my high school coach and asked if he would work with me for a couple of days while I'm down there."

"I am happy you made this decision," I tell him because I don't think anyone has told him that.

"Me too."

Our eyes lock and so much passes between us. Nate's eyes lock on my lips and I have to remind myself to breathe. This summer, as short as it's been with him, between baseball and him heading back home, has been spent getting to know each other. As friends we never talked about the big things. But now that we're dating, we've let each other know our secrets and fears. Nate's fear is not living up to his parents expectations. Mine is fear of intimacy and failure. Which is probably why I'm still a virgin at twenty-one. I mean, I have no problem ogling Nate when he's shirtless. But acting on it more than what we've done by kissing, terrifies me.

"Come on," he says and breaks our stare. "Let's watch a movie."

I let out a breath and take his hand as he pulls me off the couch and towards the theatre. My parents went the opposite way in this room. While it's still dark, they opted out of the standard theatre seats and have three rows of couches with deep seats in their place. We've fallen asleep in here more times than usual because the cushions form to your body and pull you into a relaxed state.

Nate indulges me and picks out *Divergent* and turns the volume up to where the bass from the action scenes vibrate our chests. He manhandles me and sets me between his legs and wraps his arms around my waist and I rest my head back on his shoulder. The rise and fall of his chest relaxes parts of me I didn't know were tense. But now another part of me lights up.

For three months, Nate has said no. We've kissed and teased each other until I'm ready to burst. And times that he leaves me breathless, I try to relive the buildup by taking care of business myself. But after minutes, nothing. I'm tired of him taking us slow. I've been ready for the next step in our relationship for weeks. And if it's anything after our heated make out sessions, he's ready for more too.

I scoot around to get more comfortable and Nate stiffens. I wait for something from him. For him to tell me to stop. Or for him to ask if I'm okay. He seems to go back to the movie, so I scoot around again and this time I don't miss the hitch in his breath or the feel of him against my back.

"What are you doing, Jaclyn?" he breathes heavily into my ear.

"I'm getting comfortable," I reply coyly.

He snorts and pulls me closer to him. His arms drop from my waist and his hands land on my bare thighs. "Okay, same."

I gnash my teeth together and drop my head on his shoulder.

"Remember what we talked about?" he asks over the sound from the movie.

I wrack my brain to remember as his thumbs rub small circles on my inner thighs and manage a small nod. "Touch me."

"I am touching you," he responds in a smartass tone. "Be more specific."

I take one of his hands and place it over my shorts. "I want you to touch me here."

His hand reflexively curls and I swallow hard as the friction is enough to make my eyes roll shut. "Is this all you want?" Nate's voice takes on a huskier tone.

"No." I want to be bold, but I don't know how to voice what I want.

His other hand comes up and angles my head back to where we're looking at each other in the darkness of the room that's lit up by the occasional flashes of what's happening on the screen. "For this to work, I need you to be vocal and tell me what you want. Okay?"

I nod and take a breath. Holding his stare, I say, "I want you to make me come with your fingers."

Nate stills as if shocked that I said the words at all. His

nostrils flare and his fingers rub over the crease of my shorts. "Like this?"

"No," I whimper. "Pull down my shorts."

Nate swears and fumbles as he slips the button free and slides the short zipper down. My breath is coming in pants at someone seeing and feeling me for the first time. Granted, we are in the theatre that's mostly dark. But maybe it's the nervous anticipation of someone other than me touching myself that has me terrified and ready to shoot off like a rocket.

With my shorts off and legs spread, Nate hesitates. I take control and grab his hand, placing it where I want it most.

"Fuck, Bee," he groans as his fingers glide effortlessly through my center. "You're already soaked. Is this all for me?" His hand and fingers haven't moved. They're just resting on my center.

"Yes," I mewl. "Use your fingers and make me come, Nate. Please."

With his other hand he tips my head back again and drops his lips to mine as he runs his fingers through my slit again. My mouth parts on a gasp at the feeling and Nate takes advantage as he pushes a finger through my opening. I clench around the intrusion and he swallows down my moan. He adds another finger and my hips lift, searching for more but Nate pushes them back down with his free hand and rubs my clit with his thumb. The sensation of his fingers thrusting and his thumb rubbing my clit, has me breaking our kiss and throwing my head back on a silent gasp.

"Let me hear you, Bee. Tell me what feels good," Nate coaches as he teases and plays with me. It's almost laughable that he expects me to form full thoughts when he's doing this.

"That," I gasp. "And another finger." I'm writhing in his lap as that buildup I've never been able to reach is racing towards the finish line.

"Fuck," Nate whispers as he adds another finger.

I feel impossibly full as I try to ride Nate's fingers. He drops his legs and my knees fall open, spreading me even further for him.

"That's it. What else, Bee?" he grits out.

I feel his hard erection against my back and I try to move against it, but his fingers in my pussy keep me from doing anything else.

"My breasts," I whimper. "Touch them, please."

Nate's hand slides under my loose tank top and pulls down the flimsy bralette cup. His hand kneads at my breast and he kisses his way down my neck. I'm covered in Nate and it's the most glorious feeling.

"Baby, you feel so good. Taking my fingers like you've done it hundreds of times," Nate praises and I never thought I would like talking during this, but my body begs to differ. "God damn. Your pussy is squeezing the hell out of my fingers."

I throw my head back and try to close my legs as I feel myself racing towards the end. But Nate lays his legs over my spread ones and continues his thrusting.

"Nate," I cry out. Not sure why I'm crying out his name.

"You're close. Tell me what you need, Bee."

"Pinch my nipple," I tell him.

"Look at me, J. I want your eyes on me when you come for the first time," he orders and moves his fingers until he's rolling the stiff bud between his fingers.

My head falls back and our eyes meet. Molten lava to black obsidian. All it takes is a pinch of my clit and nipple and then I'm falling. Mouth agape as my first orgasm slams into me. Nate works me through it, stroking my inner walls until my legs fall lax.

His fingers leave my body and I watch in my lust-filled gaze as he brings them to his mouth, holding eye contact as he cleans them off. Popping his fingers free one by one.

Feeling brave, I lift up and fuse my mouth to his. The musky scent and taste of me on his tongue has me twisting in his hold, wanting to get closer. Wanting more.

Nate slows down the kiss and pulls back. And what I see–or what I think I see, leaves me speechless. He grabs one of the blankets that's hanging off the back of the couch and lays it over my exposed body.

My forehead scrunches, because this–I feel ready.

"You're still not ready for me, Bee. Baby steps," he tells me and challenges my thoughts.

I lay back in his arms with a huff and do my best to concentrate on the rest of the movie. His fingers travel up and down my arms in a soothing gesture. But Nate doesn't touch me the way I want for the rest of the night. And when morning comes, his bags and car are packed ready to go back home.

Standing with him next to the driver's side door, I refuse to let go. My arms are wrapped around his neck and his are wrapped around my waist. The early June sun is still rising and I wish I could hold onto him forever in this moment.

"Bee," he starts and I grip on tighter with his laugh rumbling his chest. "I'll be back in two weeks."

"I know," I pout.

He gently unwinds my arms from around his neck and I drop down from my tiptoes. "You're going to be the best return to college homecoming," he tells me.

"I know," I repeat.

Nate's smile at my response is blinding enough. He tips

my chin up and kisses me slowly, pulling away when I try to take it further. I drop my hands from his body and watch as he gets in his car and rolls the window down.

"Bye, Bee," he says after the car is started.

"Bye, Bub."

He drives away with a swoosh and I count down the days until he returns.

15

JAX

PRESENT DAY

The swoosh of an outgoing email fills my quiet office as I send off the three videos to my manager to look over and send off to the company I did some promotional work for. I've purposefully kept myself busy and avoided my phone for fear of what could be waiting for me if I unlock it.

It's been a week since running into Nate while out walking Sully. To say it's taken me the entirety of seven days to pick myself up off the floor would be an understatement.

I'd be lying to myself if I said seeing him in all his sweaty glory didn't do something to me. And that fuck ass gold chain he was wearing, made me want yank on it and pull his lips to mine. Trent never sparked that kind of reaction in my body like Nate did. Like I wanted to lose myself in him until we were forced to come up for air. He also wasn't built like Nate and I think that was another reason why I dated him. He was the polar opposite of Nate and at the time when I needed to move on with my life, I found I needed him. Trent was the artsy, sleep until noon, and smoke a pack of ciga-rettes a week type of guy and I needed that type of guy more than I needed someone like Nate.

Nate was, and from what I can tell, still is put together and confident and healthy.

But even while dating Trent, and after pushing him to the recesses of my mind—I still missed Nate like I was missing a limb. I missed what he added to my life. Forcing myself to move on from him took more strength than I gave myself credit for. Even more, forcing myself to finally stop thinking about him after three years felt like I was able to wake up one morning without the constant reminder of the ache he left behind.

And I have moved on. Or at least I thought I did until I saw him in his uniform.

I look out of my office window with the view of downtown just behind the row of homes on the back. Part of me wonders if Nate and the team are playing at home or if they're away. But then I chastise myself because I shouldn't care. I don't care. And I'll continue to tell myself that until it sticks.

I see my phone light up with a call from Kamryn. A tiny part of me wants to ignore her like she did to me all of those years ago. But that would be immature and I'm not grieving the loss of anyone like she was.

I swipe to answer and put it on speaker phone. "Hey."

"Hi, J," she says, and I can tell she was preparing for the worst.

"You don't need to call to check up on me," I tell her.

Kamryn breathes out a heavy sigh. "Yes I do."

I click my mouse on my screen and watch the transparent squares appear and then disappear when I lift my finger. I do that over and over. I think Kamryn is trying to make up for lost time, which in my opinion is a lost cause. "Well, I'm okay. So...job well done."

She snorts. "You can't get rid of us that easily."

"*Us?*"

"Yep. We have goodies for a girls night. So come open your door." She tells me and hangs up.

I stare at my darkened screen, wondering if it's actually my brain playing tricks on me until a persistent ringing of my doorbell and Sully's barking moves me into gear. I shush Sully as I shuffle to the door and whip it open.

There on my front steps are my sister, Emily, Sarah, and Sophie with Vera Bradley weekender bags stuffed to the brim and arms weighed down by food, alcohol, and pillows.

Standing to the side, I nod them in and shut the door as they make their way to the kitchen. Sully trots in front of me with her tail wagging and tongue lolling out of her mouth as she goes to join the girls. As soon as I walk in, a drink is pushed in my hands and music is playing from my TV.

"Spill the beans," someone, I'm assuming Emily, says.

I take a sip and move to the kitchen island, playing with the stem of my glass obviously stalling. "Nate and I knew each other in college. He was my great, big, first love that people talk about."

"What!?" Sophie screeches.

"My client Nate?" Sarah asks.

"Yeah."

A glass is set on the counter and a long exhale is let go.

"Okay, rewind. I'm so confused. How?"

"We met at eighteen and I gave him no choice but to become my best friend."

"I always thought assface was your first boyfriend," Sarah says thoughtfully.

I snort and take a healthy sip of the margarita that's less mix and more tequila. "Nope. Somehow in the three years we were friends, Nate confessed his crush and then after I pulled my head out of my butt, we were no longer just friends."

"Well what happened between then and now?" Emily asks.

"Yeah. You were so..." Sophie starts but stops to rethink her words because our friendship is still new.

"Cold?" I finish the sentence for her.

She cringes and then nods. "Yeah."

"Imagine you're twenty-one and planning to spend the rest of your life with someone, graduate college together, and go anywhere with them. But then they send you a seven-worded text just to drop off the face of the earth."

When I think back to that time, with how young I was and what we planned, I can see how foolish I was. How foolish we were. But when you're young you can't possibly think of anything derailing your plans. And when your plans don't flourish the way you hoped, you think it's the end of the world. You throw a fit until you finally get your way. But Nate, not coming back, made me feel abandoned in a way I had never felt before. I couldn't throw a fit and just get him back because I had no idea where he was.

"J, you know why though," Kamryn says softly.

"Yeah, I do. And if he explained that in his text, then I would have...we could have made it work," my voice cracks on those last handful of words.

I think that's why I'm more mad at Nate than anything. He never gave us the option to try. He never gave a reason for ending us.

"Men," Kamryn states and they all agree.

"Men that you all have wrapped around your perfectly manicured fingers," I point out the obvious but not in a jealous way. I'm happy for my friends and sister. Okay, maybe I'm also a little jealous.

"You could have one wrapped around your finger," Kam notes and plays with the tab of her can.

I glare at my sister for even suggesting that. In those years after Nate evaporated from my life, there was a small part of me that foolishly hoped he would reach out. And everyday he didn't that hope dwindled.

"So what are you going to do?" The question comes from Emily who's been naturally quiet.

"I don't know. Nothing?" My voice raises on the last word. Because I really don't know what I'm going to do where it comes to Nate. "I think he texted me the other day, but I've been too scared to look at my phone."

"Jaclyn!"

"What?"

"You haven't responded?!"

"Unbelievable!"

Comes from the four of them and I shrink in on myself.

"Where's your phone?" Sarah demands and pushes back from the kitchen island.

I point upstairs. "In my office."

"Hold on, how do you not know it's him?" Emily asks as Sarah huffs before charging up the stairs and I motion for us to head to the living room. The red heads stomping upstairs almost makes me laugh. I take a seat on the oversized chaise lounge and Sully joins before I'm even settled.

"Wait! Before we get into your dilemma, you know that Chance and I are having a joint bachelor and bachelorette party in Vegas and we decided that you all are invited." Sophie beams and dances in her seat.

"I'm not in a dilemma," I cry out.

Sarah feet bound back down the stairs and gets closer when I hear her huff. "Honey, you are so in a dilemma."

I look up to see her tapping on my phone and am close to scolding her when she turns her fiery gaze on me.

"Jax, he texted you last week. And I do know that this is his number because I have it memorized," Sarah says, upset for me that I left that detail out.

Would she throttle me if she knew I also have his number memorized? It's like ingrained in me and yes, I'm aware of how long it's been since he texted me. It was perfectly timed after the park. Texting Nate casually is one thing. But texting Nate after he obliterated my heart when I was twenty-two, well that's another thing. In my mind, I know the differences are glaring, but my heart refuses to let go of that pain.

"I deleted his number because it was too tempting for me to text someone who cut me out." I answer Emily.

I've looked at his message countless times until the screen blurred and when I went to respond to his simple, *hey*, I froze up. Can you be traumatized from texting someone? Because if that's the case, then that's what I am. But if I want to move forward and not associate texting Nate with doom, then I have to—at least for my sake, find a way to move past this.

16

NATE

COLLEGE, SUMMER BEFORE SENIOR YEAR

Bee: T-minus 4 days.

Me: You must really miss me.

Bee: You have no idea.

Me: I miss you too.

As fun as these two weeks have been, I am so ready to get back to Jax. I've seen my high school friends, went to a baseball game, conditioned with my old coach for three days straight, and played chauffeur for my little sister. But I'm ready to spend possibly my last free summer with the girl I'm falling head over heels for. My feelings for Jax aren't a surprise to me. I've known I more than liked her since that first kiss. But the feeling of love didn't slam into me until recently. Jax on the other hand, I think she's there too. I see it in the lingering glances and the touches that grasp before slowly falling away.

I'm flipping through the pictures she's sent of some

drawings she's completed and of butterflies and bees circulating her balcony when I hear my dad having a coughing fit. It doesn't end and I heave myself off the kitchen chair and go in search of him.

"Dad, are you okay?" I ask as I find him in his office.

He waves me away as he attempts to catch his breath. "I'm fine, Nathan. Just choked on my own spit."

"Do you want some water?"

He shakes his head and sits back in his chair. The hinges squeak as he tests its movement. But it's the one consistent thing he's always done. Every day when he'd get home from work, he would journey to the office and clock in for a few more loose ends he was unable to tie up at work. And every day, whether I'd just be getting home from practice or as I sat at the kitchen table doing homework, those hinges squeaking became an essential soundtrack in this home.

Listening to my dad, I shake off my concern and turn to head back out to the living room, but he stops me.

"How's Jax?"

We've never talked about girls. Mainly because I've never dated anyone worth introducing to my parents. And throughout high school, mainly my junior and senior years, I was at parties most weekends while they were raising my baby sister. I lost my virginity in the bathroom at a house party and kind of went from there with girls. Until I met Jax and stopped looking at other girls altogether.

But this—having a girl I'm madly obsessed with occupying large spaces of my brain, is new. And this. Talking about girls with my dad is new.

I backtrack my steps and take a seat on the gaudy printed loveseat to talk with my dad. "She's good. Ready for me to come back up there."

"I'm surprised she didn't join you."

I snort as I remember her not-so-subtle hints about joining me. "She wanted to, but didn't push. I figure next year I'll drag her down here."

"Next year, huh?" My dad asks and his dark brown, almost black, bushy eyebrows fly to his hairline.

"She said the same thing."

"Well, if anyone can make a relationship last, it's you. You've been obsessing–"

"I haven't been obsessing," I cut him off with a smile.

He chuckles and continues, "as I was saying, you've been obsessing over her for three years. You think your mother and I didn't notice every time you name dropped her?"

I lean back on the couch and scowl at my dad. "I didn't name drop her that much."

"The lies our son tells," I hear from my mom as she floats into the office and kisses my dad on the lips. She takes a seat in her matching office chair and slips her heels off. "Jax this, Jax that...we thought you would come down here with a ring on your finger."

I open my mouth to sass them, but stop when they let go of the laughter they were holding. Crossing my arms, I wait for them to stop. This is what I've been surrounded with for twenty-two years. Love and laughter have been the pillars of the Holloway household. It's how I want my future household to look.

My dad's coughing fit returns and my mom sobers up, rubbing her hand down his back until he calms back down. In this moment, I don't miss the tension that lines her face. My mom told me that kids don't need to worry about grown-up things until they're older. But now that I'm older I feel it's in my nature to know if something is happening. Especially with my parents. Because whether I'm a child, an adult, living at home, away at college, or married with kids, I'll always worry about my parents. Worrying about living a life without them in it, is something I find myself severely unprepared for.

"Dad, are you sure you're okay?" I ask again.

"I'm fine, Nate," he rasps and clears his throat. "When you get older you'll find it's easier to lose your voice after laughing."

"Okay," I say skeptically.

I watch my parents interact. How my mom hovers over my dad with worry covering every surface of her face and his nonchalance to his second coughing fit.

The truth is that we like to believe that our parents are invincible. That they'll live with us until it's time for us to pass together. But the startling realization that your parents are getting older and you can't do anything other than help- lessly watch is something that nobody prepares you for.

My mom meets my worried stare and gives me a reas- suring smile. Knowing I can't do anything, I wordlessly get up from the sofa and head back out to the kitchen. Some- thing is wrong, but knowing my parents they'll brush off my concern. Maybe they're right and I'm just overthinking. But something is gnawing at me that they're lying.

"Hey, Nate?" My little sister Kayla asks from the couch.

I turn and face her. "Yeah, munchkin?"

"Can we go get ice cream?"

Shaking my head with a smile, because since I've been home, we've had ice cream just about every day. Sometimes twice. I'm not complaining though because it's been hot at the beach and the small businesses make some of the best ice cream.

I walk to the bowl that holds the car keys and find mine. "Let's go."

Kayla scrambles off the couch and runs to get her shoes on. I pop my head back into the office and see my parents with their heads together having what looks like an intense conversation. They didn't notice me so I back out and knock on the wall to alert them.

"Hey, I'm taking Kayla out for dinner and then ice cream." I tell them as I pop my head back in.

My mom looks at me with clouded eyes and a bright smile. A dichotomy if I ever saw one. "Okay, sweetheart."

Again, I ignore the weird feeling I'm getting from them and head out to the car. Kayla hops in the backseat and I wait to hear the seatbelt click before pulling off. I drive the familiar path to the diner I loved coming to as a kid. It's nothing too special, but it's cheap and, next to fair food and baseball stadium food, they have the best hot dogs. Thinking back to when I left Jax, I could have brought her with me. I should have brought her with me. My friends hounded me about my girlfriend and it would've been a good opportunity for her to blend in with my family. But in order for us to work, we need time apart. And let's be real, this will prepare us for next year.

Finding a parking spot, I get out and open Kayla's door. She grabs my hand as we cross the busy path and shuffle inside. The cooks instruct us to find an empty table and Kayla picks one right in the middle.

"What are you getting?" I ask.

"Mmmm, maybe a hotdog and fries."

"Sounds like a plan," I tell her and when the waitress comes over I do just that.

I listen to my sister talk about whatever it is eleven year

olds are into these days and I listen intently. She carries our conversation and for that I'm thankful because I can't seem to find anything to say without wanting to scream that something's wrong. I've never been a suspicious person. But even I can't ignore how, whatever is happening with my parents, is bigger than they want to let on.

17

NATE

PRESENT DAY

Bryce screams as he's chased around the field by the youth group camp that's being held here this week. Even though we're in the thick of baseball season, we always find time to give back to the community. Our baseball camps have some of the biggest turnouts and seeing the kids chase Bryce reminds me of Kayla, although she's far from that age.

"So I learned something interesting this past week," Chance starts as he comes to stand next to me.

"What's that?"

"That you and a certain someone used to date. Or, how did Sophie put it? In looooovvvvvveeee," he exaggerates the last word and I shove him lightheartedly with his maniacal laughter turning the heads of some of the parents.

"How does she know?"

"My future wife and your ex are besties now. Plus, they had a girls night recently and apparently that's when the beans were spilled."

I'm not in the habit of clobbering my teammates, but Chance makes it so easy. Although knowing Jax talked about us, eases my worries that there may be hope for us yet.

"If you want my advice–" Chance starts.

"I really don't." I tell him and pull the brim of my hat down further, but he ignores me like I said nothing.

"Don't wait. I had a front row seat to what happened with Liam and Kamryn. The man was a wreck when he saw she moved on with Mason. Which, to be fair, Mason was a hot commodity in college, so I see why he acted out. But I don't want to see that happen with you on the off-chance that she does finally move on from her ex and you."

"Is there a point to your story?"

He slaps his hand down on my shoulder and I look at it before looking at him. "Yeah. Don't wait. Life is too short to not spend it with the one you love."

Chance walks away to help out the catchers while I stay posted up by the dugout. Since running into Jax a few weeks ago, I haven't stopped thinking about her. Granted, I haven't stopped thinking about her since I was eighteen; but this is different. I feel like I need her in a visceral way. Like once she finally gives me more than five minutes to talk to her, the puzzle pieces will click into place.

The rest of the day is spent helping the younger ones learn how to catch a ball in the outfield, how to throw to the cutoff, how to crow hop, and the best way to shield your eyes from the glaring sun. I laugh more than I have in years and it's a strange feeling that rattles in my chest. Like the muscles I used to laugh are squeaking as they're used for the first time in years.

Since my dad passed away, it's like I've been underwater. Sounds are not as clear, colors have lost their vibrancy, and life has not been as enjoyable. But after one hit of Jax, I feel myself about to break the tension as I finally come up for air.

I busy myself in picking up the equipment we used for today's drills and drop them in the trunk that's in the dugout.

"Before I forget," Chance starts as he, Bryce, and I walk off the field and towards the tunnel. "Soph and I are doing a joint bachelor and bachelorette party in Vegas once the season ends. Naturally, you two are invited."

"Why so soon?" Bryce asks.

"Because we get, what, like three months with no baseball before we're off to Spring Training? Even then we're not technically off. And then it's preseason."

Bryce and I nod our heads like it makes sense.

"We're in," I answer for the both of us. "When are you thinking?"

"The week after Thanksgiving."

"Sounds good," Bryce says.

We push out of the doors and to the parking lot. Saying our goodbyes, I hop in my truck and just sit. Thinking about my next move.

I SHOULDN'T BE HERE, I say to myself as I find myself in front of Jax's place. By listening to Chance in my battle to not wait, and Kamryn telling me to fight for her, I went to the store and bought the candies she likes. Or at least I hope she still likes them as I put them in a basket. If not, she can let them sit on her kitchen counter until they expire for all I care.

What Chance doesn't know is that I would blow through every red light to be with her. But Jax is holding onto her hurt like it's her lifeline and I'm the pit of snakes at the bottom. I turn off my truck, grab the basket and hop out. As I'm walking up the few feet of pavers to the front door, I hope she's home. I haven't seen any movement inside, but she could've seen me sitting at the curb and assume I'm a stalker.

Taking a breath, I ring the doorbell. To avoid the crushing realization that she might not be home, I turn and focus my gaze on her front entryway. To the pot of flowers that are reminiscent of those we awed over in college. With those, the fire that lights the match for us gives me hope. And my heart leaps to my throat when the door unlocks and flies open.

"Hi," I breathe out and swallow. I'm twenty-eight years old, the getting tongue-tied around pretty women should've stopped. But nope! Jax looked beautiful in anything and that hasn't changed even in an oversized shirt that hits her thighs and the sweatpants that look like they've seen better days.

"Hey," she says slowly and manages to keep her eyes on my face, unlike me who's taken in every little piece of her.

I hold out the basket for her, nearly tossing it in her direction. "I got this for you."

Her eyebrows scrunch but she tentatively takes the gift. "Thanks."

Her dog bodies past her and comes to greet me with its tail wagging and tongue falling out of its mouth. I drop down to my knees and greet it. "Hello, to you too. Your Mommy doesn't like me very much so I don't know what to call you."

Jax snorts but I keep my eyes on her dog. "Her name is Sully."

"Hi, Sully. Maybe you can put in a good word with your Mom because I'm quite positive that she and I are meant to be." I continue petting Sully and see Jax shuffle on her feet, realizing I've likely overstayed my welcome since I rang the doorbell. Standing up to my full height, I look at the girl who's had my heart for almost half of my life. "If I text you, will you respond?"

"Depends on what you text me," is what she responds.

Six words. I hold onto those six words like they were personally made for me.

"Noted. Enjoy the candy." I leave her standing in the doorway as I trot down the stairs and to my truck. When I glance over, she's eyeing me like I'm a stranger. And in a sense I am. But she is too.

The Jax I knew was full of warmth and radiated sunshine like the first day of summer. The Jax I'm seeing now is a partly cloudy day, where there are glimpses of the sunshine I *used* to see peek out. Now I want to get to know every new detail of Jax—every sunny and rainy day. And *if* I continue to play my cards right, maybe she'll let me in just enough to do that.

18

JAX

COLLEGE, SUMMER BEFORE SENIOR YEAR

I'm putting away the last of my clean laundry when I hear a car door slam shut. My heart leaps to my throat when I rush to the window seat at the top of the stairs and peek out the window to see Nate's car out front. Rushing down the stairs and out the front door, his bright smile greets me before I'm flying into his arms. My legs are around his waist and my face is buried in his neck soaking in the patchouli scent that always follows him around. I feel my body relax for the first time in two weeks. And to most, two weeks is nothing. But when you finally go from friends to more with the person who's been by your side for the last three years, two weeks away is too long.

"Hi, Bee," he says with his voice muffled.

"I missed you," I tell him and swallow down the tears that decided to creep out.

"I missed you too." We stay entwined on the street next to his car until Nate slowly bends and my legs loosen from around his waist before I drop down to the ground.

I back up as he grabs his bags out of the trunk and together we walk back into the house like an old married

116

couple. It's weird, as I say that, because most would run scared at that thought. But me? I've walked alongside Nate for three years and I don't see that ending anytime soon.

My black lab Jersey greets Nate when we come back inside. Apart from me and my dog, it's just been us since this morning.

I head back up the stairs with Nate trailing behind. Walking back into my room, I finish putting away my clothes when he comes in and drops on my bed. Once my bed is free from clothes, I join him and cuddle up next to his side. We lay like this, like it's the most natural thing in the world–his arm around my back and my leg thrown over his waist. Nate kisses the top of my head and I hold tighter to him.

"Where's your parents? Your sister?"

"They're on a group trip with some of their college friends. And Kamryn is...I actually don't know. I haven't talked to her much lately."

When my parents found out the trip coincided with my birthday, they were a breath away from cancelling. But with my insistence that they go and that I'll have another birthday they can make it up to me with, they flew off late last night. I can't even tell you what's going on with my sister and Liam. One day they're in love and the next they're fighting. I had hoped the best for them, but at this rate they'll be lucky to get through this summer unscathed.

"And they left you alone before your birthday?" Nate asks, confused.

"It's just a birthday. Plus, I knew you were coming back." I say and snuggle further into him with lightness in my voice.

"You did, did you?" Nate asks and shocks me by tickling me.

The problem with being friends for so long is that he knows where all of my ticklish spots are and he hits all of them. I do my best to scoot away from him, but he pulls me back and sits on my legs.

"Okay, okay," I breathe out through my laughter.

His hands position on my sides in warning before he's resting them on the bed and leaning down into my space. In the span of seconds, the air has changed and I'm more aware of the position we're in than ever before. I bring my hand up to his face and trace the angular features. My thumb brushes along his full bottom lip.

"Welcome back." I tell him before erasing the small inch of space between us and kissing him.

"Happy birthday, baby." Nate says as he moves and settles between my legs. His tongue licks at my bottom lip before he's sucking it into this mouth. I turn to jelly when he does that and my mouth parts on a whimper. He takes advantage and plunges his tongue into my mouth. I wrap a leg around his waist and revel in the feel of him pressing against my core. My hands roam over his body and I pull him into me. I tense in anticipation as his hands roam down my body.

Suddenly, he breaks the kiss and trails down my body. Laving kisses on my neck and licking at my collarbone. My breath comes in embarrassing pants as he slides his hands up my shirt. Nate's hands engulf my body as he places kisses on my stomach. He follows where his hands are, kissing a trail up my torso and licking the underside of my breasts. There's something sensual about his head being covered by my shirt as he teases me.

My hands claw at the comforter as Nate sucks a nipple into his mouth. He teases the tip with his tongue, flicking and tugging until I'm squirming underneath him. His other hand plays with the other nipple, twisting and pinching.

"Oh, God," I breathe out. I didn't know it was possible to make someone come like this. I didn't know my nipples were this sensitive.

Nate continues his ministrations until I'm quivering beneath him. He slowly releases me and kisses down my body and pops out from under my shirt with a smirk.

"That's one," he says and my eyebrows furrow.

"What...?"

"Do you remember what I told you?"

I try to think back to what he said months ago. But my brain is still three minutes behind and nothing is coming to the front. That is until Nate's thumbs rub circles on thighs.

"Yes." I tell him and hold his eye contact.

He bites back a smile and places a kiss on my t-shirt covered stomach. "For this to work, I need you to tell me what feels good."

I nod my head. "Okay."

Nate sits up on his knees and drags his hands to the waistband of my shorts. "May I?"

"Yes," I say, even though I'm beyond nervous. Him touching me with his fingers was one thing. But using his mouth? That sends my nerves into overdrive.

Nate drags my shorts down and I lift my hips before they're flying off my legs. He falls forward and kisses me thoroughly before he's sliding my shirt up. Giving my body attention until he's sliding back down the bed. Nate places kisses on my inner thighs, sliding up until he's moving to the other one. Driving me up and pulling me back.

"Nathan," I groan.

"Yes, Bee?" the cheeky bastard asks.

"Stop teasing me."

"Okay." He says and licks me from bottom to top.

I moan my approval as he teases me with small licks at my entrance and stiff licks against my clit. My hips swivel trying to chase the friction, something, anything that my body is craving.

"Spread your legs wider for me, baby." Nate says before he's diving in and making my hips lift off the bed. I feel his fingers enter me and his mouth plays with my clit. "What feels good?" he asks with the huskiest voice I've heard from him.

"That." I choke out as he flicks my clit with his tongue. "Definitely that," I whimper when he sucks it into his mouth. Mimicking the action of kissing me there. "Oh, God," I say as he pushes his fingers inside me again. "That feels so good."

"What else? Harder, faster, slower, softer?" He asks as he drops kisses on my thighs. "Less fingers, more fingers, tongue? You tell me, J."

"I liked what you were doing," I start.

"Liked?"

"Love what you were doing," I tell him and my breath catches as he drops his mouth back to my pussy. "And another finger." I say and gasp as he groans against me but adds a third finger and I feel deliciously full. "That. Oh, that feels so fucking good."

"You feel so fucking good, Bee," Nate praises.

He works my body and listens to my cues, licking and sucking, bringing my body closer and closer to the edge.

"Relax, baby," Nate instructs. "Let me make you feel good."

I blow out a breath and unclench my body. Nate begins to work my body like an instrument. Using his fingers and mouth to wrench my pleasure from me, my breathing comes in pants and my body coils ready to spring.

"Scream my name when you come, Bee."

Nate curls his fingers and my body is weak to the motion. I scream his name when I let go. His mouth stays fused to my pussy as my orgasm slams into me. My hand falls to the back of his head as I rub myself against his mouth for the friction. When my body falls from the high, I fall back onto the comforter and stare up at the ceiling boneless and breathless. Nate places a kiss on top of my mound and crawls up my body.

"Thank you." He says when he settles next to me and takes me into his arms.

"Shouldn't I be thanking you?"

"No. Thank you for letting me be the first you experience this with."

I place a kiss on his chest and lay back down. "The pleasure is all mine."

We fall into a fit of giggles. What I thought would be awkward silence, Nate makes me more at ease with him in my half-nakedness than anyone ever could. And if our need for each other continues, then maybe he'll stop planning and finally be my first.

That is if I don't die from sexual frustration.

19

JAX
PRESENT DAY

"I need those mock sketches by the end of the day," I hear my sister shout as I exit the elevator lift in a hurry.

One could say my sister is strict, but she just knows what she needs when she's working. I wave to some of her team and Olivia waves me into her office. Kamryn is hunched over her drawing desk and I know not to disturb her when she's working. I did that once and walked on eggshells for the rest of the day.

I drop on the couch and take my laptop out of my bag and power it up. Once a month, Kam and I have a one-on-one meeting to discuss trends in terms of marketing and how to weave it into promoting her designs. Every six months we meet to see if the traffic on her website has increased. And then once a year I give her website and social media pages a complete makeover to reflect what's to come. Because social media is like wading into the ocean. One second it's waves you can ride and the next there's no waves at all.

We like to find the happy medium so that current

customers stick around and new customers find a reason to give her brand a chance.

"Oh, I need a massage." Kam groans and comes to sit next to me on the couch. Our meetings don't usually last long unless I see a significant dip in traffic being driven to her sites.

"I'm sure your retired football husband would be happy to oblige." I say off-handedly as I tap away at the keyboard.

"Hmm. I bet he'll do more than that."

"Kamryn!" I whine.

She shoves me as best as she can while we're on the couch and laughs. "When you finally pull your head out of your butt with Nate you can gross me out."

I shake my head and pull up the back end of her site. The dream I had last night was the first time he made me come before my birthday. I woke up reaching for my vibrator and getting off in less than thirty seconds. A record if I do say so myself.

"What was that?" my ever observant sister asks.

"Nothing," I say quickly.

"Nuh uh," she starts and closes my laptop when I hold it up in her face. "We can talk about work after you tell me what got your face all twitchy."

"Twitchy?" I ask deflecting.

Kamryn snaps. "Focus. Now, spill."

"You're annoying." I say in an exaggerated groan and drop my head back. "Fine. He came by my house a couple of weeks ago and dropped off a basket of candy."

"Cute."

"He also said he would text me but I'm still waiting." I'm not sure why I sound sad about his lack of communication. Nate did tell me that his promises aren't something I should hold tight to. And he was right. But try telling my heart to not expect more than what he actually tells me.

"If he does text, are you actually going to text him back? You're all about patterns. At least that's what you told your listeners." Leave it to my sister to use my words against me.

"I hate that you hold me accountable." I tell her as I cut my eyes her way. "I wouldn't know what to say to him." I admit and sigh.

"A simple 'hey' never hurt anyone."

I give Kamryn a look because I'm not bold like that, but instead I say, "Maybe when I get home."

My sister shakes her head and allows me a pass, handing me my laptop back so we can get started. I show her the reports of where we're struggling to reach customers and where the customers seem to engage more and then where they drop off.

Working with my sister in the fashion world is not the path I saw myself on, but I am grateful for the doors it's opened up for me. But working on a sliding scale when it comes to social media trends proves that I can never get too comfortable because what might work one day, won't work that next week.

When I leave my sister's office, I have a few more freelance clients I have meetings with and by the time I drive myself home, I want nothing more than to pour myself the largest glass of red wine, order a pizza, and watch the sunset. I'm the typical cliched millennial and I refuse to change that pattern. But when I turn down my street, I see the familiar truck of the man from my past sitting at the curb. Parking in front of my garage, I look in my rearview mirror and see Nate standing at the end of my short driveway with his hands in the front pocket of his hoodie with his eyes trained on me.

Time has done Nathan Holloway extremely well.

I purposefully didn't look at him when he first reappeared. Because I would have ignored all of my anger and hurt, and folded on the spot. Now, with the sun setting and casting him in an ethereal glow, I can't deny that he got more handsome with age. If I thought Nate was big in college, that time has nothing on him now. It's like standing in front of a new man.

Even in a hoodie, I can tell he fills out every inch of the material. And those legs I refused to pay attention to when he was running that day he caught me and Sully, are encased in form fitting joggers. And I do mean form fitting.

New patterns, I tell myself and I blink as I lock my car doors, stepping out and rounding to the passenger side of my car.

"Hi." I greet as I meet him at the end of my car and tuck my hand on the straps of the bag on my shoulder.

"Hey, Bee."

God, that nickname falling from his lips. With Trent he never gave me one and I never bothered to give him one either. Because as much as I can admit it to myself, nicknames and pet names were always reserved for Nate. But maybe I was always one foot out with Trent and I just needed a reason to bring the other foot.

"What are you doing here?" I ask softly. It's not that I hate seeing him here. But Nate disarms me in the best and worst ways. He always has. And the years between us hasn't lessened that in the slightest.

His hands tuck back into the pocket of his hoodie and my eyes greedily follow the movements before I move back up to his face. He shrugs before looking off to the side and then back at me. "I wanted to see you."

Yeah. He definitely disarms me in the worst way.

I shift my bag on my shoulder and move from one foot to the other. "Have you been here long?" My question must shock him because his eyes widen just slightly before he's replying.

"About ten minutes. I rang your doorbell and only heard Sully barking."

"And you decided to wait around?" I ask, but not in an accusatory way. Any other guy would've left after no response. But not Nate. He's always been patient when it comes to me.

"Like I said. I wanted to see you. So I waited." He tells me. One brick falls down from the simplicity of his statement.

"I was in meetings all day." I tell him instead and move towards the front steps, but turn and look at him. "D-do you want to come inside?"

He tilts his head as he surveys me and is probably wondering if I'm joking. I'm not. But I am scared shitless about bringing him into my space and my life again. *Baby steps.*

"Only if you want me to."

I nod my head and turn towards the door. I hear the clacking of nails against the floors as I push the key into the lock.

"Hi, Sully girl," I greet when I walk inside.

She leaves me when she notices I'm not alone. I turn and bite my bottom lip to stop the smile from covering my face as she gives Nate all of her attention. When I adopted her, the shelter workers said she was fearful of men. But animals, as I've come to learn, are a great judge of character and with the way Sully gravitates towards Nate, that has to mean something. I slip off my heels and stifle a groan when my feet are no longer in an upright position and then set my bag on the entryway table. I head towards the kitchen, thinking I can't handle watching the man I've always loved, loving on the dog who practically saved me.

Heading to my wine fridge, I pull out a bottle of red. And as I'm reaching for a glass, a whistle from Nate spooks me.

"Nice place," he says as he continues to take in my home.

"Thank you. Do you want a glass?"

He furrows his brow and shakes his head. "No, thank you."

Right. He's in season. I nod and slide him one of the bottles of water I keep on my counter. I use the uncorking and pouring of my wine to avoid looking at him. When my glass is almost filled to the top I have no other reason to avoid him.

"I think I want to be friends. With you." I tell him and I move over to the kitchen island.

He regals me with those eyes that I have purposefully avoided. "You think?"

"Yes. We were friends before, right?" Friends is such a tame word to describe how we actually were with one another.

I don't miss the slight widening of his eyes because even Nate knows that calling us friends is too tame, but he recovers quickly.

"Yeah. Right. So, tell me, friend. What have you been up to?"

"I work with my sister on the marketing end. Plus, I dabble in the back end of her website to see where customers are clicking the most..."

His hand resting on mine stops me. "I didn't mean about your work, Jax."

"What do you mean?"

"I mean, what have you been up to and not through your work life?"

"I don't–" I break eye contact and look down at a spot on the kitchen counter before looking back up at Nate. "I don't really know how to answer that."

"Okay." He nods and takes a swallow from the bottle and I have to curl my toes in on themselves as I watch his throat bob. "How about the last six months?"

I take a healthy sip of wine and look past him towards the city skyline. "I have been rebuilding my life."

"What do you mean?" he asks, turning that question back on me.

"I guess restructuring my life would be the better word. Less depending on others and learning that I'm enough, that I can live on my own."

"Huh." Nate starts and takes another pull of water. I watch the way his throat bobs with each swallow and I have to forcibly drag my eyes away. Drinking water is not sexy. But it is Nate...so.

"What's with the 'huh'?"

He shakes his head and caps his bottle.

"No. If we're gonna do this friend thing, then it's only fair you tell me what you were going to say." I tell him and take a healthy swallow of wine.

"Are you sure?" he asks and I nod my head. "I always knew you didn't actually need me in your life."

I open my mouth to object because I needed him more than anything. "How can yo–"

"Jax, there's a difference between need and want. Needing means that you can't survive without it and wanting means that you can survive without it but you choose not to. So no, you didn't need me, but you wanted me in your life. And I wanted, still want, you in mine. As for the missing years, I wish I could understand how you felt you needed someone to make you feel like you were enough. Because you were always enough. For yourself, for me. When did that change?"

My forehead scrunches as I think about what he said. When *did* I need Trent to make me feel like I was enough? The silence surrounding us is weighted. What do I say after that? What *can* I say after that? As we sit in my kitchen, the truth is that I don't know when I needed someone like Trent to make me feel like I was enough so I can't answer Nate's question.

Nate pushes back his chair and disrupts the silence as I've said nothing for the past minute. When he stands to his full height, the only thing in my line of sight is his chest. A firm chest, but that's not my main focus. It's him. His body heat and patchouli scent I loved so much is dizzying to my wine-muddled brain. My body warms as he wraps a gentle hand around the side of my neck. I don't look up and he doesn't make any move to lift my head. I stay perfectly still as he leans down and presses a kiss to my forehead. And I almost whimper from a simple act. I never realized how starved I was for affection like this until he did this.

Nate rests his forehead against mine and if I thought my feelings for him were strong back then, they're nothing compared to right now as they come rushing back like a fastball to the plate.

"I think who you're becoming is exactly who you're meant to be," Nate says against my forehead and I could weep because his words have always been what I needed to hear in moments like this. But Nate has always had a beautiful way with words. It's something that I've been searching for for the last eight years. Turns out, maybe I just needed him.

We stand like this in my kitchen. My hands rest limp at my sides and his hand stays hooked around my neck with his forehead resting against mine. And if I were an irrational person, I would lift my chin and kiss him for the first time in almost eight years. I would lose myself to him in this moment. But I don't think he would allow that.

"Thank you." I tell him.

His thumb strokes along the pulse point in my neck and I know he can't ignore the racing. "You're welcome. I'm gonna head out."

Wordlessly I nod and follow him to the front door. And when he gets in his truck and drives away, do I finally take the deepest breath and let it out.

20

NATE

COLLEGE, OCTOBER, SENIOR YEAR

Jax slams the door to my dorm room and flops on my bed. Her shoes clonk onto the floor shortly after.

"Hi, Bee." I greet from my spot at the desk. Fall baseball season wrapped last week. So while I still have my workouts, they've been less strenuous. But bonus is that Jax and I have spent all of our free time together. My feelings for her still burn as bright as the moment I realized I had a crush on her.

"I can't wait to graduate," she groans.

I finish highlighting this section in my textbook and turn to face her. Her curly hair is splayed over my pillow and her sweatshirt rides up on her toned midriff. She is my dream woman. "And where would you go?"

"Anywhere you're at."

I smile as big as humanly possible and get up to move onto the bed. I crawl between her legs and rest my head on her chest with her hands instantly running down my back. If men could purr I would be doing that.

"Anywhere, huh? What if I'm in Alaska?"

Her hands stall their movement and I smile against her. "I'd rethink my stance on following you anywhere."

"So you'd leave me to freeze?"

"It's not cold all the time there."

"Just six months out of the year," I note.

"Exactly."

Silence falls over us as it normally does. It's not a we-ran-out-of-things-to-talk-about silence. In fact Jax and I can talk about anything under the sun. Well, she talks and I listen with a smile on my face. But we can also sit in the quiet and not feel the need to fill the quiet with noise. And that's good when some people refuse to stop talking.

"What would you want in your dream house?"

She gasps and drums her fingers on my back in excitement. "Are you starting your senior project?"

"I am." I say and pinch her side resulting in her to squirm. "Now tell me what you'd want."

"Oh that's easy." She tells me and goes back to rubbing my back. "An all-weather sunroom that overlooks a lake, that way we can see the seasons change from that one spot. A kitchen and dining room that's big enough to host our families and friends."

"We don't have a lot of friends," I say.

"We will when we're older. Now hush. This is my dream home." She says with a laugh and I can't help but chuckle.

I listen in comfort as she lists every room that's downstairs, because according to Jax we need a two-story house. But in listening to her list what she wants in her dream home, I'm also locking everything away for our future because I want this life with her.

"Oh, and a playroom."

"A playroom, huh?" The thought of kids never scared me. I love being an older brother. While most of my friends tolerated their younger siblings, I took every chance to be around Kayla. Now imagining kids with Jax makes me want a time machine so we can get to that part of our life faster.

"Mm hmm," is what she responds with. "But it won't be a playroom at first."

"Of course not," I go along. "What would it be?"

"An empty room, silly goose."

"Oh, pardon me. What about the second level?"

Jax describes in detail what she'd want the upstairs to have. The primary suite would be on one end of the house for privacy and because every house should have a spa-like bathroom and department store sized closet.

"Is it just our room on that level?" I tease.

"Nope. It would be a very big house. Speaking of, how many kids would you want? Hypothetically speaking."

I sit up and her eyes meet mine. I move next to her and prop my head on my closed fist, toying with the string of her hoodie. "Hypothetically, two or three. But knowing my luck I'd end up with four kids."

Jax's eyes widen to a comical size. "Four?"

"Your choice if you're able to carry them."

"How considerate of you." She says and turns into me.

I say nothing back as I survey her. The light smattering of freckles is spread on her button nose and tops of her cheeks with her wayward curls framing her perfect face.

God, I have it so bad.

"I like you a lot," I tell her.

"I like you a whole lot, too."

Leaning forward I press a kiss to her lips. Jax sighs as our lips touch and I bring my other hand up to cradle the side of her face. I let her lead and Jax leans into me, pushing me back on the bed and crawling over me. Her legs straddle my hips and my hands slide up her legs and rest on her waist.

Jax's tongue licks at my lower lip and I open, letting our tongues tangle. I push her hips down on my erection and I revel in the breathy whimper she lets out. She's tentative to move her body and I assist her by moving her back and forth.

"Nate," she whines as I roll my own hips up into her.

"Just relax, Bee. Do what feels good."

"I want to try," she starts and cuts herself off.

"Try what, Jax?" I ask and push her hair back.

"To pleasure you."

In any other situation, I would tease her for the furrow in her brow. But this? I've been all about focusing on her pleasure, that I never worried about myself. Because it never was about me. But Jax wanting to do this for me is making my brain empty.

"Bee, you don't need to."

"I know." She says and sits up, resting her full weight on my still hard erection. Because when the girl you're utterly obsessed with says she wants to pleasure you, all blood heads south and thoughts fly out the door. And it's clear she's fully aware of the effect she has on me. "But I want to. Please, Nate. I want you to teach me how to make you feel good."

"Fuck, Bee." I throw my head back and groan before abruptly sitting up and taking her mouth in a bruising kiss. Jax yelps before I take advantage, pushing my tongue into her mouth and I'm weaving my hands through the spiral tresses. I break the kiss and trail a path down her jaw and to her neck. Nipping and soothing the sting with a kiss.

"Is that a yes?"

"Yes. But we're gonna take this slow too." I tell her and back her up on my lap. Jax's arms rest on my shoulders and the look on her face is one of surety. "Okay. Pull down my sweats and take out my cock."

A blush covers her face as she looks at me before down to my pants. Jax's hands go to the waistband of my pants and tugs them down. My dick springs and bobs against my stomach. I'd find it amusing by the look on her face if I wasn't about to come from just a look.

I grab her hand in mine and bring it to my dick, wrapping her small hand around my length. "Grip it like this," I say through clenched teeth.

Her touch is feather-light as she moves up and down. "It's surprisingly soft."

I'd laugh if a very important piece of me wasn't in her hands. "What were you expecting? I ask and try to hold a simple conversation about the texture of my cock.

"I'm not sure," she muses. "But I like it."

"It likes you too."

Jax's touch gets firmer, the way I like it before she retreats and is back to the feather-light touches.

"Tighter," I instruct and her hand stalls. "Don't be afraid to grip it tighter."

"Like this?" Jax asks as her hand strokes me harder.

"That's it." I say and drop my head back on a groan. My hands bunch into the sheets as Jax pumps me in her hand. My eyes roll back when she swirls her thumb over the tip of me, smearing the pre-cum that's pooled at the top. "Fuck."

"Is that okay?" Jax's innocence shows through and it's the biggest turn-on.

"Yes, J, this is perfect. Use my cum to help your strokes." I breathe heavily through my nose as she does what I tell her.

"What else do I do?"

My head falls forward and I meet her eyes. "This is perfect, Bee."

Jax uses my cum to ease her strokes. Fast and slow and every time she twists the tip of my dick with her hand my balls retreat.

"I'm gonna come, Jax."

She keeps at it with her pace until I'm swearing her name. My cum shoots onto my stomach and all over her hand. And I groan as she continues to stroke me.

Ultra-sensitive to her touch, I stop her movements and pull her hand away then look down at the mess. My first instinct is to look for my t-shirt or a tissue, but Jax surprises me once again as she licks my release off her hand. I wait for her reaction because a man's cum isn't what a lot of women like tasting.

"Salty," she tells me with a furrow in her brow.

"It can be."

She leans over and grabs a tissue and cleans me off. "How long are you going to deny me this?"

"Delayed gratification is worth it. Plus, I have one more lesson." I pull my pants up over my softening erection.

Jax's eyes widen. "Tell me."

"Nope."

"Not even if I take my top off and beg?" She asks and inches her hands to the hem of her sweatshirt.

Maybe. "Nope."

"Fine." She pouts and hands me my shirt.

With a chuckle, I put the shirt on and haul her back into my arms. "You're precious to me. And I don't want to rush any step because it's your first time."

"You've been preparing me for months."

"Bee, my fingers and dick are two different things."

"Doubtful," she says with a pout.

"Fine. You wanna go right now?" The color drains from her face and I lean forward and take her lips in a bruising kiss. "That's what I thought."

"You don't play fair."

"Me taking your virginity that you're willfully giving me is as fair as one can get. I don't know what it's like for girls, but it's easier for us; not painful."

Her body relaxes back in my arms and I drop us back to the bed. Jax nuzzles into me and places a kiss on my throat. For the rest of the night, she tells me of her house plans and I file every room, down to the tiny detail into a folder. Not just for school use, but for my future with her.

21

NATE

PRESENT DAY

I shut and lock my front door then drop my duffle by the stairs. The late afternoon light filters throughout the windows in my home casting a golden glow throughout the space. A lot of single baseball players would laugh at my buying a house. But the apartment life was never for me. I like my own space and not catering to others' rules. My home is my haven. And it's an architecture junkie's dream. It's all angles and smooth lines. And exactly the home I would have drawn up and had contracted to build if I had the time. So when my realtor sent me this listing, I put in my offer that day. Having a house this big when it's only me gets lonely. But it's my dream. For now at least.

I head to the kitchen to pull my steak out of the fridge. I've been in a mood and maybe it has to do with our losing streak. It's tough to get up everyday and play the game you love but not get the results you want. To not get the results your city expects. And to disappoint your fans. I love the game more than anything, but I wish we'd have something to show off for our success. But we only have a month left of the season and after that, I plan to use that time to train.

While my steak comes to room temperature, I start working on the sides. I'm constantly thinking about my next move, that when I have the downtime I don't know what to do with myself. So I usually cook to busy that part of my brain. I'm rinsing off the broccoli when my phone dings with a text and I almost drop the vegetables in the sink when I lean over and see who texted me.

Bee: Hi, friend.

Telling Jax it's okay for us to start again as friends was painful. And so necessary because I'd rather have her in my life as a friend than nothing at all. *Baby steps*, is what I've been telling myself for the last few months. It's taken us months to get to this stage. Which is a stark difference to how it was when we were younger.

When I first texted her after my run a handful of weeks ago, I expected a late response, not her completely ignoring me. And when I took candy to her house a few weeks ago, I was hoping for a little bit of communication. An ice breaker of sorts. But nothing. I'm guessing she has her reasons, but her lack of it still stings. I wipe my hands off and pick up my phone.

Me: Hey friend.

Me: How's the busy life?

Bee: Surprisingly not so busy. I'm caught up on all my work for the rest of the week, so I have nothing but time to twiddle my fingers.

I stare at my screen in shock that she replied that much. Maybe this is the way to get back into her life. Sometimes we can't speak what we mean, so we type it instead.

> Me: So, you have time to support your favorite baseball player at his games?

> Bee: He plays for Atlanta so I'm afraid that can't happen.

> Me: You're hilarious.

> Bee: I keep telling people that.

I laugh and then realize she can't hear me. My thumbs hover over my screen debating if I want to ask what I want to ask. *Fight for her*, is what rings through my head. Thank you, Kamryn.

> Me: Do you want to come keep me company?

The bubbles pop up and disappear. Over and over until my phone goes dark after five minutes. Maybe I pushed my luck. Pushed her. Brushing off her dismissal I get back to starting on my dinner, rinsing off potatoes and slicing them for fresh fries. I'm seasoning my steak when my phone dings.

> Bee: Can I bring ice cream?

> Me: Yes.

I send her my address and do a general overlook of my house. I have a cleaner come by once a month so nothing is out of place or messy. And it helps to keep my space tidy when I'm on the road most of the month or at the field from sunrise to sunset for practice or games.

I'm placing my steak on the griddle to cook when my doorbell rings. Suddenly I'm nervous. Like I'm seeing her for the first time. And in this case it is like seeing her for the first time. She's in my space and I'm suddenly more nervous than being up to bat with bases loaded, two out, the strike not in my favor, and the other team is up in the score. I wipe my hands on the dish towel again and make sure my burners on the stove are off or on low before walking to the door.

I pull open the heavy door and smile at my visitor. Curly hair in beautiful spirals frame her face and fall down her back and dressed in jeans with holes on the knees, an over-sized graphic short sleeve tee with a long sleeve underneath, and worn-in Doc Martens, is Jax. Her casual attire blows me away. I'm not sure what or how much I expected her to change in the years we were apart. But it's good to know this side of her, the one who wears graphic tees like they're all that's available at the store, still exists. I'll admit that I loved seeing her in her work attire of heels and pressed pants. But Jax dressed down is my favorite.

"Come in." I tell her and step to the side.

Her jasmine and vanilla scent I loved so much in college, and is such a contradiction to what she wears, follows her into my house. "Wow."

I close the door and turn to meet her. But her stare is everywhere, not staying on one spot. It's like she's getting to know me when we've barely scratched the surface.

"Nate, your home is beautiful."

"Thank you." I tell her and move past her to head back to the kitchen. "Have you had dinner?"

"Uh, no?"

"Are you confused by that?" I ask and pop an eyebrow in her direction before I'm flipping the steak. It has a perfect sear and my mouth waters from the aroma alone.

She blushes having been caught in a pickle. "No. I mean I was just going to have ice cream for dinner."

"Don't be silly. I'll split my food with you and then you can split your ice cream with me." I tell her as a way to barter.

"Are you sure? Looks like you only made enough for one."

"Positive. I'll take your ice cream and pop it in the freezer." I hold my hand out and take the ice cream carton from her.

Our hands brush in the exchange and I look up to see her gaze unfocused. Once you crossed a line with someone, felt what we felt and the way we did, those feelings don't just stop. No, they only lay dormant because you're no longer together. But once you find yourself in their space again, those dormant feelings come rushing back. Sparked alive and refusing to dim.

Just this one brush of skin against skin with Jax has those feelings burning brighter than the sun on a cloudless day.

Jax clears her throat and crosses her arms over her chest, likely thrown off kilter the way I am from that simple touch. I take that moment to put her ice cream in the freezer and let the cold air chill me before I move onto the food. The steak is a perfect medium so I remove it from the eye and place it on a tray to rest.

"You still like steak?" I ask and grab a carving knife before placing it on the counter.

"Is the sky blue?"

I snort, because I shouldn't have expected anything less. "Smartass."

The timer on the oven goes off signaling the broccoli and fries are done. I set those to the side and get out a couple of plates. I'm privy to my audience but don't want to make it obvious that I like her watching me.

Jax pushes away from the kitchen and does a slow walk-through of my living room. "Nathan, your house, I know I've said it's beautiful. But that's such a tame word. I bet your college-self is shitting his pants."

I let out a sigh mixed with a laugh because every dream I had, Jax was a part of. But this house is a mere stepping stone to where I really want to live. "That was the selling point."

I slice the steak into bite sized pieces and plate the rest of our food, then head to the dining table. The floor to ceiling windows allow us the view of the fading sunset and it's a stunning sight. How the purples and blues push away the lightness of the oranges and yellows from the day as the sun dips below the horizon. Movement in my peripheral, signals that Jax has made her way over to the table.

"Here." I tell her and pull out her chair.

"Thanks."

"Of course."

I try not to let my nerves show that she's sitting right next to me. Which is a stark difference from when we first sat next to each other. I head back to the kitchen to grab us silverware and we eat in mostly comfortable silence.

"This is really good," Jax tells me. "You'd give my friends' boyfriends a run for their money."

"Tell me about them."

She wipes her mouth and sits back in her chair. "Emily is soft-spoken but loyal to a fault. We lived in the same apartment complex for a while before she moved in with her boyfriend. We're not as close as her and Kamryn, but she's still someone I can talk to when I want an unbiased opinion. Sarah is out-spoken and also loyal to a fault. She's a kickass publicist and she's one of the people who pushed for me to leave my ex."

"Wait. Sarah? Like my publicist, Sarah Callahan?"

She wipes her mouth on her napkin and places it on the table. "Huh. She did say that she had a baseball player on her client list. Did I forget to mention we're friends?"

"It must have slipped your mind," I admit and then shake my head. "Small world."

"You have no idea."

"Well, it sounds like you have a good circle," I note.

"They're the best." She says and takes a sip of water. "I'm also getting my sister as a best friend so that's also a bonus."

I'm glad you have your sister," I tell her.

"Me too. So what about you? What are your friends like?"

"Would you believe me if I said I don't have a lot of friends?"

Jax looks at me with her head tilted, but I shovel the rest of my food in my mouth. We both finish at the same time and push our plates away from us.

"No. I don't believe that for a second. What about your friends from high school?" Jax asks, coming back to my comment.

"Kind of hard to keep friends when you're away at college, your dad dies, and then you get drafted by the major league."

"Nate..." she begins but I shake her off.

"I don't want your pity, Jax."

"Good," she says and places her hand on my arm. "Because you're not gonna get it. I don't know what it's like to lose a parent and I am so deeply sorry that I didn't know about your dad."

"I pushed you out of my life. So there's no way you would have known." It does sting and makes me a bit narcissistic that she never looked me up. If she had she would have seen how fast everything fell apart those few months I was at home. Because I know Jax would have dropped everything to travel to Virginia to help me and my family out. That's the type of person she is.

"You really want to do this now?" She asks with a sigh and I don't miss the tight tremble in her voice.

"If not now, when?" I ask back and sit back in my chair. The motion pulls my arm out from under her hand and I want to sit back up and put her hand back in that spot just to feel her warmth.

Jax looks at the hand still resting on the table, then mirrors my pose and sits back in her chair, meeting my gaze with fierce determination. "Okay. Why?"

"I didn't want you to have more than you needed to on your plate." I tell her.

"That wasn't your decision to make, Nathan," her voice is hard and I flinch at her usage of my full name in this tone. "Did that year before not teach or show you anything? I would've been there for you."

I shake my head because that's exactly what I didn't want. "Do you know what it's like to go home and see your parent collapsed on the floor for God knows how long? Do you know what it's like to go to the hospital looking for answers, just for the doctor to say the tests were inconclusive? Because I do, Jax."

She mumbles something under her breath, but it's too low that I can't hear her over the thundering sound of my heart.

"What?"

"For better or worse. That's what you told me."

"Yeah, well, we weren't married so that doesn't apply to us," I spit.

Jax's body stiffens and I realize I said words that I can't

take back. The silence is thick. And not in a good way. The silence is thick enough to suffocate me. But I can't take those words back. For better or worse was what we started saying soon after we made us official because we knew we were forever for each other. Who knew that those words would be my downfall.

She stands up from her chair and takes her plate to the kitchen. I follow closely behind with my plate in-hand and feel like an absolute douche-canoe.

"Bee." I start and reach for her, but she moves out of my way at the last second.

"I would have said yes. I would have stayed with you." She says and rinses her plate off before setting it down in the sink and using the dish towel next to her to dry her hands off. Jax doesn't need to clarify what the yes was, because I know. I have those four words inked forever on my body.

I crowd her as I put my plate in the sink with hers. Jax's body freezes at the point of contact and I know I need to smooth things over. But no relationship, whether romantic or platonic, can go without stepping on the other's toes. This is an unfortunate truth I have to come to terms with. Better we do this now than later.

I hurt her. I can admit that to myself and one day, when we're not clouded by anger, I'll tell her. I broke her heart. But in turn, I also broke mine. And it's clear that as we've both moved on, we did a shit job at repairing the inner hurt. It's like we put a Band-Aid on a wound that needed to be stitched.

"I know you would have, Jax. But we both know we would have crashed and burned if we made that commitment so young."

She backs away from me as if my body is fire and she's ice. "So that's your reason. Run before it gets tough?"

"No, Jaclyn. I would have stayed with you and fought through the hell that was my life when I left Pennsylvania. I would have stayed with you and it would have ruined us."

"You are not a fortune teller, Nate!" She yells and pushes me. "You don't get to predict what the future will be and then save yourself from the pain. Life doesn't work like that." Jax continues to push me through it all as tears of anger fill her eyes. "Life is messy and hard and the only way people get through the messy and hard times is with someone by their side. You didn't give me a chance. You didn't give us a chance!"

Jax and I stare at each other in my kitchen. My defeat mixed with her anger and hurt over my choice is one I'll have to live with. Her chest is heaving and her eyes are wild with anger at me and unshed tears of sadness from what we could have been. I pushed Jax and I have to live with that.

After the standoff I swallow a few times before speaking. "What can I do to make us right?"

"I don't know."

We go back to staring at one another. So many words were said tonight but I can't find the right ones to string together. I can't find the ones to tell her how sorry I am. But words aren't enough for this. And in seconds I watch the fight leave Jax's body. It's like standing on the beach with the sun shining down on you and out of nowhere rain clouds take that light away.

She walks around me and heads for the door. But before she gets to the stairs, I say the words that might cut more than what I've already said.

"For better or worse, huh? I thought you meant them?"

Jax freezes on the spot but doesn't turn around to face

me. I watch her shoulders lift and fall as she breathes through her anger. Her head turns so I can only see her side profile. "I meant them. Did you?"

She flies down the steps and out the front door leaving me once again staring at where she was standing. It was like the first time seeing her all over again. Except this time we left with the heaviness of the last hour hanging around in my house.

Kamryn said I have to fight for her. But how long do I have to fight with her before our past is one we can no longer work through? How long do I have to fight before I throw in the towel? How hard do I have to prove that the words I tattooed on my body mean something? For better or worse are words you use in a marriage ceremony. But they were also the words we used to pledge our love to one another.

But after tonight, who knows if those words hold weight anymore. And suddenly the words I have branded on my body feel meaningless.

22

JAX

COLLEGE, NOVEMBER, SENIOR YEAR

Nate's body is dead weight on mine as I read the latest book in a trilogy I've been anxiously waiting for while he sleeps. What we must look like with a man almost a foot taller than me covering my body like a weighted blanket. I have an actual blanket thrown over us and with my balcony door wide open letting in the November air, I'm more comfortable than I've ever been.

We've been in different study groups for the last two weeks preparing for finals and with it finally being Thanksgiving break, we both have a chance to relax before our actual finals begin. But with Nate now firm on his decision to enter the draft, his workouts have been bumped up to two a day. So this moment, with him laying on me, is the first time we're able to spend uninterrupted time with each other without him having to run off to train.

I place a light kiss on his forehead and finish up this last chapter. I'm putting my book to the side when he stirs.

"Has anyone ever told you you're cute when you sleep?" I ask softly.

He makes a mumble of protest at me calling him 'cute' and burrows his face into the crook of my neck. "I'm so tired."

"I know. Just think–this is just a tiny taste of what you'll get when you're a super famous and successful baseball player."

Nate snorts. "I don't know about super famous. But definitely successful."

"Hmm." I hum and massage along his upper back. "Well, rest assured to know I'll have your poster on my wall."

"Just the one?"

"I think more than one of you on my wall would make me out to be a stalker?" I joke.

"A hot stalker," Nate corrects at the same time a knock on my door sounds.

The door creeps open and my mom pops her head in. "Dinner is ready if you two are hungry."

"Okay, we'll be down in a little bit, Mom." I tell her and she leaves with a knowing smile.

Nate and I make no immediate attempt to get up. I like laying with him like this. Where the world is silent and the moments are peaceful. It's just us.

"Okay." I start and begin to move from under him. "Let's head down."

Nate stops me and scoots his body up. "Kiss first."

"How can I resist?"

"You ca–" I cut him off and press my lips to his. I pull his bottom lip between my teeth and moan into him when his tongue slides into my mouth. Nate grinds himself against my center and it takes my breath away. He's been very diligent in his lessons and we've still yet to go all the way. But I want to. I've made that clear more times than I can count. The pain–I think I can manage, because soon that'll give way.

Nate hikes my leg over his arm and opens me up. He swallows my whimper as he brushes against my clit. My hands roam all over his body as I try to regain some power. But it's like we're in a dance. Where one gives and one takes. The power eventually comes back to me. I push back on him and he falls to the side before landing on his back. My legs fall on either side of his waist and I drop back down to kiss him. My hair curtains us as I lick into his mouth, claiming him as mine when his hands land on my waist and he pushes me down onto his stiff erection. My body stutters as I feel his full length from this angle. My hips move on their own as we continue to kiss. Devouring each other like this is our first and last time.

"Jax, Nate! Dinner!" My mom shouts from the stairs.

I break our kiss like we've been caught and push up on Nate's chest to catch my breath. It doesn't do well that I put my full weight on his cock and I watch Nate's eyes flare.

"Hungry?" I ask.

"Mm hmm. Just need a minute," he tells me.

I give him another kiss on the lips before rolling off him. My phone buzzes on my nightstand and I see it's a text from my sister.

> Kammy: Miss you.

> Me: I miss you!

> Me: You know you live like twenty minutes away.

> Kammy: I know. Things are weird with Liam.

> Me: All the more reason to come home.

> Me: But hopefully you two work it out.

I put my phone back on the charger when Nate slides off the bed. He's mostly composed himself and while the sweats are a good choice, they're definitely not ideal when you have a girlfriend who wants nothing more than to jump his bones. Well...bone.

"Don't look at me like that." He chastises and leads me to the door with his hands on my shoulders.

"Like what?"

"Like you want me to fuck you so hard you forget your name," he whispers into my ear and I stumble over one of Jersey's toys, because yes I do. Nate laughs and holds me up. "In due time, Bee."

"Will that be before I turn thirty?"

He smacks me on the butt and kisses me on the cheek. Nate leaves me without an answer when he hops down the stairs. *At least he's teaching me something*, I say to myself as I trail after him and to the kitchen to serve my plate. I'm especially grateful that my parents let him stay here during breaks. They were lax with Kamryn, so I didn't expect much pushback from them. But they surprised me my first year when they said I could have a friend from college stay here if they were from out of town. Guess they never expected that friend to be a boy.

My parent's boisterous laughter greets us as we walk into the kitchen. From day one they've been the prime example of the love that I want. They met in college, got engaged when they graduated, married two years later, and have been married for almost thirty years. That's what I want. And I feel like I'm close to getting it.

Nate and I fix our burgers and add fries to our plate

before joining my parents. My dad and Nate talk about the upcoming baseball season and I'm glad my dad has another person to talk about the sport with. His go-to was Liam, but with the way his future hasn't panned out the way he wanted, their talks have significantly decreased. I have to hand it to my dad for being emotionally aware of others' struggles. He doesn't push, but I know he was hurt when Liam stopped coming by for their monthly catch-up.

"Nate, are you ready for winter break?" My mom asks once we've all finished eating and can't find it in us to clean up.

"As ready as I'll ever be."

On the outside, I'm as happy as a clam that Nate is going home to spend time with family. On the inside, I'm selfish that I want him to stay here. When he gets back our time will be more limited. And while I know I'm with him for the long haul, I don't want to miss any more time with him.

"You're still entering the draft?" My dad asks with pride beaming behind his eyes.

"That's the plan."

After the sixth month of bringing Nate around, my parents got sick of him addressing them as Ma'am and Sir, despite it being a huge sign of respect. So now he calls them by their first names, speaks directly to them, or calls them Mom and Dad. Which if that's not the best sign of our future that they accept him calling them that, then I don't know what is.

A throat lightly clearing from across the table pulls my attention to my mom who's giving me a knowing smile. I haven't told her much about my feelings for Nate as I'm not as open about my relationship like my sister is. But from the look she's giving me, I know she knows how I feel. It's strange that Nate and I haven't uttered those three words.

But we haven't needed to as with every look, every touch, and every moment spent together has said more than those words needed to. My mom announces that it's getting late and I volunteer us to clean up.

"I wash, you dry?" I ask Nate as I turn towards him before standing up. I gather my moms dishes while Nate gathers my dads.

I turn the water on to hot and get to washing. Nate and I work as a well-oiled machine to get everything cleaned and wiped down.

"You're quiet." He notes and hands me the dish towel to dry my hands.

"I love you." I blurt out and meet his brown eyes unashamedly. "I know we haven't said it, because personally, I don't think we've needed to. But I love you."

Nate stands in front of me speechless until a smile blooms on his angular face. "I love you too, Bee." He frames my face and angles it up so we're eye-to-eye. "Will you tell me why you were so quiet?"

"Because I'm scared," I admit.

Nate shocks me by picking me up and putting me on the counter. He steps in between my thighs and gives me his full, undivided attention. "Scared of what, J?"

"Of saying those words. I've loved you as a friend for longer than us being a couple." I say and fiddle with the strings of his hoodie. "Plus, with baseball–"

"Hey, we'll make the long-distance, if that's what it comes to, work. I'm not losing you." He tells me and I feel his eyes all over my face.

"Okay."

"Now, if we're done down here, let's go to bed."

I nod and a smile curves my cheeks as Nate turns around

and taps his back. The silent message is clear and I climb onto his back.

"The air is so much clearer up here," I joke as he turns toward the stairs.

He snorts and easily walks up the stairs with me like a backpack. "It is a wonder how you can reach anything."

"That's why I picked you." I tease and kiss along his neck.

Sometimes it's laughable to see us standing next to each other. Nate's 6'2 towers over my 5'2, but the love we have for each other surpasses both of our heights.

Nate snorts. "Is that the only reason?"

"No. I also picked you because you're younger than me and will stay limber longer."

Nate laughs and drops me on my bed. "By two months ya goof. Doesn't quite make you a cougar."

I slide off the bed and trail after him with a laugh to the bathroom and we go through a nightly routine to get ready for bed. Nate joins me moments later and we lay facing each other. My room is swathed in darkness, save for the moon that shines through a sliver in the blackout curtains. But my eyes adjust and I'm able to make out Nate looking at me with a soft smile on his face. Tonight I told him I love him and my heart hasn't stopped racing. Those three words are terrifying to tell someone, but knowing he feels the same way eases the nervous feeling.

"For better or worse, it's you and me Jax," Nate declares after moments of silence and us looking at each other.

My heart leaps at him saying those words and I reach out to trace his lips. "Those are–"

"Words you say in wedding vows? I know. It helps that I know there is no one else for me but you. So I say those four words and I'll always mean them."

Yep. I totally love him.

"For better or worse, it's you and me, Jax," Nate says.

"For better or worse." I tell him and close the few inches of space and press my lips to his. I don't take it further than this and he doesn't press. When I pull back, I curl into him and let his heartbeat lull me to sleep.

PODCAST

"Hi, everyone, it's Jax and I'm your host of *Life Not Simplified*. It's been a few months since I announced I was introducing new patterns into my life. If this is your first episode of mine, I don't mean bringing patterns into my wardrobe.

"I got into a rut. A huge rut caused bumps in my personal life. No matter what I would do I would find myself doing the same thing over and over. And I was just unfulfilled.

"So I challenged myself over the summer to do one thing a month, which turned into one new thing a week. I met a new friend at the dog park and I went to a baseball game. This is where I reverted back to my old ways. I saw someone from my past. Someone who took up a huge chunk of my heart when I was younger. You all may be thinking "I know where this is going" and I would tell you that you're way off base. It's hard for me to let people in. As open as I am to those in my life, I'm not as open to those who make a reappearance. And this person is on the receiving end of my frosty exterior.

"I don't know how the rest of this challenge will play out.

As soon as I uttered the words that I was doing this, I wanted to take them back. I *still* want to take them back. Because doing new things scares the shit out of me. But I see the messages and comments from you all that you've also challenged yourself to introduce new patterns to your routine. And I've never looked at myself as an influencer, but seeing that so many of you needed that push, is the reason why I can't and won't give up on this. No matter how hard I want to.

"This is unfortunately a short check-in episode and I hope you all enjoyed it. Four months of this new patterns challenge is done. I hope those of you who are participating, are finding new things that stick. And if you're terrified of starting right now, remember that there is no set date. I hope to catch up all on the next episode of *Life Not Simplified*. Bye, guys."

23

JAX

PRESENT DAY

y alarm goes off too early and I smack my hand over my phone with a groan. When I peel my eyes open, I see it's still dark out as evidenced by the sun not peaking through the edges of my blackout curtains. I stretch my cramped body and run into a solid lump at the foot of my bed. Sully yawning is how I've felt for the last few weeks.

Things were going well with Nate. I was slowly letting him back in and trying to move past the past. Until he wanted to dive into why he gave up on us and things were no longer going well. I get angry all over again as I remember him making the decision for me. For us. How dare he? I knew we would have to get ugly before we came out united and shiny. I knew that we would have to talk about the way he ended us. But I was so unprepared for the reaction he would bring out of me that I've been working non-stop for the last few weeks just to avoid thinking about him.

I punch my mattress as my alarm goes off for the second time. Turning it off, I fling the covers off me and head to the bathroom to get ready for my flight.

Am I dreading a long weekend in Vegas? No.

Am I dreading a long weekend in Vegas with my ex? Yes.

But this weekend is for Sophie and Chance. That's what I repeat to myself after I finish packing the last of my clothes and toiletries and I roll my suitcase down the stairs as I wait for Kamryn to pick me up.

Kammy: Here.

Me: Coming.

I hook Sully onto her leash and grab her food bag with a few toys before heading out to the car. The street is quiet, save for the car idling on the street. Mason gets out and grabs my suitcase while I let Sully into the backseat and slide in after her.

"Couldn't drive on your own, could you?" I joke with a yawn.

"Please," Kam starts as Mason gets back in the car. "He wouldn't let me anyways."

"You spoiled princess."

She throws a smirk over her shoulder as Mason drives us towards the airport. I've always loved the city at night and especially in the early morning. It's still in a way life never is. Of course, I'm rarely awake during those times so to see the city with sleepy eyes is a new experience. I quickly take out my phone and record a bit of the drive so that I can revisit this moment when life gets too busy. And when the familiar signs of the airport make itself known, I begin preparing myself for what's to come.

The rules of this trip are simple: get the earliest flight for more debauchery. Not my idea, but I can't deny that the happy couple has a point. It's so easy to get lost and caught up in the hype of Vegas. You drink too much, spend too much money, or God forbid you come home with a horrible tattoo. I for one, won't be participating in anything that follows me around.

We have the first flight of the day and I see a few other cars are here at the same time we are. The car in front of us opens and out comes the groom-to-be with his bride-to-be and his butt buddies. I straighten in my seat at seeing Nate unloading his things, along with Bryce and Chance's bags, from the Uber. Curse our timeliness to be early. But I can't deny that the idiot is fucking sexy as hell in joggers and a sweatshirt so I'm able to stare at him unabashedly.

Mason pulls forward and puts the car in park.

"Be good for Uncle Mason." I tell Sully and give her a kiss.

Kamryn and Mason snort at my reaction to saying goodbye.

"What!? Like you don't do the same to Lucy and Poppy." I say pointedly to Kamryn and climb out of the backseat but put the back window down before I shut the door.

"You two made it!" Chance bellows and rushes over, taking us in his arms.

"We wouldn't miss this," Kam tells him.

Sophie rushes over and tackles me in a hug like I haven't seen her in a year. Which to be fair, I haven't seen her in a while due to working as much as possible to avoid Nate. But from what I've seen on socials, they all do a lot of group outings when they have days off. Which is rare, but since the season ended they've all gotten closer and I've made so many excuses as to why I can't hang out with them. Over Sophie's shoulder, I see Nate watching us with a look that can only be described as wistful. And maybe a little bit of regret.

"Woah." I hear Sophie say and she pulls away from our

hug and moves a few steps away. "You're Mason Brooks." Chance laughs and comes up behind her.

"Guilty," he responds.

"I'm a huge fan," Sophie gushes.

I move back over to Mason's car and give Sully some pets behind her ear. It's not that I'm sad to leave her for the weekend. But I am nervous about how this weekend will go.

"Alright gang are we ready?" Chance asks after introductions are made and he's pulled a drooling Sophie away from my brother-in-law.

As we've all gathered off to the side at the front of the entrance to the airport, the sun has begun to rise and I conclude I need coffee as soon as possible.

Once we're all checked in, I make a beeline straight to a cafe. And when I take that first sip of caffeine, I close my eyes in caffeinated-bliss and my mind stops running. I head towards our gate to find a spot along the window and take a seat. Good thing about early flights is that it's relatively empty. Bad thing is that I have a lack of options to look at for people watching.

I look at my phone to mindlessly scroll and when I feel the seat next to me jostle, I assume it's Kamryn so I look up from my phone to look at her and the words fail to launch.

"Are you going to ignore me this whole trip?" Nate asks.

"Are you deciding that I should stop ignoring you? Or am I allowed to make that decision for myself?" I ask and I know I can't mask my anger.

"Bee." Nate starts and I look up to see him look around to make sure our friends aren't eavesdropping. "If I could go back in time I would. You have no idea how much I regret ending us over text. Making that decision for you...because if any guy did that to Kayla I would beat their face in."

I look blankly at my phone as he says this and it takes

everything in me to not cry. Unfortunately when I get angry, I cry. It's a character flaw that I deeply hate.

"What do you want me to say, Jax?" Nate asks pleadingly.

"It's not about what you say Nate. Because as you said, your promises, which are also your words, don't mean much. And you can say you're sorry until you're blue in the face. But it's your actions that hold more weight than your words ever could," my words come out as a whisper towards the end. We sit in silence. It seems to be our default setting as the world around us in the airport moves on. "Why didn't you come back to me?" I ask and feel the familiar stinging of tears as they threaten to make an appearance the more I speak.

His expression drops and Nate opens his mouth to respond, but the call to board our flight is made. I quickly stand up from my seat and pull up my ticket on my phone. I smile to the attendant and make my way down the breeze-way, tossing my empty coffee cup as I go.

"Hey." Kamryn says as she catches up with me. "I saw you and Nate talking. It looked tense."

"We got in a fight." I keep my voice low as I tell her.

"What? When?"

"Keep your voice down," I scold her and step in front of her as we go to step on the plane. I was comfortable with riding economy, but Kam upgraded us to First Class. And it seems everyone else was of the same thought process and when I sit in my seat, I see the rest of our group takes up the other seats. Kam sits next to me and we accept glasses of champagne despite it not even being eight in the morning.

"So tell me what happened," she whispers to me. Though it's not needed as the engines start and nothing can be heard over us as we take off.

"We got in a fight a few weeks ago about him making the choice to end us."

Kamryn's eyes widen and I know she's thinking of when Mason broke up with her in college. Although, the decision wasn't all his but he still went through with it. His college coach made him end their relationship to focus on getting drafted. When he and Kam got back together and she unloaded about her past with Liam, Mason spoke about what his college coach did to his NFL coach where he was told that was extremely unethical. We all knew it at the time, but who's going to take a college student's side over a decorated college football coach? So Mason eventually went to the board at their alma mater, after all those years, and outed his coach. Served the man right as it turns out that wasn't the first instance of that happening. Mason was just the first to finally speak up.

"Where does that leave you two now?"

I finish off my champagne and place it on the tray in front of me. "I don't know. Friends? People who know of each other? I told him his actions need to start backing up his words."

"Good for you, JJ." Kamryn praises me and finishes off her champagne as well.

"You don't think I'm being too unreasonable?" I ask my sister because as I've stewed in my anger and seen the devoid look on Nate's face, I'm starting to wonder if my anger is unjustified. Or if I'm being too unreasonable and too hard on him. But then I remember that we could have still been an *us* yet he made the choice to end it. So while I'm doubting that this anger is productive, it is exhausting.

"I think as women we're told that overreacting is dramatic, emotional, unnecessary. Or it makes us a bitch, callous, cold. But how many of those instances stemmed from someone causing us to react that way? So, no. I don't think you're overreacting. In fact, I think you're reacting with the right amount of anger and hurt. Because when someone hurts you, it's not up to them or anyone else to decide how you feel or when to get over it."

I let Kamryn's words sink in. And I realize that on top of being angry at Nate, I'm also hurt. He hurt me, my feelings specifically, and I don't think I've gotten over that. I don't know if I can. Because no amount of words or his actions that prove otherwise, can mask that hurt with a Band-Aid.

"How do you–" I clear my throat to push back the emotion. Through the crack of the seats, I see Nate looking our way and it's as if he can tell what I'm talking about by the furrow in his brows. "How do you move forward? I won't say our situation is the same." I tell my sister and I don't expand on our situation. "But how and when did you decide to let Mason back into your life?"

Kamryn blows out a breath that ruffles her lips as she gathers her thoughts. "I–I think I was just ready to let go of the years of hurt. I was in the same spot as you were where he never called once he was gone. He was just gone. Like disappeared into thin air, gone. I was hurt. But it was after celebrating another fashion week...oh I was angry at seeing him. Thinking he could just approach me, talk with me, and think that's it. But I also realized that I missed him more than I was angry at him."

"That was that?" I ask incredulously. Because if missing someone was all it took to have them back in my life, then Nate would have never left.

"No. I needed a little more work on myself before I decided to let him back in." Kamryn regards me carefully. "Speaking of–when was your last session?"

I look down at my fingers and pick at a non-existent scab. "A while ago."

I stopped going to therapy because I felt like I talked more about my life and feelings on my podcast than to my therapist. It's cathartic. But maybe there are some things where talking to no one can't solve and I need more help than I realize.

"JJ, maybe you need to make an appointment?"

"Yeah. I'll think about it." I tell her and sit back in the seat.

The rest of the flight I think and I think and I think until I'm ready to drink so much when we land that I forget what I'm thinking about. When we finally land and head to baggage claim, check in at the hotel and find our rooms, I'm ready to crash from all of the thinking.

24

NATE

The door to my hotel room slams shut with the typical boom and I shove the plastic card in my pocket as I stand in the middle of the room. It's a standard hotel room but with the classic Las Vegas flare. The bathroom is where they're typically placed, right by the front door and it has a nice walk-in shower and a good lighted mirror. The bed is a single king-sized bed with a dresser and TV on top of it, then you walk down two steps to get to the small living room area which has a massive bay window that looks over the city.

Orders from the bride and groom to be, were to rest up before dinner and hitting the strip. Because knowing how those two feed off one another's energy, we'll likely be out until the sun rises again. And after my tense talk with Jax and the flight where I knew she was hurting because of me, taking a nap is all I want to do. But a knock on my door sends my heart to my throat thinking that it's her. Checking the peephole, it's not the Rawlins sister that I expected, but the other Rawlins sister and I open the door.

"You idiot!" She shouts and shoves me back into my

room. Now I see where Jax gets it from. Because for their petite heights, they're freakishly strong. "Nate, I said fight for her! Not send her back to how she was with her ex. Rules out on which ex I'm referring to."

I wince because I don't even know the guy and I hate being remotely compared to him. "I'm at a loss here, Kamryn." I say completely defeated.

"Look, when I say you and her ex screwed her up, that's not an exaggeration. I was in my own grief with losing Liam but I still had my eye on my sister. And she was broken. For me and for her. But Jax was far past hurt and I think it's because the one person she loved more than anything left and broke her beyond repair."

I look up at the ceiling and then wander back over to the window that looks out over the strip. For a city that never sleeps, it sure is empty. But it's nice to know that even in one of the most iconic cities in the states, people still need rest.

"I don't know where to start," I admit. And for someone who starts every blueprint with a blank page, not knowing where to start with Jax is like I need to chop down my own tree and head to a paper mill to create a blank page to move forward.

Kamryn heaves out a heavy breath behind me. "Have you tried telling her you're sorry?"

I turn around and rest my body against the window. My eyes meet Kamryn's and I'm sure she sees my answer. "Not in those exact words."

She drops her head into her hand and groans. When her head pops back up it's with renewed fire for her sister. "Then start there. You have no idea the impact those two words can have on someone." Kamryn turns to leave but stops before she opens the door. "Oh. Her room is right next to yours." She points to the wall to the right and my head perks up. "Do with that what you will."

When the door closes my heart goes into overdrive. With this information, I need a plan. But I need to sleep before I do something stupid like stomp over to her room and kiss her as soon as the door opens. *Yeah, totally stupid*, I tell myself. I flop down on the bed and think while trying to listen for any movement next door. Silence. I pull out my phone and pull up Instagram, moseying my way to Jax's account to see if she's posted anything telling. Nothing for the last few weeks. I toss my phone beside me on the bed and stare up at the bare ceiling.

I'm aware of everything. The sound of my air turning on with a low hum and a door closing in the hallway and the occasional blare of a horn from down on the street. But I'm most hyper aware of the temptation next door.

Don't do something stupid, I tell myself.

I fly off my bed and out the door to the room next door. Knocking on the door with a force to wake up anyone who's still asleep, I wait. I hear the door lock unlatch.

"What the hell–"

I don't let her finish her question before I'm pushing into her room and taking her lips in a burning kiss. The door closes as I push her up against the wall. I pour eight years of wanting into this very kiss. I kiss her like I've never kissed anyone. Her hands are on my chest, positioned to push me away until a beat passes and she's curling them into the fabric of my hoodie. Jax pulls me closer and I eliminate the small breath of space between us. This right here is what I've needed. Her in my arms and our hearts beating in sync. I slow the kiss down before I'm breaking it altogether, leaving her with one final kiss.

When my eyes open, I see the scrunch in her brow and

her kiss bruised lips. And when they open, they search my face for something. An ulterior motive possibly.

"I'm sorry." I tell her and I watch her face relax. "I'm sorry for ruining us. I'm sorry for deciding what was best for you. What I'm sorry most for is hurting you. I swear on my life that that was the last thing I ever wanted to do."

Jax's eyes flutter and fill with tears. And a weight I didn't know I was carrying finally lets up. Who knew that saying those words could free me? Whether she accepts the apology or not is up to her. But Jax's hands come back up and land back on my chest, pushing me away this time. I swallow down the rejection with a small smile.

"Thank you. But that doesn't mean all is forgiven," she tells me.

"I know." I say and nod my head.

"Eight years, Nathan." She says and her chin trembles with emotion. "Do you know how hard it is to reconcile that you lost eight years with someone?"

"I know, Jax. I hate myself for that," I plead with her. "You said second chances don't always work. But *this* could be our second chance if we want it to be."

Jax blinks her tear-filled eyes and I watch, painfully, as one trails down her cheek and I want to hit myself for making her cry. But she quickly wipes it away, shaking her head and doing her best to erase all evidence. "I do want us to be friends again. But I don't know if I can let go of my anger so easily."

"I don't expect you to, Bee. Be angry with me, fight with me, and laugh with me. Because there is no one else I would rather do that with than you. As long as you do all of that with me, I'll be happy."

She's leaning against the wall with her hands behind her

back, staring at me and taking in all of my words. Her decision is written clear on her face. But I don't push her.

I take her not throwing me out on my ass as my cue and head to the door. "I'll see you later for dinner."

The door locks behind me and I walk back to my room with a smile on my face. When I get back into my room, I look at the time on the clock and decide now is the time I'll take a nap. We have about seven hours until dinner so I close the curtains, set my alarm, and drop into bed.

I FINALLY FEEL REFRESHED after my nap and as I step out of the shower I feel like a different person. I wipe my hand over the fogged up mirror and stare at my reflection. I haven't seen the light in my eyes in a long while and after one interaction with Jax it's like seeing someone else staring back at me.

I go about my skincare routine, because Kayla said it was criminal that I only used bar soap and body lotion. *A moisturized man is a desirable man.* Her words, not mine and I lotion up my torso and legs before heading out to the bedroom to get dressed. My black jeans are laid out on the bed, along with a cream sweater and undershirt. It's not as cold in Vegas as it is in Cincy, but sometimes the wind will come and hit you with a chill. My black boots with cushioned inserts are off to the side because who knows how much walking the married-to-be pair will make us do. Looking at the time I see I have about fifteen minutes until I have to be in the lobby. I pull on my watch, spray some cologne on the hot spots, grab my phone off the charger, and beeline to the door.

It seems I'm not the only one on the same schedule as I

see Jax exit her room at the same time as I do. And my goodness she's a vision. Her hair is smooth with soft waves that fall down her back. A black mini skirt with what looks like pantyhose and black cowboy boots cover her feet but when she turns I swallow my tongue. A deep red lace bodysuit hugs her petite figure and she has a matching sweater that dips low in the front so it shows off the lace detail of the suit. Laying across her torso is a small black purse that looks no bigger than her phone.

She takes a few steps and stops when she sees me lingering outside of my door. "Neighbor?" She asks, pointing to my door.

I can't find my voice so all I can do is nod. Jax smiles at my speechlessness and it feels like we're back to the college versions of us. The versions of us where she left me speechless after every interaction.

"Come on, friend," she begins. "Let's not keep the pair waiting."

Jax walks past me towards the elevator bank and I lengthen my strides, which is not hard to do, to catch up with her. She hits the button and I stand next to her with my hands in my pants pockets, waiting for the doors to open.

"You look beautiful," I tell her and look over at her.

She looks up at me with a small smile as a blush covers her face. "Thank you. You look very handsome."

When the doors open, I hold my hand out to Jax and follow in closely after her. I hit the button for the 'Lobby' and lean against the other side of the elevator car. Jax manages to avoid looking at me as she looks all around the elevator, but I keep my eyes on her. She's an expert at avoidance and thankfully we have three more floors until we're off.

"So…" I start and push off the wall, taking a step closer to her.

"So…" she says and matches my step. The familiar scent of jasmine and vanilla fills the small five by eight space. But this time, the scent is deeper. Like she found another version that's a more mature version of the scent she loves. Jax's lips, that I expertly avoided looking at moments ago, are painted a deep red color that when she smiles, all I see is joy. But I'm also wondering if it stains. "You're staring."

"Mm hmm." I tell her with a nod, refusing to lie. My heart is racing and if I don't get it together I'm gonna need to be resuscitated. On second thought, if it gets Jax to put her mouth on mine again to revive me, maybe I should consider it.

"Friends don't stare at friends like this," her voice is merely a whisper heard over the sound of the elevator beeps as we pass each floor.

I swallow roughly. "Well, it's good we're barely friends, because I'm not thinking friendly thoughts right now."

We've unconsciously drifted closer to each other and the air has thickened to levels of pure lust. Jax's chest heaves with each breath and I think she's about to say something or do something reckless, like test the limits of her lipstick, when the elevator comes to a stop and the doors open. The lust-filled bubble we found ourselves in is popped by the now bustling sound from the lobby as it filters into the elevator car and we both break apart like we were doing something we shouldn't have.

Jax walks out first and I follow behind her, blowing out a breath, to where Bryce and Kamryn are chatting. He nods when he sees me and raises his brow at Jax who's now talking with Kamryn. I shrug and look around the lobby. Now that it's not so early for Vegas standards, this hotel is the place to be. People in various states of dress walk about and it's a reminder that Vegas is a people watchers dream come true. I've only been to Vegas a handful of times and I've never been able to afford such luxury like this hotel provides until now. And when I have been able to afford a stay at a hotel like this, I never found a reason to travel out here.

"Alright party people! Are we ready?" Chance booms when he and Sophie come off the elevator. They're dressed in typical white and black like a bride and groom would. And a handful of guests turn towards the loud voice and look around to see who he was shouting to. What must we all look like? Baseball players in Vegas during the off-season? Could we really get more cliche than this?

We follow the happy couple out to the limo they rented for the weekend. The strip is now full of tourists, families, and bachelor and bachelorette parties as we weave through the clusters of groups to get to the car. Can't blame the amount of people out as it's the perfect weather in November and I can't decide which I like more: a sleepy city or a busy city.

"What's up with you two?" Bryce asks. He doesn't need to keep his voice down as other chatter and yelling at all volumes around us, drowns him out.

"Nothing," I respond quickly.

"You can't bullshit me. I saw you two when the elevator doors opened."

I let out a breath and slow my steps when we get closer to the car. "I kissed her earlier."

"Atta boy, Nate," Bryce praises.

"Shut up." I lightheartedly tell him and gently push him towards the open door to the backseat.

The sound of a champagne bottle being popped open

greets me and I hurriedly shut the door. Bryce helps Kamryn hand out the glasses, before a toast is being made.

"So Kamryn, what's it like being married to The Mason Brooks?" Bryce asks.

"Ugh. Don't make her answer this." Jax pipes up and downs her champagne in one swallow. With a smile, I hand her my untouched glass and she takes it from me with ease. Downing the amount in one go.

"What's wrong Jax?" Sophie asks with a teasing tone to her voice.

"She's just traumatized—" Kamryn continues telling us all the times she walked in on her and Mason while Jax plugs her ears and scrunches her eyes closed. The playful side of Jax is a sight to behold.

Kamryn throws a piece of ice at Jax and she jolts from the chill. "Are you done?"

"Are *you* done?" she tosses back.

They share a silent and loaded look with a conversation passing between them that the rest of us look on in amazement. It really is a shame that I never saw this when we were younger so it's like getting to know Jax again with a sibling dynamic. An elbow gets jabbed into my rib cage and I look over at Bryce who makes a very suggestive face. I shake my head and brush him off.

The driver navigates the streets without issue and pulls up to a restaurant that's at the other end of the strip from where we're staying. I nod to the driver who opened the door and wait off to the side. Jax's eyes meet mine as she slides out of the car and I keep it very respectful by keeping my eyes on hers.

"You can't be buzzed already," I observe when she gets closer to me. I try to keep my tone light as I feel we're slowly wading back into friendship territory. But it's hard when all you want to do is wrap your arm around their shoulder and pull them into you until no space can pass between.

"Not even close, Natey baby." She says and is pulled away by Sophie.

I'm left dumbstruck on the sidewalk at the use of the nickname she shot back at me.

"He's so gone," Chance observes.

"We only knew it was only a matter of time," Bryce notes.

I look to my left and to my right at my two friends. They're wearing twin grins like this was their plan all along.

"What are those looks for?" I ask when I can't take it anymore.

Bryce puts his arm around my shoulder and leads us forward. "Nate, I love you like a brother, but you are a grumpy, broody bastard. And have been since the day we met."

I narrow my eyes at him. "Thanks I guess."

"You're welcome," Bryce accepts the fake gratitude, "but you've been a little less grumpy and less broody and we think it has to do with a certain 5 '2 someone."

I look at Bryce like he's insane, but don't call him out because, and I'll never admit it, he's right.

"Don't even deny it." Chance tells me. "I saw you eyeing her in the limo."

"The longing, the yearning," Bryce calls with a hand on his chest but groans and folds in half when I elbow him in the stomach.

"What Romeo means—" Chance starts and we tip our head to the door being opened for us. "—is that if anyone can make you less grumpy and less broody, it's Jax."

"Gee," I muse. "What gave that away?" I ask dryly. I'm as

much of an open book than anything, except for my relationships. But these two know me too well.

"Nate, we sense your sarcasm and because we love you, we're gonna let it slide." Bryce says and moves past me with a pat on the shoulder when we get to our table.

"We really only want what's best for you." Chance gives my other shoulder a squeeze before heading to the table as well.

I shake my head and follow the sunshine twins to the table. When I get there, their twin grins are something out of a horror film when I see the only seat left is next to Jax.

25

JAX

I shoot daggers at the table. I knew something was up when Sophie and Kamryn had the hostess take away the extra chairs. And as they hide their smiles behind their drinks I think of ways to get back at them. I certainly can't poison their food. Plus, I'm too pretty for prison. But I'll think of something. And I keep thinking until my sort-of friend Nate takes the only empty seat next to me. I knock back my rose and set the empty glass on the table. I really should eat something as the alcohol is starting to make my head fuzzy.

"Are you catching on?" Nate whispers to me only.

I let out a sigh and keep the others in my sight, but angle my head to him. "They're Parent Trapping us."

His soft snort is one of confirmation. "Yeah, I can see that now."

A server comes over and drops off a few complimentary bread baskets on the table before taking our orders. My stomach rumbles loud enough for Nate to hear, if the smile on his face is any indication, and he reaches forward to set up our pre-appetizer.

When he sets the small plate in front of me, I look at him with a raised eyebrow.

"Play along," Nate tells me so only I can hear and holds out the piece of bread to me.

He's in my line of sight but I don't miss the others in the background with their attention on us. I lean forward and take a bite of the small piece. My lips brush against his fingers and I see his eyes solely focused on the spot they touched. I sit back in my seat and chew the piece, keeping my eyes locked on him the entire time. Nate's eyes stay on my lips and trail down to my throat when I swallow and I've never needed a glass of water more in my life.

"Anyone else a little flushed?" Someone whispers and we finally break our stares.

I pick up my newly refilled glass of rose and use that to cool me down. Nate sits back in his chair and with his spread thighs, one presses into mine. I could move my leg, but I don't. I revel in the feel of him pressed against me and when I finally lift my eyes to the rest of the table, I feel like I'm under a microscope.

"Yes?" I ask, as if Nate and I have been friendly since forever and him feeding me bread is perfectly normal.

"Did you two want some privacy?" Chance asks with a teasing tone in his question.

"I needed to feed her," Nate begins, "Jax's stomach grumbling was aggressive enough to cause an earthquake."

I reach under the table and pinch his thigh. Or at least I try to. The man has thighs as solid as a rock. God bless baseball.

"It was not that loud. He's being so dramatic," I finally speak up. I polish off the rest of my glass, because seriously, the microscope keeps getting more intrusive. "Tough crowd," I murmur so only Nate can hear me.

He chuckles and leans forward on the table. Giving his attention to whatever Bryce is waving his hands about. While Nate and I had our moment this morning, I'm still walking on eggshells around him. Letting him in and just giving into the history that we have–it would be so easy to drop all of my walls around Nate.

Our server brings out our food and my mouth waters at the pasta sat in front of me. But my gaze can't help but notice the pizza on Nate's plate. Jerk. He knows my food weaknesses. Specifically pasta and pizza.

"I'll split my pizza if you share your pasta," he says when he looks at my food and then to me with a smile that can only be described as dazzling.

"Deal."

We start on his pizza first and then move on to the pasta. When we've polished off the entire meal, I'm stuffed to the brim and the alcohol is all soaked up. Kamryn's knowing smile from across the table is one that I'm choosing to not acknowledge. When we were in high school and our parents would take us to dinner, sharing meals like this is what we would do to have the best of both worlds. Her seeing that I'm doing this with Nate, no matter how small the exchange, shows that the bricks I had up to keep him out are finally coming down.

"How did you remember?" I ask Nate as our dishes are being cleared from the table. He tilts his head as if he doesn't know what I'm talking about. "The food," I clarify, although it could also be said for the candy basket he brought me.

"I remember everything," Nate tells me and our eyes lock again.

It's like that moment in movies where everything blurs: people, sound...life. There is this energy running through me at the thought of finally kicking down that last brick wall. Sure we said friends. But a tentative friendship at best. Only, when he says stuff like that, I want to bypass the whole friendship route and try to pick things back up to where we were in college.

"Alright, gang!" Chance booms once again and it's enough to break the connection between us. "Let's go."

Him and Sophie pop up from their seats, eager to get the rest of the night started. It's fun seeing these two so excited to get married and all the celebrations that come before getting married. One by one we all push up from our seats and head back out to the strip. In the two hours we were at dinner, it seems like Vegas is finally waking up.

Chance and Sophie lead us to a cocktail bar that is filled to the brim with all kinds of celebratory parties that we all have to sandwich ourselves to stay together. The closer I get, I'm hyper aware of Nate and his patchouli scent, and something else that I can't quite place. People bump into us from all around like a pinball machine. Hands locked together, we manage to find an empty table and flag down a cocktail waitress to order some drinks. I'm not sure how long we'll manage to last here. Or how we'll find our way out.

Thirty minutes later our drinks are being delivered.

"Shots? Really?" Kamryn yells over the noise.

We're all adults so we can agree that shots, no matter what's inside, leads to bad decisions.

"Do we need to call your husband and have him fly out to save you?" I joke.

She gives me a devious look and I plug my ears again to avoid hearing all the things my sister and Mason get up to.

"It really can't be that bad," Nate says and his voice rumbles over my body and sends tingles to my core.

I look up at him and meet his eyes. "Picture walking in—nope, I can't even say it."

His laughter sends vibrations over my body and I feel his torso brush against my arm. *God, pull it together Jax. It's an arm*, I tell myself.

"Okay, cheers. To an amazing group and hopefully an unforgettable night," Sophie cheers loud enough to be heard over the sound of the music and the lively crowd.

I eye the brown liquid like it's a pit of snakes before my glass is tapped by the one next to me. My head turns and I meet Nate's eyes.

"Bottom's up, Bee."

Our eyes stay locked as we take the shots. My mouth would go dry if I wasn't downing fire in the form of liquid.

I cough and set the glass back down on the table. The room comes back into focus and I grab my cocktail and take a sip of that. While this place is busy, it's definitely not the party scene. And once we leave some cash for our waitress we're onto the next place.

"Oh, the light show," Kamryn says when we get to the Bellagio.

We stay standing on the sidewalk to watch the rest of the fifteen minute show before heading into the first casino we can find. Walking to the entrance and through the lobby, the sound of slot machines echoes throughout the room. People of all, hopefully, legal ages fill the area. Sophie and Chance run off shouting Blackjack while the rest of us look around with our eyes as big as saucers. Kamryn takes a step away but pauses when she realizes I'm still here.

"Go ahead," I tell her.

"Are you sure?"

"Positive. Go wipe the floor with them."

Her glee is infectious as she kisses me on the cheek. "I'll see you later. Text me when you're ready to head out."

I watch my sister run further into the casino with a Poker table in her sight. And then it was just me, Nate, and Bryce.

"Huh. I see some very single ladies begging for my attention," the black haired baseball player says. "You two have fun." And then he's off leaving Nate and me.

"Could they be any more obvious?" I ask. I'd be offended if Nate and I weren't on speaking terms. Because as it stands, I've gotten more comfortable around him as the night has progressed. Or maybe that's the alcohol.

"I don't know, Bee. They might need a skywriter to spell it out," Nate teases. "Come on, let's go do what Bryce said and have some fun."

"Are you a gambler?" I ask as we walk into the pit.

He shakes his head. "I can't say I picked that up. Unless you count playing Go Fish or UNO with Kayla and bartering Oreo's."

"Cute." I tell him, although I feel a bit of melancholy when he mentions the sister that I never got to meet. It's going to be tough to move around this elephant that's taking up space with him. It's hard knowing that we missed out on so much. But I want to. Move past this, that is. I just haven't told him yet.

"She was a tough opponent," he says and our feet take us in the direction of the slot machines.

We walk down the row of machines, determined to find one that's not occupied. I've never been a big Casino fan. What I've seen has been solely in movies or TV episodes. It seems time can pass people by the longer they sit in front of a machine and tap incessantly on a button. Luck is on our side when we turn down the next row and find an open one.

Luck is not on *my* side when we only see one chair in the area.

"You can sit on my lap. I won't bite," Nate says and there is no hiding the smile in his voice.

"Sure you won't." I say and follow him with my heart beating a mile a minute.

Nate takes a seat on the chair and pats his leg with a smirk, a raised eyebrow, and an unspoken dare. Shaking my head, I move to stand between his legs, his eyes meet mine like they did all of those years ago, before I turn and take a seat on his leg. His hand automatically wraps around my waist and I will myself to not turn and meet his eyes. This position is already intimate as it is and all it would take is the slight turning of my head to fuse our lips together. Add on the dim lights of the casino, save for the lit up machines, and yeah. My thoughts are running before I know I'm ready to walk.

I jolt when he moves and I have to wrap an arm around his shoulder to keep from falling. Although I know he would never let that happen.

"One dollar in and then we pull the lever. Seems easy enough," Nate says and I barely hear him over the blood rushing through my ears. Is it from our proximity or the deep tone of his voice hitting me in the chest? I don't know. "Ready?" He asks and taps me on the hip when I'm slow to respond.

"Yeah," I think I tell him loud enough but I can barely hear a thing over the sound of my heart beating louder than normal.

We play the game for the next thirty minutes, or maybe it's an hour. Time really has flown past us. I've gotten looser around Nate. My body has sunken into him and my hand brushes along the exposed skin of his neck. Drinks have been flowing since we sat down and before I know it we're calling it quits and heading to the next spot in the casino which happens to be the bar.

"You've changed," Nate notes and I turn to him with my eyebrows furrowed.

"Good change or bad change?"

"A bit of both."

I take a sip of the margarita and look out onto the floor. "I don't know how to get the other me back. The happy me. The fun me. The one who never second-guessed her moves."

After Nate and Trent, my mind and who I used to be in general, went on a vacation. I used to jump into everything head first, damn the consequences. Now I do a lap, before dipping my toe in, and then taking the stairs to lower me down.

"Maybe you just need to remember what brought you joy," Nate notes as we continue to sit at the bar.

I finish the rest of my drink and place it on the bartop behind me. "And you have a plan for that?"

He finishes his own drink and stands, holding his hand out for me. "I do. Let's go."

Tentatively I place my hand in his and let him pull me off the chair and he leads me to the entrance. "Where are we going?"

"Somewhere only we know." Nate says with a wink.

26

NATE

I don't know what prompted me to take Jax to the gardens. But in my mind, taking her places that brought her joy, the gardens, is the key to Jax becoming her again. We walk through the casino and head towards the double-doors and I brace myself for the cool Vegas night air because it's gotten chiller the later it gets. Through the alcohol induced haze, I retrace our steps back to the Bellagio. When we stopped to watch the water and light show, I kept my wits about me and looked around. And seeing the Botanical Gardens sign felt like fate.

"Here again?" Jax asks skeptically when we get closer to the fountains.

Still holding her hand, I turn and walk backwards. "Not quite."

Jax starts to drag her feet. "Nate, where are we going?"

"Do you trust me?"

She hesitates and I'd be hurt if I didn't know the reason. I hurt her. Left her. So she has every reason to balk at my question. I give her hand a light squeeze to let her know it's okay if she doesn't fully trust me. With a lot of work on my end, I do hope that one day I can get her trust back. Jax gives me a small nod and I have to tamp down the urge to throw my hands up in victory like I hit a walk-off Grand Slam.

I take a tentative step backwards and drag her along with me. Seeing the smile teasing at the corner of her lips has mine threatening to take full formation.

When the sign for the Botanical Gardens comes into view, I see recognition fall on Jax's face. And maybe a bit of sorrow? It has me worried that I'm way overstepping. I don't know if she's been to one since college, I know I haven't.

"Nate..."

"Trust me?" I ask softly again. When Jax meets my eyes, I let out a breath when she nods.

Wordlessly we walk up the pathway and through the sliding doors. This is one of the most iconic hotels in Vegas and I'm slightly upset our group isn't staying here. Jax and I navigate our way to the Gardens, which isn't on as large of a scale as the one in Philly, but still holds a bit of nostalgia for the both of us.

With it getting later into the night, it's thankfully not as busy as reported so Jax and I take our time walking through the exhibit. Stepping foot in here, it's like I could see the weight of the past lift off of her and witness joy take its place. I've followed her around, like I used to, as she explored, taking pictures of flowers and the themes, while my eyes have never left her. If I had my camera, the lens would have had her as my main subject.

We get to the end of the exhibit and take in what we saw. The quiet was one of the reasons I wanted to bring her here. It seems Jax thrives in areas where she can get her bearings.

"Where to now?" She asks as if I had a grand plan all along. I didn't. But it's nice that she's looking at me like this instead of like an enemy.

I shove my hands in my front pockets and lazily shrug. "The rooftop?"

"Okay," Jax agrees nervously and looks around for the elevator bay.

I point to the opposite side of the lobby and we head that direction. Our steps are both lighter having been paired up for the last handful of hours. When we file into the elevator, we take up opposite sides and I watch as Jax leans her head back and closes her eyes.

"Are you okay?" I ask, mildly concerned that she's about to display her dinner.

"Mm hmm," she responds without opening her eyes. "Just not a fan of elevators going this high."

"Since when?" I ask. If I can keep her mind off the small car taking us up ten stories, I'll do anything.

"Since forever. I've always had this weird fear of the elevator stopping and plummeting to the ground. What a morbid way to go, huh?"

"Well, I didn't have that fear until now."

She peaks an eye open and looks at me with a grimace. "Sorry."

"Don't be. Tell me another fear."

"Waking up and realizing I've missed out on big moments because I'm scared."

I look at Jax. And really look at her. The hard swallow, the tenseness in her jaw, how her shoulders cave inward– what happened to her?

"The Jax I knew wasn't scared of anything."

Her eyes blink open and she tilts her head down so we're looking at each other. "The Jax you knew, had you by her side."

I open my mouth to tell her that I never left, when the doors open. But the truth still stands that I did leave her.

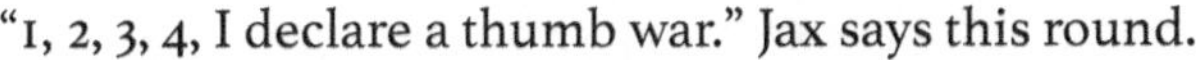

"1, 2, 3, 4, I declare a thumb war." Jax says this round.

We've been playing this childhood game, but made it adult with alcohol, for the past hour. And for every game one loses, they take a shot. So far we're tied. Plus, we've been asking each other questions so it's not been too bad of a time.

"My favorite color is still yellow, but it verges on shades of pink now and again," Jax says.

I pause our game by tucking my thumb and looking her outfit up and down.

"Okay, besides this outfit. Untuck your thumb," she scolds with a smile.

"When did you add black to your wardrobe?" Her tongue peeks out as she tries to maneuver my hand. "Don't cheat."

"I'm not." She tells me guiltily. "Um, probably a few months after we moved to Cincinnati and Kamryn's designs really started to take off. She was getting ready for a date with Mason and came up with the idea of doing an entire line of black clothes, just because she wanted to and somehow every piece from that line ended up in my closet. Ugh."

I smile as I pour a shot for her to take. We've almost gone through this bottle of tequila and I'm wondering if we'll need another or if we should switch to water soon.

Jax slaps her hand in mine and I count us off.

"Least favorite food?" she asks this time.

My thumb flexes to trap hers but she dodges it. "Um, brussels sprouts."

Jax laughs at my distaste for the vegetable. "Fair."

I look at her sitting between my legs and smile at how

far we've come. Jax never liked big crowds. Save for baseball games, so tonight was a lot. But getting her one-on-one has done wonders for her opening up to me.

"I'm not big on vegetables."

"Still?" she asks.

It's weird the things we remember when something manages to jog our memory. Jax remembering that I'm not a big fan of vegetables is that one thing that continues to spark the flame of hope.

"You sound like my mom and Kayla," I pout.

"Don't pout," Jax scolds, "besides, don't you need the veggies to be a big, strong baseball player?"

"You've been checking me out?" I ask and groan when she moves her thumb at the last second.

"I didn't say that. Yes!" She cheers as she pins my thumb down.

My hand falls to my lap as she pours the next shot, effectively emptying the bottle.

"Bottom's up, Natey."

I smirk and wink at her before taking the shot. My eyes don't leave hers once as I swallow down the liquid gasoline. When I place the shot glass down, Jax leans forward and presses her mouth to mine. Blame it on the alcohol, but my mind glitches for a second before I'm reaching for her. I tangle my hands in her soft hair and tilt her head, swallowing her moan when I lick into her mouth. Kissing Jax is like hitting a walk-off grand slam in the bottom of the ninth inning with two outs and the bases loaded in the World Series.

I never want this feeling to end.

I pull her onto my lap and keep her sideways, because we're still in public after all and she's wearing a skirt. I kiss Jax like my life depends on it and it seems she's doing the same. The little moans she makes as her hands fist my sweater, pulling me closer than I already am, and my arms wind around her like ivy, eliminating every inch of space has me wanting to maneuver her so her legs bracket my waist. Cheering from the rooftop is like cold water poured on top of us. I slow the kiss down. Alternating between lingering kisses and pecking her top and bottom lips.

When I pull back, her eyes are still closed in concentration and I see the lipstick I hoped would smudge, did just around the edges. Using my thumb, I wipe the color off her skin while she watches me with those honey brown eyes.

"How drunk are you?" I ask, breaking the bubble.

"Not drunk at all." She tells me.

"Are you up for a walk?"

Wordlessly she nods and I shift her off my lap, helping her to stand and adjusting her skirt. Our bottle was already paid for so we head back to the elevator. Jax isn't as tense on the ride down. Could be the alcohol or the kiss still playing on a loop in her head. I know it is for me. When the doors open, I hold my hand out for her to take, giving her the option to follow or stray. My cheek twitches when she takes my hand and links our fingers together.

Look at me. Getting giddy that I'm holding her hand.

Pushing out to the street, I walk us to the curb where I flag down a cab. I'm all for walking but that would take us over an hour. When a car stops, I open the door for Jax and slide in after her.

"Where to?" the driver asks.

"Fremont Street Experience, please."

I sit back in the seat as we're whisked away. Some could say I'm doing this to win over Jax. And they'd be right. But I'm also doing this for me to live out the wild tales that I never got to experience because of baseball.

"Where is it we're going?" Jax asks softly.

"A place I think you're going to have a lot of fun at."

"You mean the rooftop wasn't fun?"

I lean over and kiss along her neck. Just light kisses before placing one by her ear and I don't miss the light whimper that escapes. "Anywhere with you is fun."

I sit back in my seat and wrap my arm around her shoulder. Jax relaxes into me and wraps an arm around my thigh. Blood rushes through my ears at the contact because apparently I've never been touched before and this sort of contact gives me tingly feelings. I watch the lights blur by until our driver slows down.

"Here you go." He says and pulls over to the curb.

Once we pay and get out, we just stand on the sidewalk. Neon lights illuminate the street and those in its vicinity.

"What do we do first?" Jax asks and I look down at her. Her face is the definition of awe as the lights bounce off of her face. Like this is her first true living experience. Then again, maybe it is if what I've heard from her sister is any indication.

"Get a drink and then walk around?"

"Sounds like a plan."

Together Jax and I experience this side of Vegas that's full of joy. I watch her laugh more times tonight than I have since she waltzed back into my life. We watch another light show and a live performance. We dance and sing, drink more and eat a little bit of food. This version of Jax is the one I've been waiting to see.

27

JAX

*O*uch. That's the first thought that enters my head as the sunlight shines through the curtain I forgot to close before our night out. I scrunch my eyes closed as if that'll eliminate the light and plunge me back into darkness. How much did I drink last night? We polished off an entire bottle of tequila last night, that I vaguely remember. The kiss? Of course I remember that. Nates lips on mine. How could I ever forget that? But I don't remember much of anything after we left the rooftop.

I stretch and recoil when my foot hits something solid. Slowly, I turn my head to the left and see Nate lying face down in my bed. But it's only then I realize that this is not my room. What the hell happened last night? My bladder is screaming at me and I go to flip off the covers when something catches my eye. *No.* No, I am not seeing that. I scrunch my eyes together again, hoping that it's just the remaining alcohol coursing through my bloodstream playing a trick on me.

On the count of three, I'll open my eyes and I won't see

what I think I saw. *1, 2, 3. FUCK!* And I can't stop the gasp that escapes when there is no mistaking the ring on my finger. What the hell did we do last night?

I stay perfectly still as I feel Nate start to wake up. *Don't freak out. Don't freak out. Don't freak out.*

Nate turns his head and meets my eyes. If he's shocked I'm in here, he played it off, although I didn't miss the slight widening of his dark brown eyes upon seeing me in his bed. His eyes have a slight redness around them probably from how late we stayed out and the alcohol.

"Jax?" his hoarse voice does something to me. *Focus, Jaclyn!*

I give him a small wave and then his eyes narrow on the diamond sitting on my finger. Nate sits up rather quickly for someone who drank more than I did and the jostling of the bed proves motion sickness is here.

"What the hell is this?" He asks and grabs my hand, inspecting the ring I'm most certain he put there if the gold band on his ring finger is any indication.

"I'm assuming that's rhetorical?"

Nate places my hand back down and rolls off the bed like we didn't polish off more alcohol than humanly possible last night. How is he moving so easily? He paces and gets this furrow in his brow that I would find cute now if we weren't married. *Married!?* How the hell did this happen? Fucking tequila that's how. I'm never drinking again, says everyone who ever woke up after a night they can no longer remember.

I'm realizing that last night the wall I had up came down in spectacular fashion. Or I at least created a little doorway. We laughed, we drank, we kissed...we kissed a lot–but other than that, I'm failing to see how we both ended up with rings on our fingers.

"Nate, what are you doing?" I ask on his third round of pacing the room. I understand people's need to work things out, but his pacing is threatening to make me barf.

"Trying to remember what we did last night."

"Well, can you stop? It kind of makes me want to barf."

He stops and looks at me with a wince before a frown mars his dark brown skin and he's moving to the living room pit to continue his pacing there. I roll my eyes and finally slide out of his bed. My dead phone is on the nightstand so I gather that up along with my shoes.

"Where are you going?" Nate asks from his spot with a hint of panic in his voice.

"To my room to shower. And to brush my teeth. I feel like something died in my mouth."

He nods because he's probably realizing he feels like ass too. "Yeah. Okay."

"I'll be right next door. If I'm not back in an hour, come over." I turn from his nodding form and push out into the hallway. Seriously. What happened? I pull my room key out of my small clutch and push into my room. Tossing my things on the other bed, I head straight to the shower to feel somewhat put together. While the water warms up, I undress and then stare at the ring on my finger. Even in his drunken state, Nate knows me better than any man. The oval cut engagement ring is framed by smaller diamonds wrapping halfway around the band. Maybe he remembered me talking about what kind of ring I would want? But that's impossible as I said it offhandedly and we were still in the friend zone. Shaking my head, I slide the ring off and set it on the vanity before washing the night away.

There is no way he remembered this was my dream ring, I say to myself as the warm water washes over me. There's no way.

SOMEONE KNOCKING on the door when I'm finishing up my skincare routine has me jumping on the spot. I place my moisturizer on the counter and wait, thinking someone got the wrong room. Only it continues until I check the peephole and open the door.

"Jax! Oh my God! Where were you last night?" Kamryn asks when she flies into my room like a tornado and then turns to look at me. "Are you just now waking up?"

"Nate and I went out after you all ditched us to play games and must have lost track of time." I tell her and take the towel off my head. My curls are back in action after a deep conditioning session and I've never felt more like myself. While Kamryn loves her blowouts, I for one hate going to the salon for anything other than a trim. Last night was an exception to the loose curls that swept to the middle of my back. I toss the wet towel back into the bathroom and move sit on my bed.

"You and Nate? You and your ex-boyfriend? Hung out? Like all night?"

"Yes. Did you think I'd walk around Vegas by myself? Have you seen the earlier seasons of *C.S.I. Las Vegas*? No thank you." I attempt to joke with my sister but it falls flat when I see said joke failed to land and I sober up. "I'm sorry. I should have called you. Or at least sent a text. But then my phone must have died and I didn't even realize it."

Kamryn moves and sits on the other bed across from me. Dressed in a black bodysuit and dark wash jeans, my sister is the definition of collected. I admire her confidence and resilience more than she'll know. "Well, I'm glad you're okay. Did you two do anything fun last night?"

Got married, I say to myself but I'm not ready to tell my sister Nate and I got married and that neither of us remember it. So I settle with, "Not really. We people watched mostly and he took me to the Botanical Gardens at the Bellagio."

"That was sweet of him," she observes with a tilt of her head because even she knows that the Botanical Gardens is one of my favorite places to visit.

"Don't give me that look."

"What look?"

I give her a *get real* look. "Don't think we both weren't onto what you guys were planning," I call her out for their blatant need to push us together.

"What? We just gave you two the push you needed." Kamryn stands up from the bed when she sees I'm alive and well and turns towards the door. "But I am glad to know you two got through last night unscathed."

Just married. "Me too." I say and walk with her towards the door. "Have Sophie and Chance said anything about today's plans?"

She shrugs. "No clue. I lost them after they ran off to the Blackjack table."

Opening the door, I make a note to text Sophie and see Nate strolling down the hall in a pair of black joggers that mold to his muscular thighs and a matching black hoodie. *Drool.*

"I heard you two had fun last night."

Nate looks at me and I widen my eyes, slightly shake my head indicating that Kamryn doesn't know everything.

"Just a bit of people watching," Nate says. And I'm glad he unknowingly said what I told my sister.

Kamryn looks between us as if she can read what we're

hiding. But we give nothing away. If Nate and I are indeed legally married, then what? We get a divorce? An annulment? The thought of going through that process makes me nauseous.

"Okay. You two are acting weird. So, I'm gonna go call my husband." She says happily and floats back to her room. When she turns the corner to go down the hall, Nate and I let out a breath as I let him into my room.

"I found something." He tells me and I watch as his eyes trail down and land on my chest. Following his gaze, I see my robe has gaped open giving him a perfect view of my cleavage.

"I'm gonna get dressed." I tell him and walk past him to my suitcase.

"Don't change on my account," he says cheekily and the dimple in his left cheek pops out.

I throw a sock at him and head into the bathroom. Pulling on a bralette and an oversized tee with loose, dark washed distress jeans, I feel more me than with the outfit from last night. I rake some leave-in conditioner through my hair and rub an oil on the ends, praying that the air drying Gods are in my curly hair's favor. I pause before leaving as I look at the ring on the vanity. Do I put it on? Put it in my pocket? The me at twenty-one would yell to put it on. But only if she knew that Nate and I went on different journey's. Decision made, I put the ring in my pocket and head back out to my room.

"So what did you find?" I ask as I come to sit next to him on the couch, tucking my leg under me as I sit facing him.

Nate unlocks his phone and hands it to me. My eyes go wide as I see pictures of us with a marriage license, standing with Elvis, and showing off our rings. The signed marriage license is then placed on top of his phone. And clear as day, our signatures are more legible than anyone in our possible inebriated states should've been.

"What the hell did we do last night?" I ask again for what feels like the hundredth time today.

"Better question is what was in those drinks?" Nate asks.

"100 proof alcohol that's for sure. So we're married," I conclude. My heart races at the thought of being married to Nate. This was always where the road would lead us. So why does it feel wrong?

"It appears so," Nate starts, "I would suggest a quickie divorce or an annulment. But even suggesting those makes me wanna hurl."

At least we're in the same boat with that. It's not that either of us are against divorce. It was one of the things we talked about in college. But a divorce from each other would put the final nail in the coffin for us. I nod and blink hard as tears threaten to expose me.

"Hey. Come here." Nate holds his arm out and I slide over, burying my face in his shirt. "I'm not taking offense because I know this is not the road we were even close to driving on. Hell, we're still in the shop. And while I was hoping that one day we would get to this place, I wanted us to remember it."

His words are a comfort and the tears pour out. I always dreamed that my wedding day would be one of the most memorable days of my life. With the white dress, my dad walking me down the aisle, the man I love waiting for me at the altar, and the vows–the promise that the life we're promising to spend together is one full of laughter and love. And to find out that neither of us even remembers what happened last night is crushing.

"So what do we do now?" I ask through my tears.

"We date. I assume you don't want to live together right away?"

I snort and I'm pretty sure a snot bubble is smeared into his hoodie. "You'd be correct."

"I'm a great roommate," he says as he begins to plead his case for us to live together.

"I'm aware." Slowly the tears stop and I wipe the remnants away.

He places a kiss on the top of my head and I feel that all the way to my toes. "We'll fight because the past is our painful reminder. But we'll stay because this time I'm not letting you go."

I nod and wrap my arms around his waist. Those walls I had up around Nate are completely gone now. Well, not completely. They're still up, but I can walk back and forth if need be until I can finally take a sledgehammer and knock it down for good.

"So we date?" I ask for more clarification.

"Yep."

"You haven't asked me."

His chest rumbles with a silent laugh and I smile against his chest. "Jaclyn Marie Rawlins, will you go out with me?"

I make him wait longer than necessary. "I guess."

"Okay. What do you say we go find some food? Because I'm starving."

At that my stomach rumbles and we both laugh. "Will you text the guys and see what they're up to?"

"Mm hmm. Go get your shoes on."

OUR DRINKS ARE DROPPED off along with baskets of fries long before the sunshine couple joins us.

"You guys look like you had a long night," I say to Sophie and Chance when they finally join us at the burger place across from the hotel. Our hostess set us up at a table on the patio. We almost immediately balked at the idea until just walking through the restaurant made us all gag. Thankfully the table is big enough for the six of us. Nate sits at one end of the table and I'm on his left, Bryce is across from me and Kamryn is sitting next to me. My foot is hooked around Nate's leg and it's thrilling to have a secret that no one is aware of.

"We didn't go to sleep until almost four." Sophie tells us as they take the only two empty chairs. They both have sunglasses pasted on their faces and look like they threw on whatever they could find.

"Did you two even shower?" Bryce asks with a wince and leans away from them.

As soon as he says that a breeze pushes their scents towards the rest of us.

"Fuck off, Bryce. The alcohol has decided to ooze out of our bodies." Chance scolds.

"Ew," Kamryn says and decides to take mercy on them and pour them both glasses of water and shoves over the other basket of fries that was delivered their way. We all watch on in amusement as they take tentative bites of the salty potato.

"So what's the plan for tonight?" Bryce asks. We leave tomorrow and after last night I doubt anyone wants to go as hard as we did. I for one want a chill night, but in Vegas anything is possible.

Sophie and Chance look at each other before swinging their gazes to us. "Probably just dinner and then call it a night."

"We're game." We all agree and finally place our orders for lunch when our waitress comes back to our table.

We recap each other on our respective nights. Seems we all don't remember much of what happened once we entered the casino. Once we all have food in our bodies, I for one feel better. And when the afternoon turns to evening, we regale on the weekend and look forward to the future.

28

NATE

COLLEGE, DECEMBER, SENIOR YEAR

I toss on my beanie before I step out of the Empire School of Design and into the cold December afternoon. The weather has been calling for snow for the last week and it seems that today is the day. Light snow falls from the sky but not enough to stick just yet. My last final of the semester is done. Now I need to buckle down and get my senior project in motion. The house I'm designing is coming to shape and with the little details Jax has talked about they've made the blueprints all the more real.

I'm planning to spend a week with Jax and then spend the rest of my break back home before coming back up here for our final semester. Jax and I have gotten used to my coming and going during the holidays. But it still doesn't make it any easier. Jax does her best to hide her feelings regarding me going back home, but like the trooper she is she doesn't voice a thing. That's what makes her perfect for me.

I shake off the snow and trudge to my dorm. My roommate, who is on the golf team and rarely in our shared room, is all packed up and already headed back to his hometown. Do I know where that is? No. And that makes me a terrible roomie. My goal is for us to at least be friendly with each other next semester. Better late than never.

> Me: Packing up and then I'll head to your house.

Jax: 😢

Less than an hour later and I'm headed to Jax's house. The snow has continued a steady fall. Big, fat snowflakes fall faster and I'm a bit worried that we'll get snowed in.

"Hi, baby," I hear from Jax when I close the door and I see her standing on the stairs.

"Hi, Bee."

I am deliriously in love with this girl. She is my future.

"I have your Christmas present." Jax tells me as she hops up and down with barely contained excitement. One thing about my girl is that she loves giving gifts. I think she likes others to feel joy.

"Can I guess what it is?" I ask and step closer to where she's standing on the stairs.

She shakes her head and rests her arms on my shoulders. "Nope. Go put your stuff away and then I'll give it to you."

"Okay." I lean forward and peck her on the lips before moving around her and up the stairs and dropping my stuff right inside of her room.

"Did your stuff even land on the floor before you sprinted back down here?" Jax asks with a laugh.

"Nope." I proudly say and drop onto the couch next to her. The fireplace has warmed the sunroom and the large bay windows let in all of the natural light, bathing Jax in a soft glow.

She grabs a rectangular box from the coffee table and places it in my waiting hands. I try to shake it but nothing moves. My eyes flick up to hers before I'm tearing the wrapper off.

It's a picture. I can't even describe in my mind what or how she did it. On it is the baseball field with the Botanical Gardens in the background. It's us. And in perfectly written cursive is 'Somewhere Only We Know'.

"Jax, this is–"

"It's us," she finishes for me.

"Yeah, Bee. It's us." And it is. It's where all of our big moments happened, where big feelings were felt, and where life changing decisions were made. "I love it."

With my birthday in September and Christmas a few months behind, I told Jax only one present. Not that I need anything from her, because being with her is the only gift I need. But her tendency to spoil those she loves knows no bounds so I know that me putting a limit on what she could get me probably angered her.

"Merry Christmas, Natey."

"Thank you, Bee."

Jax cuddles into my side and we watch the snow fall as it blankets the backyard turning it into a winter oasis. Moments like these, the quiet ones where we can just be, are ones that mean more than any championship or big accomplishment.

"It's hard to believe we have a few more months of college left," Jax breathes out.

"I know. Pretty soon we'll be wishing for the structure of a class schedule," I tease.

Her body shakes with a laugh. "No way."

I kiss the top of her head and pull her closer than she already is. "I am ready for the future with you."

"Yeah," she whispers. "Me too."

I ZIP up my suitcase and turn to the brown-eyed beauty with sleep-filled eyes watching me get ready to leave. This is our last school break separation and if we can survive this, then baseball season and what comes after will be a breeze. I crawl back up on the bed and lay out on Jax. Her legs wrap around my waist and her arms loop around my shoulders as she lays kisses all over my face.

"Last break." I say and lean up on my elbows. I wrap a curl around my finger and let it slowly unravel.

"These few weeks better go by faster than light."

I know Jax still gets nervous when I head home. But she plays it off because she knows how important it is for me to spend time with family.

"I'll be back before you know it," I say to ease her worry. "Now kiss me so I have something to hold me over for the next few weeks."

Jax lifts her head and erases the bit of distance between us. I breathe into this kiss, letting it fuel me. Her tongue licks at my bottom lip and pulls it between her teeth, sucking it between her lips and then plunging her tongue into my mouth. A groan travels up my throat and I hook an arm under her leg, opening her up to me and rolling my hips into her clothed center. We kiss and roll our bodies into each other until we're panting and moaning. Jax claws at my clothes, pushing her hands under my shirt, signaling she wants this to go further.

But it can't. And not before I'm about to leave.

I break the kiss and trail kisses down her neck, bringing us both down. Because I don't want us to part like this.

Dropping her leg from my arm, I wrap my arms around her and sit up, flipping our positions so she's in my lap.

"You're good at that," Jax says breathlessly. Her curly hair is wild from my fingers and her lips are swollen from my kiss. It's a picture every man loves to see. It's a picture I'd love to look at everyday: Jax ruined by me.

"Soon you'll know what else I'm good at." I tell her. With baseball and then midterms and then finals, that part of our relationship did not progress. It could have. But I wanted more than a quick session with Jax.

"You are the biggest tease ever."

A smile spreads across my face. It's not that I enjoyed waiting, far from it. But I am all about timing and it has never been right for us.

Jax looks over my shoulder and her body deflates. I know that means it's time for me to head out. She kisses me one last time and crawls off her bed.

"Three weeks and then I'm back." I say when we're standing next to my car. The snow disappeared the next day but it was good for me to see it as the beach doesn't get a ton.

"I love you."

I kiss her on the top of her head and wrap my arms tighter around her. "I love you too, Bee."

Jax winds her arms tightly around me and I do my best to soothe her when I feel her body tremble from the sobs she's suppressing. With a final kiss, I hop in the car and drive away from the curb.

I MADE good time on my drive and pull into the driveway just after five. Grabbing my suitcase from the trunk, I head in through the front door and set my bag by the stairs.

"Dad?" I call out as I walk through the foyer and towards the kitchen for something to eat. The TV is blaring which is normal because Dad always has the TV volume up to an obscene level. I don't see anyone in the living room, so I move to the remote when I see him face down on the floor. "Dad!"

I curse gravity as it slows me from slamming into the floor. Carefully, I flip him onto his back and check his pulse. It's there, but weak.

Fumbling for my phone and almost dropping it in the process, I dial 911 and tell them what happened and our address.

I give him chest compressions, because that's the only thing I can think to do. In all of the preparation my parents gave me for Kayla, they never prepared me to have to use life-saving measures on them.

I hear the sirens pull up but I don't stop.

"Hello?" I hear someone, I'm assuming a paramedic, call out.

"In here!" I yell. "Come on, Dad. Wake up."

Footsteps coming closer alert me that help is here. A hand touches my shoulder and I flinch. Not pulling away until someone drags me away. My body feels like it's no longer mine. Like I'm no longer tethered to this space. That gut feeling I had over the summer was right. Why? Why would he hide this from me?

"My partner has him," one of the medics tells me. "What's your name?"

I know I'm only being asked for legalities sake, but I could care less about myself. "Nate."

"Okay, Nate. I'm assuming this is your Dad?" I nod in lieu of a response. "Can you tell me what happened? How long was he like this?"

"I–I don't know. I just got home from Pennsylvania," I tell the medic and feel completely helpless.

"Okay. How old is your Dad?"

"Uh. He just turned fifty-five."

"Any underlying health issues? Concerns?"

"I was home over the summer," even to my own ears my voice is monotone, "and he was having a coughing fit. He brushed it off."

"Okay. That's good to know."

I grab dads hand as they continue to look him over. I'm angry. That's the feeling I settle on. My parents want me to be a grownup, but when it comes to their problems, they treat me like a child. But I'm also scared.

"Nate, we're gonna have to take your Dad to the hospital."

The color leeches from my face. "What?"

"It's standard and since your Dad is still unconscious, it's protocol."

I feel like I'm gonna be sick. "Can I come with?"

The paramedic gives me a sympathetic smile. "Of course."

In a daze, I stand back as my dad is loaded onto a stretcher and follow them out to the ambulance. I feel helpless.

How was I just kissing the love of my life hours ago and come home to this? This ugly reality that my parents lied to me when I asked them point blank if I needed to worry.

The ride to the hospital is almost one that you want to forget but you'll unfortunately remember for the rest of your life. How many turns it takes and the undisclosed number of potholes we unfortunately hit. This ride is one I'll unfortunately remember.

When we pull up and unload, I follow them into the ER

until my dad is admitted to an actual room. He's still unconscious and that does not do well to ease my fears. It's then that I need to call my mom. Kissing my dad on the cheek, I step outside and dial her number.

"Nate, you're home!"

I tamp down my anger and tell her what she needs to know. "Dad and I are at the hospital. He was on the floor when I got home and unconscious."

"Shit. What hospital?" She asks hurriedly and I hear her packing her things up to leave work.

"VB General."

"I'll be there soon."

My mom hangs up and I stare at my phone. It's also when I realize someone needs to pick up Kayla, so I call one of the gymnastics moms to see if she can stay with them for a bit.

"Hello?" Mrs. Greenfield answers.

"Hi, Faith. It's Nate. Um, something came up, but do you mind if Kayla goes home with you all?" I try to come off unaffected, but my throat feels like sandpaper and I'm sure she can tell.

"Sure, honey. Is everything okay?"

I bite down hard on my back teeth, I fear they'll crack. "No. But I don't wanna worry her."

"Okay, honey. She can stay as long as she needs to." She says softly and the way she says it makes me want to punch a brick wall.

"Thank you." I hang up and stand out in the breezeway. Waiting for a sign. Waiting for my mom. Waiting for someone or something to wake me up from this godforsaken nightmare I've found myself in. How?

"Nate!" I hear called out to my left. Her short hair is styled in a tinkerbell cut and her body is covered head to toe in layers to brace for the winter cold. Even in the winter, my mom's umber skin is warm like she spent hours in the sun despite being at the office when I called. She rushes up to me and it's clear the strain from this secret dad and her have kept from me has eaten away at her.

"Mom." I say and stand up to my full height. I level her with a stare that tells her I'm angry and scared shitless. "What is happening?"

"We don't know," she tells me and I quirk an eyebrow at her. "Nate, I promise I am not lying to you."

"But it's something?" I ask, grasping for some information.

My mom nods. "Yes."

I look over her head and to the parking lot. Rows of cars litter the asphalt, the sound of jets taking off from the nearby Naval Station, and the sound of semi-trucks brakes squeaking as they come to a stop at a stoplight is one of familiarity in Virginia Beach. Only, I've never heard them from the hospital. And it's now, as I'm standing outside of a hospital, that I hate the sight and sound of all those things that feel like home.

Letting out a breath, I angle my head to the side. "Okay. I'll take you to his room."

After my mom checks in and gets a name tag, I take her back up to his room. I go to the chair by the window and watch as they have a moment. Dad finally woke up and is hooked up to machines with an IV drip administering something that's above my knowledge. They talk in low voices and I see my dad's eyes flicker to me a few times. That look does very little to ease my concerns over him.

A knock sounds and in comes the doctor with a nurse following close behind. Every muscle in my body coils as I wait for what he's about to say.

"Christopher, we compared your tests from your last visit and everything still looks the same."

My spine straightens as I level a glare at my parents and then swing it to the doctor and then back to my parents.

"I'm sorry," I interrupt while not sorry in the slightest, "did you say 'last visit'? When was this?"

The doctor has the nerve to look taken aback and he looks to my parents who finally give him a nod. "Nathan, your Dad is sick."

"Yeah, I can see that. But from what? Because this is the first time I'm hearing about any of this."

"Nate," my mom tries to calm me down.

"No! I asked you both last summer if everything was okay. And you lied to my face." I tuck my hands in fists and feel the bite of pain from my nails. I will not cry. Crying makes me look weak. But not knowing what's wrong with my dad, the man I've looked up to my entire life, makes me feel helpless.

"That's because we don't know what's wrong," the doctor chimes in.

I turn my attention to him. "What do you mean?"

The doctor leans against the wall and directs his attention on me. "While your dad is sick, we've run so many tests and have come up with nothing. But my guess would be IPF."

"What's—what is that, exactly?"

"It's more common in older men, but idiopathic pulmonary fibrosis mainly attacks the lungs. Which explains the coughing."

I slide my eyes to my parents and they're looking at me with sympathy. "Is there a cure?"

"I'm afraid not."

My mouth opens and closes like a fish gasping for breath. "Does he have a timeline?"

The doctor looks at my parents and I see them nod again from the corner of my eyes, giving him the okay to tell me. "Right now, with you finding your dad unconscious and him being down for an unknown amount of time, he has a few months. Give or take."

I gnash my teeth together so hard I fear they may crack in two. A few months? No. He's supposed to meet Jax and watch me become a father. There is no way my dad is dying. I'm not ready to join *that* club.

The doctor speaks to my parents, but I don't hear a word he says so I stare at the floor trying to make sense of this nightmare I find myself living. And when the door closes, I let the silence linger. I know my parents are worried about me. But they don't need to be.

"I'm staying here," I say as I keep my eyes on the tile floor.

"What do you mean, you're staying here?" My mom asks.

"I'm gonna withdraw from Phil U and transfer here."

"No." My dad says, albeit weakly.

"What do you mean, *no*? You two kept this from me for months, when I asked you if I should be worried. And to find out you now have months? No. I'd rather transfer here to be close."

"Nathan, what about baseball? It's your final semester too."

A cold sweat coats my skin as I think about what I'm giving up. My chance at the Major League. An internship at the top architecture firms in the country. All of it slipping away for a chance to stay close to my family. And Jax. I bury my head in my hands as I know this is going to crush her. The plans we've made, disappearing faster than cotton candy on your tongue. I won't put this on her. It's not fair to put this on her. It's not fair to put this on anyone. But I can't tell her right now. Honestly, there is no right time to tell her I'm not coming back.

"I'll figure it out. But there is no way I'm going back to school five hours away. No."

"Okay. If that's what you want," my mom says.

"It is." I tell them.

A WEEK HAS GONE by since I came home for winter break. Since I found my dad facedown on the living room floor. And a week since I've ignored every one of Jax's texts. Everyday I've gone on a run until my legs turned to jell-o in an attempt to build up the courage to tell her I'm not coming back. But every time I pick up the phone and look at her countless unanswered texts, I close out of the app, promising to myself that the next day will be the day I tell her. Today is that day. Today needs to be that day.

> Me: I'm not coming back to school. I'm sorry.

After the message is delivered, I turn my phone off and decide to run down to the beach. Doesn't matter that it's December. Doesn't matter that this is my second run of the day. I just gave up three of the most important things in my life to stay home with my family. And while I love my family, I'm more hurt and lost that I now have to start over.

29

NATE

PRESENT DAY

"Remind me why we booked our flights for the asscrack of dawn?" Bryce asks with a yawn.

We're at the airport before six AM again and it really is a question for the masses.

"So that we can get home before traffic?" Kamryn poses.

"Sure," Bryce agrees, "because traffic is my biggest concern right now."

We're all in the waiting area seats of the airport. You'd think this one wouldn't be so busy. But Vegas is proving to prove me wrong at every turn. My phone buzzes in my pocket and I pull it out.

Bee: So about this date…

I flick my eyes up and see she has the perfect poker face in place as she continues to scroll through her phone.

Me: Considering we're still on the mend. I propose, you, me, and a classic movie night.

Bee: Your place or mine?

Me: Your place. At six.

Bee: Can't wait.

The announcement to board our plane comes and wearily we all gather our things and head to the gate. We're far from the lively bunch when we first arrived. But the fun we had here will be briefly remembered forever. The saying is 'what happens in Vegas, stays in Vegas'. I always found that saying cheesy, because there is no way the things that you did, don't follow you back. Like, getting married. Oh yeah. That's absolutely following me back.

AT SIX O'CLOCK ON the dot, I knock on Jax's door with a box of pizza and sparkling apple cider in my hands. Her wreath with lights signals that she's already decorated for Christmas and hopefully the inside will reflect the same because I know how much she loves this time of year. Barking and nails tapping on the floors brings a smile to my face. And when the door unlocks, revealing the only face I've dreamed about for the last eight years, my heartbeat goes into overdrive.

"Hi," she says sweetly and is almost pushed over by Sully. "Ugh, Sully. Get back in here. Come in."

I sidestep her into the house and the sound of the door closing is instead the opposite. It's like opening the door to a new us.

The inside definitely reveals she's decorated for Christmas. Holiday decor is tastefully placed with her classic tree in the front room and if I look past her, I see her balcony decorated with white lights.

"She won't stop until you give her some attention." Jax notes and takes the pizza and cider from my hands, then walks to the kitchen.

I drop to my haunches to get up close with Sully and give her chin a good scratch. "Thanks, for the good word with your Mom. I think it went better than expected." Booping her on the nose, I toe off my shoes and head towards the kitchen. My steps slow as I look at some of the pictures she has framed on the wall. Mainly of her family, a few from what I'm assuming is Kamryn's wedding, and a group photo with her girls. But in them, I don't see the Jax who's in the kitchen. This version of her looks like a ghost. There's no color in her complexion, no joy in her eyes, and she looks almost sick. Like whoever she was dating shamed her for what she looked like so she changed herself to make him happy.

"I wish I could go back." Jax says as she comes next to me. I look down at her and see her main focus on the wedding photo. That's where she looks the least like herself.

"What happened?"

"I guess we'll have to talk about this sooner than later, huh?"

"Oh, yeah." I tell her and turn to her. "I want all of it. The good, the bad, the ugly, and the beautiful."

A blush covers her face and I like this side of her a lot.

"Can I tell you while we eat? Because I'm hungry."

I nod and take a step until I'm wrapping her in my arms and walking forward with her backwards steps and laughter sounding like music to my ears. The sound of Jax's laughter is less innocence like it was when we were in college. It has a husky undertone to it that adds to the allure of who she is as a woman now.

I kiss the top of her head and release my hold on her to wash my hands.

"I met my ex right after I finally moved on from you, or so I thought I had. Which took me about three years," Jax starts when we're both settled at the table. "I was leaving Kamryn's office one day and my purse spilled on the sidewalk." I snort and she smiles. "Total cliche right? I was blinded by his kindness and after leaving a meeting with Kamryn that left me frustrated, I think I needed that. I needed a light to show me that I made it through the darkest part of my life and he was that."

Jax takes a bite of her pizza and I follow suit. For a simple pizza, the flavors explode on my taste buds and I don't come up for air until I finish my slices.

"So how did you two...date?" The word tastes like acid on my tongue.

"He gave me some line about how he'll help me clean up all my messes. Somehow that worked on me. I blinked and three years had gone by."

I hook my thumb over my shoulder towards the hallway with the pictures. "And how did you get to that?"

"The comments would start little—" a red haze covers my body as I fear this story is going to take a turn "—until they weren't. Comments about my weight and how come I don't look like this fake Instagram model or if I ate less and worked out more, he could lift me effortlessly."

"I'll kill him." I say and mean the words entirely. To hell with baseball. Any man who makes a woman feel less than for the curves on her body deserves a life of misery.

Jax smiles softly and surveys me with careful eyes then points to my face. "I like this look on you."

"What look? Charming, chivalrous, possessive?"

"Yes, yes, and yes."

The look that passes between us is loaded. It's more than the small dreams we had as kids. This is the look where we realize our dreams we made is now the future that we dreamed it could be.

"So movie," I say, shaking myself out of my daydream. "What'll it be?"

"I basically have all the apps, so our options are endless."

We clean up from dinner, reminiscent of college, then shut off the lights and head to the living room. Jax turns on the battery operated candles, the strip lights on the back of the TV, and then joins me on the oversized couch.

I flip through the apps before picking one and doing another scroll before landing on *Pitch Perfect*.

"Seriously?" She asks with a teasing lilt in her voice.

"Kayla is obsessed with it and you can't deny it's a funny movie."

We lay back and the beginning credits begin, covering our eyes when Aubrey throws up on stage and laughing when Amy does the mermaid on the ground.

"How are we going to work?" Jax asks when the auditions start on the movie.

"Like the dating part or the married part?"

I still get tingles when I remember that Jax and I are legally married. At least one of us is thinking clearly, because I'm clearly thinking with my heart.

"The married part," she clarifies and reaches for the volume remote to turn the TV down.

"I should probably alert my agent and publicist that I'm married. Along with my accountant and lawyer."

"So many people." Jax groans.

"Yeah," I say, "we could have fun with the publicist part."

"Are you suggesting we tell Sarah we're married?"

I pull back and look at her. "Do you not want to?"

"I do." Jax says and I smirk at her word choice. She gently hits me on the chest and sits up. "I thought I would tell my sister first, but knowing her she would blab about it in our group chat before we had a chance to tell anyone else."

My eyebrows lift as I watch Jax run herself into a panic. "Bee, breathe."

She does her deep breaths and relaxes. "Okay, I'm good. I want us to tell Sarah. Your team should be ahead of this before the media anyways."

"Good plan. I can't wait to date my wife."

"How long have you been wanting to say that?"

I do the math and tilt my head, looking up at the ceiling. "About nine years."

"You know, with dating comes other things..." Jax says coyly and draws a random pattern on the couch.

I grab the remote and pause the forgotten movie. "You're right."

"This marriage is off to a great start."

I throw a pillow at her face, muffling her laughter. "Okay. Let's talk about it."

Jax drops the pillow from her face and pushes her hair back. "You first."

"Zero," I tell her. "Not since before you."

"What?"

I hold my hand up in a zero for my silently repeated answer.

"How is that...what about the cleat chasers in every city?" Her beautiful face scrunches up as she tries to understand.

"They tried. E for effort on their part."

"But you have needs."

I hold up my hand again as if that's explanation enough. Yeah, it's pathetic now that I'm in this moment. I haven't had sex in over ten years. Have I missed the act? Of course. But having it to have it with a random hookup never appealed to me. I'm a relationship man through and through and the only person I've wanted is right in front of me.

"I got by. Enough with me and my celibacy."

Jax adjusts, folding her legs under her and sitting on her feet. "Just my ex. But not as much as he wanted."

"He didn't..." If she says he forced himself on her, I will find him and make him wish he was never born.

"Force himself on me? No. Was any of it enjoyable? Also no."

My body is throwing a malfunction code. The man in me wants to throw her over my shoulder and show her what she's been missing. But I fear that would come off as retaliation and that's not how I want mine and Jax's first time to be. Plus, I'd come after two seconds and that'd be more embarrassing than admitting I haven't had sex in over a decade.

"What a prick." Is what I settle on.

"I don't miss him. So I don't ever want you to question that."

"It never would have crossed my mind."

Jax snorts and repositions on the couch, settling into my side. "Now that that's settled, we'll tell your team first. Can we do that sooner than later?"

"Yeah." I tell her because I want that too.

"Monday?"

"You really do want people to know," I tease her.

"I just want to date my husband out in the open."

"Fuck I love those words falling from your lips." I groan and grab my phone with Jax laughing at my hurriedness.

Me: Hey. I need to see you both on Monday.

Me: It's important.

Sarah: Woah. Yeah. I have time at ten. Does that work for you Mallory?

Mallory: I'll have to video chat in. I'm in California for the next week.

Me: That's fine. See you Monday.

"Done." I state and toss my phone to the side.
"Good. Now press play. They're at the riff-off."

30

JAX

I'm putting on my black cowboy boots, yes the ones I wore when Nate and I allegedly got married, when I hear my front door open and close.

"Jaclyn Marie, are you ready?"

I slide my ring on my finger before spritzing myself with some perfume from Jo Malone and then grab my peacoat that I tossed on my bed. It's been colder than usual in Cincinnati so the thick, dark patterned floral maxi skirt I have on swishes around my legs as I walk down the stairs. I have it paired with a black sweater and a black belt with a gold buckle. My curly hair is styled to perfection as the diffuser was finally on my side today and humidity is low. Small wins for those of us with curly hair. I see Nate playing a soft game of tug-of-war with Sully when I hit the last step and smile.

"I'm ready." I tell him and I pull on my coat.

We made a game plan last night. Nate will head into Sarah's office and I'll stroll in five minutes later. Once we leave Sarah's office we're planning to head to Kamryn's office.

"You look beautiful," Nate says as he looks up at me.

"Thank you. You look very handsome yourself."

Nate ruffles Sully's ears and stands up. I don't think I'll ever get over his height. He was tall in college but now that he's had years in the league it's like he's continued to grow. And I know that's impossible, but now I'll get to reap the benefits of his training. Lucky me.

"Stop looking at me like that," Nate scolds.

I shrug and head towards the front door but I'm hooked around the waist and turned into his chest with a gasp. His patchouli scent surrounds and comforts me. It's the one scent I avoided after he never came back. But now that he's here it's like I can bathe in it. Last night we had a classic first date. And when I mean classic, I mean old school. Nate didn't touch me apart from wrapping his arm around me. And when I confessed about not enjoying sex with my ex, I thought he would throw me over his shoulder and prove just how enjoyable sex can be with the right man. But no. Now I'm back to waiting like I was in college and I hate it.

"I'm not looking at you in a way." I tell him, finally finding my words.

He kisses me on the forehead and thousands of butterflies take flight. "Yes, you were. Now let's go."

Nate walks around me to the front door and I suck in a deep breath before moving and walking across the threshold then hearing the door lock. I canceled work for the day, telling my manager I had personal things to do. I'll email her back and tell her the real reason. The passenger door is opened for me and I climb up inside. I look around at the clean interior and the new car smell hitting me.

"Is this new?" I ask Nate when he gets in and starts up.

"Nope. But I did get it a few years ago. I just like to keep it clean." He tells me and pulls out onto the road with one hand on the steering wheel. *Hot.* "Stop looking at me like that."

"Well, stop looking like that." I say and wave my hand up and down.

Nate's smile lifts his cheeks and he rests a hand on my thigh. He has a tattoo that covers his right hand and I'm finally able to get a good look at it in the sunlight. It's the classic lion. But where one half is the lion, the other half is a garden. I trace the floral ink with my pointer finger reveling in the way his forearm twitches.

"How many tattoos do you have?" I ask now very curious. The road turns open as we hop on the highway towards Sarah's office.

"I lost count after ten." Nate says with a shrug. "You are more than welcome to do a full body inspection."

"I bet I am," I say dryly.

Nate turns up the volume to the music and we sit in companionable silence the rest of the way to the office. He finds a spot and whips in with one hand and I blow out a breath.

"Nervous?" Nate asks when he parks and turns off the truck.

I shake my head slowly. "Far from it."

Nate picks up my left hand and thumbs the ring. Who would've thought playing with jewelry would send my heart into overdrive? He kisses my hand and places it in my lap. Am I breathing? I quickly check my pulse and feel a heartbeat.

"Let's go ya goof."

I get out and take Nate's hand and together we walk into the building that holds Sarah's job. Nate heads to the elevator and hits the button to go up as I wait off to the side.

This is the plan. But I completely forgot about the elevator and my hands get sweaty.

"Bee, it's a quick ride up and then we're coming back down together."

"Yeah. Short elevator ride. Got it."

Nate is, rightfully so, unconvinced at my act. "Let's just scrap the plan and go in together."

I chew on my bottom lip as I weigh my options. We tell Sarah at once or we tell her when I join them. "Are you sure?"

"Yes." Nate says and the elevator doors open. "Besides, the sooner we tell her, the better right?"

"Right." I say and the doors open up to It's A Match PR.

"Hi, Tessa," Nate greets the receptionist. "We're here to see Sarah."

"Hi, Nate. You two can head back."

We smile at her and head through the double glass doors. The office is at half-capacity today. I'm assuming most of the agents are on vacation or traveling to their clients' games. I'm still not entirely confident I know what they do. But it must be good work if they're constantly traveling. Sarah's corner office is straight back from the entrance. My hand starts sweating in Nate's hold and he gives mine a reassuring squeeze. I let go of his hold when we get closer to her office. At least this part of the plan will work.

Nate knocks on her door and opens it when he hears her call out. "Hey."

"Nate. Come in," Sarah says.

Before he does he holds his hand out to me and I take it. His fingers weave through mine and together we walk into Sarah's office.

Her face lights up and I don't think I've ever seen her so

happy. Well, apart from when she's with Riley, her fiancé. Nate leads me to a chair and takes the one next to me.

"Jax, did you pull your head out of your butt? Are you two finally back together?"

Nate and I look at each with twin bemused expressions as we sit in the chairs in front of her desk. But I raise my eyebrow to let him know this is his show. "Actually, we got married. In Las Vegas."

The air cuts out, Sarah stops moving in her chair, and it's so quiet you could hear a pin drop. That is until she laughs like Nate told the funniest joke. I'll admit, he's funny when he wants to be. But this? No.

Sarah gasps when she sees us not laughing with her. "Oh, you're serious?"

We hold up our left hands and her eyes about fall out of her head.

"Oh my God. Shit, we're supposed to video in Mallory. Hold on."

Is she mad?, I mouth to Nate.

He shrugs just as confused as I am. I guess I thought she would yell, try to make us cry, or try to make us claim it's fake and then demand we get a divorce. Nate and I have barely been married for a week and already this feels more real than my last relationship. I already feel so solid that I'm wondering why we didn't do this in college. *You were both broke*, I tell myself as if that's a valid reason and not that we loved each other. But maybe Nate was right and had we stayed together, it would have ruined us.

"Mallory? Hey, I have Nate and his wife." Sarah says and flicks her eyes up to me.

"Hey, Sarah. Hi, Nate. Um...I'm sorry. I must have forgotten to Q-tip my ears this morning," Nate's agent says on the other end. "Sarah, did you say Nate's wife?"

"I did. And she's sitting right here." Sarah turns the camera towards Nate and I and I mouth *I hate you* to her before coming face to face with Nate's agent. She just shrugs and sits back in her chair.

"Hi, I'm Jax. Or Jaclyn if you prefer that."

Her mouth opens and closes like a guppy. "I–you, Nate. You're Jax. This answers so many questions." She says and sits back in her chair.

"Huh?" I ask and see Sarah just as confused. I swing my gaze to Nate who's glaring daggers at the screen. "What is she talking about?"

"Nothing. We wanted to tell you both before the media found out."

"How considerate. But, yes, Nate can explain all of that to you. It's nice meeting you, Jax. Sarah, I'll call you later today. Congrats you, two. Oh and happy holidays."

We sit in Sarah's office. Me staring at the now darkened computer screen, Sarah looking utterly confused, and Nate burning a hole in the side of my face.

He breaks the silence first. "That went better than expected."

"Yeah," Sarah says softly. "Make sure you tell Kamryn before someone else finds out. We know how she hates being left in the dark. And if you two managed to keep this from her when y'all were in Vegas, then you know how she's going to react."

I wince as I remember her reaction to Emily and Adam dating after they had already been together for a couple of months.

"She's our next stop. And I'll text Emily since she's teaching."

Sarah turns her computer back around to her and leans

forward on her desk. "Seems like you both have your ducks in a row."

"We're getting most things situated," Nate chimes in.

My quiet husband.

"You've both told your families?" Sarah asks.

Nate and I turn to each other with wide eyes causing Sarah to laugh.

"I won't say a word. Have fun you two."

Nate stands up and holds his hand out. "Later tater."

Hand in hand we walk back to the elevator with more excitement than we walked in here with. Nate presses the button and wraps his arms around me when we're in the elevator car.

"What?" I ask softly as we head to the ground level.

"Just thinking that maybe we should plan trips to see our families."

I wrap my arms tighter around him, eliminating the space between us. "I was thinking that too. I don't want my parents to freak out."

I think my parents will be happy that Nate and I found our way back to each other. He's the only guy I brought around that they genuinely liked and respected. My ex on the other hand never cared to meet them and Kamryn's wedding was their first introduction. Safe to say, they threw a party when he and I split.

"What does your schedule look like Mrs. Holloway?" Nate asks with a smirk.

A blush heats my face and the smile turns massive. "I have some meetings, a couple of podcasts to film, and some brand videos to film. But if I spend all day tomorrow getting everything done, then I'll have the rest of the week free."

The elevator doors open and Nate takes my hand, swinging them between us as we walk out to his truck. "You let me know how long you want to go and I'll book us tickets to see our families."

"Sounds like a plan, Mr. Holloway."

IF I WAS nervous to face Sarah, nothing compares to sitting in Kamryn's office while she rests on her desk and stares at us. Nate has wiped his hands on his jeans five times in the fifteen minutes we've been sitting here and I crossed, uncrossed, and recrossed my legs more times than I can count.

"So you lied to me?"

"Um," that comes out higher pitched and she narrows her eyes at me. "Yes."

"Why?"

"You are," I pause as I think of the right words to use. Thank goodness Nate is letting me take the lead on this. "Pushy. No. That's not it. Kammy, you command respect in every room you walk in. That's just how you are. You expect everyone to be upfront about everything and that's something I admire about you. Not everyone is like that. Some of us need to sit in our choices before we tell other people. But Nate and I getting married in Vegas of all places and not remembering it was something we needed to iron out before we told anyone. How would you feel if you married Mason and didn't remember it?"

My sister deflates and nods her head finally seeing my point. "Okay, I get it. You two really don't remember?"

"Nope. The last we both clearly remember was going to Fremont Street Experience and then waking up the next morning."

"Which is why you two were acting so weird," Kamryn notes.

"Yep."

"Well, hey I finally get another brother."

Nate looks at me weird and I pat him on the leg. "Mason has two younger brothers and a sister."

The door to Kamryn's office opens and Olivia pops her head in. "Damn. I have to go. Holiday season is my busiest time, so thank you for bringing this to me now."

I roll my eyes and pull Nate up from the couch. "No problem. See ya later, Kam."

Nate and I head back to my place where we make a larger and more solid game plan for how married life will work. Neither of us want to lose who we are as individuals so until we're ready, we'll continue to live in our respective homes with sleepovers. Is it what most married couples would do? No. But Nate and I aren't most married couples. Plus, most married couples remember the part where they got married.

"What did your agent mean?" I ask as I look at the calendar that has all of our dates marked in for the next six months. With baseball spring training in February that was a surreal thing to write down.

"Long story short, I'm friends with her brother. And one drunken night I spilled about how I'll never date anyone because Jax is the only girl I'll ever want."

My heart aches and soars if that's possible. "When was this?"

"About a year after I was drafted." Nate tells me and I continue to look over our joint schedule. "Bee, stop looking at the calendar. It's not going to change if you look away."

He's on the other side of the counter chopping up the

chicken for our chicken caesar salads. The oven behind him says five minutes left on the fries that are being made.

I look at him with a pout as I close the calendar and push it off to the side with a groan. "Happy?"

"Ecstatic," he replies dryly. "Will you take the fries out?"

I slide off the barstool and grab an oven mitt. The golden potatoes and salty aroma fill my senses and I can't wait to devour these. We get to work on putting the meal together and eat at the bar since our stuff is set up. I've been drafting emails and responding to a DM from Ellie checking in. I didn't think I would hear back from her, but low and behold, she had been thinking of me too.

Pushing my empty plate away, I sit back with my glass of water.

"Good?" Nate asks with a smile.

"So good. I'm keeping you."

"Noted. I wasn't going to give the option to get rid of me anyways." Nate turns me in my chair and puts my glass on the bar. His legs bracket me in as he takes my left hand in his and thumbs the ring.

I know he wants to say something, but remembering what Mallory said in Sarah's office, has me perking up. What did Mallory mean by, *You're Jax*?"

"About a year into working with her, she tried to set me up with one of her closest friends," he admits and I rear back with wide eyes. "Easy, tiger. We eventually had a long sit-down where I admitted that, in this lifetime, moving on from you wasn't a possibility. I told her your name and that if I ever got you back, it would all make sense."

My eyes water and I lean forward to give him a quick kiss on the lips.

"Do you like this ring? I mean, really like it?" He asks when I sit back in my chair.

"Yes. I was actually thinking about how you knew exactly what I wanted when I only mentioned it that one time."

His eyes are still on my ring but I see the small smile. "I remember everything you told me Jax. Do you remember my senior project?" I nod, because of course I remember that day, and he smiles yet again. "I eventually had them drafted up."

I swallow roughly because I was just telling him things at the time that probably didn't make sense for a house. But, apparently, Nate took note of it anyway. "You did?"

"Yeah, Bee. I was secure in the knowledge that one day you and I would find our way back to each other. And when that happened, I wanted to have our house plans drafted and ready to go."

"What?" How does this man continue to shock me?

Nate looks up and pushes a curl off my face. "Don't you get it, Bee? It's always been you for me. Since I was eighteen years old, it's always been you."

31

JAX

COLLEGE, DECEMBER, SENIOR YEAR

"*I knew you were coming back.*"

Six words. I remember saying those six words to him and the smile he gave me. Was it all a lie? Because I can't imagine a world where we made promises for our future just for him to text me those eight words and nothing more.

I think back to the day I told him we could be nothing more than friends. I was afraid of losing him more than anything. How he was adamant that us falling apart was all in my head. That it would never happen.

Look where I'm at now.

I sit on my covered balcony as the snow falls a few days before Christmas. Heartbroken and alone. Christmas is my second favorite holiday, but I've yet to find an ounce of joy to get me through the season.

I feel like I'm walking on a glass floor in the pointiest high heels and trying not to crash through with every step. My parents have been walking on eggshells around me too. Because after a week of texting Nate with no response until that one fated message, they found me sobbing in my room.

And through those tears I managed to tell them that he wasn't coming back. That fear I had over losing him came true.

For months he and I would spout hypotheticals about when he was on the road for games, how I would react. I always told him I wouldn't react a certain way because I knew he was coming back.

My lips tremble with the realization that he's not coming back this time. And I have to find a way to make it without him sooner than I planned to.

How did my sister do this? I thought she was overreacting when Mason left, but is this how she felt? Like she all of a sudden was missing an extension of herself?

The tears win the battle and fall in rivulets down my face. Washing away every plan we made, tear by tear.

Goodbye, Nathan Holloway.

32

NATE

I'm in my home gym when I hear the muffled thump of the front door closing and locking. A warm and calm sensation slides over me that I know it's Jax. Our plan is to visit our families before I head off to spring training. It'll also be the first time Jax meets my mom and Kayla. If it's one thing I kick myself in the ass for, it's not bringing her home at any point when we were in college. But thinking about it back then, that seemed the type of thing reserved for significant others. And we weren't together for very long until I left. But I did have one opportunity over the summer to take her home. Yet, I was a typical boy and honestly I was terrified to introduce Jax to my family. I won't deny that.

Shaking my head, I let the music that's pumping through the speakers energize me for this last circuit. Sweat pours down my face and body as I pump my arms and legs on the treadmill. When the timer beeps that my one minute is up, I hit the down arrow to slow down to a walk. Movement in the mirror breaks me out of the workout haze and I see Jax leaning against the door with a look that can only be described as lust painting her face. And even though I'm technically done, I can't help but tease her further and showing off by heading to the pull-up station and getting a few reps in. When I drop down, I head to the speaker and turn the music down from an ear-splitting level.

"Hi," Jax says a little breathlessly.

"Hi, Bee." I greet her and drop onto the mat to finish with some core work. One thing I've noticed about Jax, is that while it may not look like she puts a lot of care into what she wears, she still looks effortlessly put together even in a hoodie and leggings. Her curly hair I love so much, falls in spiral waterfalls along her back and over her shoulders. I used to fantasize about twirling the strands around my fingers. I still do. But now I fantasize about fisting them as I rut into her.

My abdominal muscles burn as I run through the last of this circuit. This one to test my balance. Growing up, I had thought that baseball was only about your arms and your legs. Oh how wrong I was. When I started incorporating more weight training and muscle specific exercises, the results on the field started to show. It's what has made me such an asset on the field. I finish up this round and then drop into my stretching, all the while watching Jax.

Damn, I love my wife. The thought pops up out of nowhere. Although it's not a sudden realization. It's been a feeling that's simmered under the surface, only laying dormant during our separation. Until now.

Is declaring the love I always felt for her too soon now that we're a married couple?

Jax says she loves the ring I drunkenly picked out for her. Hell, I've caught her staring at it multiple times with a secret smile when she thought I wasn't looking at her. I've continuously asked myself if I were sober, would I have picked out the same ring? And the answer is always yes.

"You looked good." She notes and finally walks into the room and looks at each piece of equipment.

"You're always free to join me."

Jax shivers as if the thought of working out with me repulses her and I arch an eyebrow towards her. "No. It's not you. And I'm sure working out with you would be great. Or we would end up doing a different workout, if you catch my drift." *Oh, I'm starting to.* "But me and the gym don't go together. At least not anymore."

"Does this stem back to that waste of space ex?"

"Yeah," Jax says and avoids my eyes.

There's something else. Something she's managed to hide from everyone. I don't want that. Secrets, that is.

"Bee, come here," I command softly.

She hesitates where she's running her fingers over the dumbbell rack before finding my eyes in the mirror and coming over to the mat with me. I point to the spot in front of me and when she's seated, I place her legs on top of mine, making sure she's close to me. I'm not sure what it is about Jax that I always have to touch her.

"How bad did it get?"

"About a year into him and I dating, he started making more pointed comments about my weight. Nothing too digging where I took offense. Until he would, once again, show me those fake Instagram models and ask why my stomach wasn't as flat as theirs. Or if I would ever get breast implants or a butt lift."

I curl my hands over her thighs as I hold back on demanding her to give me his number so I can track him down.

"So I cut what I ate in half. And when that still wasn't enough for him I joined a gym. I went every morning and night. My social life was non-existent at that point, I wasn't eating enough, I couldn't remember what a good night's sleep felt like, and the work I submitted to brands was lackluster."

Realization dawns on me. "Shit. That's why you and the gym don't go together." It's not a question but more a statement observation.

"Yeah. But now I workout in healthy ways. I know when I need rest and when I need to move. But now I do it at my own pace and not for an end goal."

"Do you run with Sarah?" I ask with a smile because my publicist runs a lot. So much that she puts distance runners to shame.

Jax scoffs. "God, no. She actually picked that up from Kamryn. But, no. I'm more of a pilates and spin workout girl when I want to be. Plus, my twice a day walks with Sully."

I smile as I remember running up to her that summer day on her walk. "And food?"

"That relationship was easier to heal than I thought. But sometimes his voice will pop into my head and I'll hesitate. It's hard to break patterns that were part of your daily life for so long."

I know she's past that relationship. But I can't help but feel angry for her. How a man could make a woman feel like she needs to change how much she eats, or how much she weighs so he can lift her easily. I'll take Jax anyway I can get her. I'll be the best support system for her when the doubt creeps in.

"I'm glad you broke up with him."

Jax huffs a short laugh. "Me too." Her gaze goes to my bare torso and I feel the path her eyes take as she looks at the tattoos covering my body. Jax's hand reaches out to touch certain spots and I know she's finding them. The tension in her face eases and her mouth parts on a gasp. "You have–you have bees. So many bees."

"You were always with me, baby. Even when we were complete strangers living in the same city."

The idea to keep Jax with me despite letting her go, some would call that a glutton for punishment. I call that holding onto hope. When I got the first bee tattooed, I knew I would get more.

Jax moves on a mission and hooks her hand on the gold chain that's looped over my neck, bringing me closer to her. Her other hand comes up to my face and traces my bottom lip with her thumb. My hands are still resting on her thighs. I won't move. Jax needs the control more than my need for her. She needs to control this. And I let her.

In a breath, our lips touch. Soft at first. But when Jax scoots closer, fusing us together, that's when the kiss is no longer soft. My hands slide up her legs and to her waist. Her arm wraps around my shoulder and then I'm taking us backward. Jax gasps at the backward motion with her body falling on top of mine and I groan into her mouth when she rubs her center over my hardening cock. Our tongues tangle and I move her hips over me. We explore each other freely with our hands while Jax's hips continue to roll over my erection.

Jax breaks the kiss and I pull a lungful of air in. She licks and nips at the sweat still lingering on my skin and soothes the spot with kisses.

"Fuck," I groan out.

"Are you gonna come like this, Natey?" She asks, and our lips brush against each others as she asks the question.

My hands fall back to her hips and grind her over my erection. "Absolutely. And you are too. Use me, baby."

Jax angles my head the way she wants and explores my

mouth. Pulling my lower lip between her teeth and sucking on it. The sensation goes to my cock and I roll my hips into her. The kiss breaks and Jax drops her hand on the floor and uses the momentum to make herself come. The little whimpers paired with her moaning when my cock slides against her clit is an erotic sound that I'll memorize forever.

"That's it, Bee. Take what you need." My hands grip her hips hard enough to probably leave a bruise.

"Nate." My name leaves her mouth on a shaky exhale.

I push her down harder for friction on her clit and that sigh does it.

"Oh, fuck," Jax says with a whine as her orgasm hits and the roll of her hips becomes erratic.

I'm right behind her. My grip on her hips gets tighter and force her mouth back to mine in a searing kiss as I move her roughly over me. Jax's tongue flutters with mine and I groan into her mouth as I come in my shorts. Her hips continue to move lazily over me as we both come down from the high. Jax peppers kisses along my neck, jaw, cheek, and nose. This, I could get used to.

"I'm not sure I'll be able to workout in here and not think of that," I say, finally breaking the silence.

"Yes you will." Jax slides off my lap and lays next to me, she props her head on her fist, keeping a hand on my chest and a leg thrown over my hip. "Just think of it as motivation anytime you step foot in here."

"Ooo. An orgasm per set I complete? I like the way you think, wifey."

"We'll see."

We lay there on the gym floor just looking at each other. This week has been quick kisses before hopping onto meetings or heading out to train. We're doing the back and forth between our houses, but we haven't gotten to the sleepover part. Despite us being married, that would be the next big step in our relationship.

"What are you thinking about?" Jax whispers.

"Everything." I tell her. And it's the truth. I can't turn my brain off. I'm constantly thinking about my next step–our next step now, and it's driving me insane. I've always been a chronic over-thinker and now that I have Jax to worry about, I fear it'll send me backwards. Erasing all of the strides I made to go with the flow in life.

Jax's brows furrow, before she's sitting up and holding her hand out to me. "Come on."

Tentatively, I place my hand in hers and let her assist in pulling me to a standing position. But let's be real. There is no way Jax could pull me up on her own. I outweigh and tower over her. With confusion plaguing me, I grab my phone and turn out the lights, before following Jax upstairs. She walks with a purpose to my living room where I see a gift wrapped box sitting on my coffee table.

"I'm all sweaty. And I have cum in my shorts. Can I shower first?"

"No." Jax demands and laughs before pulling me to sit on the couch next to her. "I did some snooping around earlier this week before knowing you needed this."

Christmas is a week away and it didn't even dawn on me that we were doing gifts.

"I didn't get you anything," I admit weakly.

"Baby, I don't care about that. Plus you know I love giving gifts." Jax wraps her hand around my neck and pulls me down for a quick kiss. "This is also for me, too."

I look at Jax, my heart already bursting from the love I feel for her. Squeezing her knee affectionately, I lean forward and grab the box. It's got a bit of weight to it and I look at her before tearing it open.

"You didn't."

"I did," Jax says with glee coating both words.

I tear the rest of the paper off and open the box. Inside is the top of the line Nikon. My other cameras are stored at my mom's place. And since baseball took over my life, I didn't find them necessary to have around.

"No. Jaclyn Marie, this is too expensive."

"Will you stop? Nate," she pauses to collect her words, "one of the things I was most jealous of when we were younger was your passion for things. Photography being one of them. You didn't see you from my point of view. Baseball, that was a given. But you behind a lens was like watching Jackie Robinson or Willie Mays up to bat. I loved seeing that version of you because there was no thought behind what you took. You just let yourself feel. And if a camera is going to help you turn your mind off, because I can see when you start to overthink, then I want you to help you get back to that."

I run my hands over the body of the camera and smile as Jax's words soak in. She's right. I did stop thinking when I had a camera in my hands. Everything shutdown and it's as if she knew that this is what I needed without me telling her.

"Jax," I start and turn to her but she cuts me off.

"Don't say something that's going to freak me out."

"How about I love you?"

She smiles, albeit wobbly, but a smile nonetheless. "Yeah, that'll do it. I love you, too."

I lean forward and close the small gap between us. Jax is trembling against my lips, emotion taking over as those three words are said as a married couple.

~

THE FIRE PIT on Jax's back porch crackles and warms us in the late December cold. We're cuddled up on one of the outdoor couches with mugs of hot chocolate keeping us somewhat warm. Tomorrow is New Year's Eve and I find myself pinching myself that we're married. That I'm coming out of this year with the girl I dreamed of marrying when I was twenty-one. Talk about destiny.

Jax and I talk. A lot. It's like we've both stored things away in the years we were apart and are now playing catch-up.

"Do you go home often?" she asks as we watch the lights in the city illuminate the river.

"No. I can't."

"Will you tell me?"

Jax doesn't have to elaborate. I know what she's asking me to tell her.

"It was a few months after I found that my dad had limited time left with us. Um, because we were in season, my coach sat down with my parents to be made aware of what was happening. He got their phone numbers in case of big emergencies." I don't have to clarify what I mean by the big emergency and I swallow as my telling this story takes me back to that day. "Luckily, we were playing at home. I must've been in a spot on the field or up to bat where I didn't see my coach take a phone call that would change everything. He made the call to have me finish the game. And when it was over, he told me my dad had collapsed again. That it was Kayla who found him. I left the field then and there. In my uniform and cleats as I sped to the hospital just hoping to make it in time. He passed just minutes after I got there."

Jax's hands wipes away the tears I didn't know had fallen. December is usually my darkest month. It's when I made the decision to leave school and the girl I loved. It's when I found out he was sick and that there was no cure. How can we make so many medical advances and not find a cure for so many things? I was mad. At my parents, at the doctors, at science. When March rolls around, that's when I feel the weight of his loss the most.

"In hindsight I know my coach made the right call not to tell me until after the game. But knowing I could have had more moments with him, is something I find unforgivable. I didn't cope the way I should have. I lost my dad. I lost the person I look up to from an incurable disease."

"Did you ever..." Jax stumbles over her words as she thinks of what to ask me.

"Want to join him?"

She nods against me. "Yeah."

"The thought crossed my mind. He was my best friend." I tell her and don't miss the wince. "But then I looked at my mom and Kayla, how they were also just as lost, and I realized that my absence would have destroyed them."

"I'm glad you stayed." Jax whispers.

I look at Jax, whose eyes are filled with a light sheen of tears, and lift up my arm in invitation for her to snuggle closer. "Me too, Bee."

"If things ever get dark again—will you tell me?"

"I promise."

The hard thing about suffering is that it's mostly done in silence. That's why they call it *suffering in silence*. The stranger you pass on the street could be contemplating ending it because no one listens to them. An outburst at work means they suffered for too long and needed to let it out before it destroyed them. My suffering was needing to escape from the grief I couldn't process.

"Will you tell me about your Dad?"

Jax and I lean further back into the couch cushions. With the fire going and the hum from downtown faintly reaching us, I tell her everything. I tell her about his after-work routine and how, like clockwork, I would hear the sound of his office chair squeaking as he reclined to finish up the rest of his work for the day. I told her that he was a quiet man, but when he spoke, people listened. His stories from when he was a kid, traveling around the country to where his Dad was stationed in the Navy, to his own stint playing college football and then the Navy as well. I tell her about when my parents met as two broke kids who said that love was more than enough. And how they were together for over thirty years until he passed away.

"I realize that my wanting to disappear would have been an act of selfishness." Jax grips onto me tighter as she lets me get the words out. "My mom lost her other half. The person that she thought she would grow old with. How can she live her life without him?"

"Maybe when we go visit your family, you can ask her?"

I kiss the top of Jax's head and rest my cheek there. "Yeah, maybe."

"Do you wanna know how I would feel? If the love of my life was no longer here?"

I think of my not being here and Jax living life without me. The thought is too much to handle. But maybe she'll tell me her experience from when we were apart. "Tell me."

"I would feel lost. And in an endless cycle of sadness. I don't know what it's like for your Mom to lose her other half. But I feel like that's what it's like for her. An endless cycle of sadness."

Jax saying that makes me think that maybe my mom is only keeping it together for me and Kayla. That she's only here because of me and Kayla. How many times has she cried herself to sleep at night? Is she eating enough? Is Kayla making sure she's getting to work?

When I got drafted, I left and never looked back. It was the only way I knew how to cope. How to heal. That makes me a bad son, but I couldn't stay there any longer. I wanted to make something of myself and I did that to honor my dad. It's why I wear number 37. I never asked why that was his favorite number. But if I had to guess it was the age he was when Kayla was born. So I wear that number with pride.

"I can book us tickets and we can go visit our families this week." I tell Jax with another kiss on her forehead and I feel her nod against my chest.

We stay on the patio until not even the fire and blankets can keep us warm. With an extended goodbye in the form of over-the-clothes groping on her couch, I head back to my empty house. Walking in with no one here, makes me want to speed up our dating process so we can get to the forever part. I love my house, but I would rather live with Jax. So it's time to accelerate the process of us living together.

33

JAX

The plane touches down on the runway with a smooth landing. We only spent a day with my parents in Philadelphia and they were more than ecstatic that they now have another son-in-law. And it being Nate of all people, soothed their hurt over us getting married in Vegas. It may have taken them our whole visit to forgive him for the way he left me the first time, but they came around.

I yawn and stretch in my seat as the only flight to get us here with enough time to not be traveling all day, without out of the way plane stops, was an eight AM flight. Meaning, my husband had us at the airport hours before we departed. Nate was on the receiving end of my less than stellar mood and got me caffeine as soon as he could. But I kissed him to make up for my crankiness, which he readily accepted. It's just before ten when the plane comes to a stop and it's then I notice that Nate's tenseness is soaking into me.

I lightly caress his chin and turn his head my way. "Hey."

Nate's eyes hold a heaviness to them that I haven't seen before and it tears me up. I know coming home is hard for him. But deep down, I know my husband needs this. *He* knows he needs this.

"Hi, Bee."

"For better or worse." I tell him, not breaking eye contact. That seems to soothe his anxiety just a smidge. Because whether it's a sunshine and cloudless day or turbulent weather is in the forecast, I'm not leaving him.

When the whirl of the engines stops, the captain announces we are safe to depart the plane, but Nate and I stay seated just a little bit longer looking at each other. He kisses me on the tip of my nose and once the aisle is cleared out, only then do we unbuckle and grab our backpacks from the overhead compartment. Hand-in-hand we make the mile long walk towards baggage claim. Okay, it's not an entire mile, but it feels that way. We stand off to the side with him holding me. His head rests on top of my head and my hands rest on his back, tracing soothing circles to bring his heart rate back down. Nate kisses the top of my head and gently unwinds my arms from around him as he goes to get our luggage that dropped.

I watch him pick up both bags, with his body tense and coiled to strike. This is not the boy I fell in love with and I can't help but think I pushed him to this. I can't help but compare Nate to how Kamryn and Emily reacted those months, and years if I'm honest, after Liam and James passed. They were definitely withdrawn and I never pushed them when they retreated into themselves because I knew they needed to heal in their own time. But I don't know how to move forward with Nate coming to terms with his Dad's passing. Because it's clear that he hasn't properly grieved.

"Ready?" He asks with fake enthusiasm when he's back over with our suitcases trailing behind him. Everything about my husband is strained and I hate it. Thankfully it's still early enough that not everyone has noticed Nate's presence, apart from the few die hard baseball fans that have gawked or weren't sure if it was him. And I'm grateful they've left him alone. But really, it could be the scowl and the hard-set line of his clenched jaw that kept people from approaching him.

"I'm ready." I tell him and hold my hand out for my suitcase. Begrudgingly, Nate hands me mine and together we walk to the rental car counter to get our keys.

NATE NAVIGATES the highway like he plays baseball. Effortlessly. And sexy as hell. I cross my legs to try to relieve the ache that's started in my core. With all of our make out sessions I feel like we're back in college. But god, I want more. I want all of him.

"You're staring," Nate says without taking his eyes off the road.

"You once told me I can stare at you all I want. So I'm taking full advantage of watching my sexy as hell husband drive."

His cheeks lift with a smile and takes my left hand in his, bringing it up to his lips for a kiss. I move closer to the center console and kiss the back of his hand before placing them in my lap. I sit in the passenger seat quietly as the trees on either side of the highway give way to businesses and apartment complexes. We pass a park with a massive hill and my eyes go wide because I've never seen anything like it.

"It's so open here." I observe.

Cincinnati is about as open as a snow globe. When you find yourself in the city more than in the suburbs, it can get a little stifling. And the longer I live where I am, the more I crave a place on the outskirts. A yard for Sully to run around in and no neighbors on the other side of my living room wall.

"Sometimes too open," Nate chimes in. "I can take you around places this week. But right now I just want to check-in to the hotel and then get food."

"Okay," I say softly.

Us staying at a hotel was a point of contention for us. I didn't think we would argue this early into our marriage. And over where to stay. But we did. After we cooled off, I saw Nate's side of not wanting to stay in his family's home. I can't imagine staying somewhere and seeing the ghost of your loved one everywhere you turn. So it's a good thing that we're staying in a hotel. It gives him a place to decompress.

As we drive further, the trees give way to towering glass buildings with windows for days and signs for the beach. I let Nate choose the hotel for us to stay since this is for him and he knows the area. But the nervous feeling of being surprised is making me bounce in my seat. Yet, when he pulls into a parking garage for a Marriott, my body relaxes.

It looks like it's a newer build and since it's the off-season, check-in takes no time at all. We head over to the elevator and take it up to the seventh floor. Nate held me the entire way as a form of support over my elevator fears and I fell in love with him a little more for that.

"Woah." I say when I see the windows open to the ocean. The sound of the door closing behind me isn't enough to get me to look away or stop drooling.

"I knew you'd like this view." Nate tells me as he comes up behind me and wraps his arms around my shoulders.

I hook my hands onto where his arms cross and place a kiss on his forearm. "It's like you know your wife."

Nate places several kisses on my neck that make me giggle. "I do."

Exhaustion hits me and I try to stifle my yawn, but Nate notices.

"Let's take a nap and then we can get an early dinner."

"In our airplane clothes?" I ask with a sneer, because that's *gross*.

Nate walks over to the bed and stands at the foot, taking his sweatshirt off and revealing the results of his workouts and suddenly I'm not so tired anymore. "I won't complain if you take your clothes off." His point is emphasized by his joggers sliding down his toned legs.

I'm not ashamed of my body. My workouts do what they need to do. But where he's hard, I'm soft. Nate makes me feel sexy even in week old sweatpants and hair I tossed in a bun for the third day in a row. I make work by pulling off my hoodie, leaving me in a black cotton bralette. I keep my eyes on Nate's as I drop my pants revealing matching black underwear. His jaw flutters and I see a swallow work its way down his throat. I erase the few steps between us and push him back on the bed. He falls and bounces a couple of times and I don't miss the swell of his dick in his briefs.

Nate's narrowed eyes follow my movement as I walk around to the other side and get under the covers. Clearly leaving him high and dry. When I get situated, I do my best to hide my amusement at his confused state.

"Good night." I say and turn on my side to face the unobstructed ocean view.

The bed moves as Nate gets into gear, finally joining me under the covers. I'll admit that my heart is pounding as we're sharing a bed for the first time since Vegas. Self-preservation is a bitch and all I want to do is share a bed and a house with my husband. But he's leaving for spring training in less than a month. I don't want to get used to a warm body and then go back to sleeping alone.

"You know I was thinking." Nate says when he cuddles up to me. Sliding his arm around my waist and pulling me closer so we're connected to each other from head to toe. "That this could be treated as a pre-honeymoon."

"You're thinking long game," I pant out as his hands start to wander over my bare skin. My breathing has become embarrassingly loud at the bit of contact. "I like it a lot."

"Yeah?" he asks as if he doesn't know.

I turn in his arms before my body turns to jelly from his caressing and he meets my lips in a burning kiss. Nate's groan vibrates through my body and down to my toes. He surrounds me and I drop my leg as he moves and rests cradled between my thighs. The feel of his heavy erection pressing into my center has my breath skipping as I moan into our kiss. Nate takes advantage and licks into my mouth. Our tongues swirl as the heat between us builds to an inferno. My hands roam over his naked skin. The warmth of him under my fingertips. The dips and bulges of the muscles in his back. Nate's body is carved to perfection and he's all mine.

"I can't wait any longer. I don't wanna wait any longer." I tell him when I break the kiss, pulling in some much needed oxygen. "I know you're once again waiting for the perfect moment. And under any other circumstances I would find that romantic. But I want to have sex with my husband."

Nate's eyes darken with desire and the look is like a signal to my pussy. "Okay, wife. Take off my briefs."

My hands hook into the waistband of his briefs and when I can no longer reach, I use my feet to shove them the rest of the way down his body. I encircle my hand around his thick length and pump him a few times. Nate drops his head to the crook of my neck groaning, thrusting into my hand as I continue to work him up. His lips latch onto my neck, sucking and licking as I swirl my thumb over the tip, smearing the pre-cum and using that to ease my hand pumping him. My body is suddenly left cold as Nate abruptly sits up, taking his warmth and the sheets with him. While I may have dressed for comfort in simple black cotton underwear and matching bralette, Nate makes me feel like I'm wearing the most expensive set I own as his gaze devours me.

His hands fall to my waist and trail down to the waistband of my underwear. I notice his hands shaking the same way my heart is threatening to burst out of my chest, but I don't tease him for it. It's clear we're both nervous. This is our first time together. The big step in consummating our marriage. I drop my hands on his and his eyes meet mine. In the moment, my breath is stolen and he gives me a smile. One that's only reserved for me. A smile that makes my heart want to run laps from the pure glee it feels. My underwear slides down my hips and thighs, baring me to him. I lift my legs as Nate slides them down my ankles and past my feet, throwing the fabric behind him.

I choke on a gasp as one of his hands keeps my legs in the air and the other traces the seam of my pussy.

"So wet for me baby." I moan as he slides a finger inside of me. "You feel better than I remember." Nate drops my legs and sucks his fingers that are coated in my juices into his mouth and then he swears, looking up at the ceiling.

"What's wrong?" I manage to ask.

"I don't have a condom. Jax, I didn't expect for this to happen."

"It's okay." I tell him.

"No it's not. I'm a planner, you know this."

"Nate, baby. I promise it's okay." I pull him by the gold chain necklace he's been wearing since college. "And I'll tell you why."

I hear Nate's swallow as the tip of his cock brushes against my clit. "Why is that?"

"I have a birth control implant that's good for another three years."

Nate is silent for a few seconds and I'm wondering if I broke him. "Are you saying..."

"That I'm protected? Yes. I got tested after my ex and I broke up, so I'm clean."

"Same."

Nate kisses me and tugs my head back, deepening the kiss. My legs hook over his hips, doing my best to get closer and rubbing myself on his cock. He breaks the kiss and sits back on his heels. My legs are spread wide in invitation and he fists his dick, rubbing the blunt head through my slit and tapping on my clit making me flinch. Nate teases me over and over by pushing himself inside of me so only the head of his cock is covered before pulling out and repeating the motion.

"Nate," I whine. "I need you inside of me."

"Not yet." He tells me and slides down my body. Nate places kisses on every bare inch of skin. Paying attention to the spots that make me squirm and gasp. He slides down the bed until my pussy is in his face and I suddenly feel extremely self-conscience. I haven't felt this exposed in a while. I haven't had a man down here in a while either. Foreplay wasn't my ex's favorite thing to do. A couple swipes of his finger through my slit and he determined I was good to go.

"Hey," Nate says, having caught on that my mind strayed. "Stay with me."

I nod my head, my hair bunching at the top of my head with the movement and I decide to lean up on my elbows. "I'm here."

"Eyes on me the whole time. Can you do that, Bee?" Nate asks as he kisses my inner thighs. His pupils have blown wide as I murmur a *yes* and he spreads my legs further. The first lick of his tongue through my opening takes my breath away. And when he mimics kissing me on my opening, I feel like I'm floating outside of my body when my head drops back. Nate releases me with a pop and my building orgasm retreats. "Eyes."

I pick my head up and watch as he kisses up and flicks a stiff tongue against my clit. A strangled moan falls from my mouth as he inserts two fingers inside of me. I try to close my legs because the pleasure is too much, but he locks an arm over my leg.

"Nate," I breathlessly say his name as I feel the tingling in my toes from the beginning of an orgasm. "I need, fuck–"

"I know what you need, baby. Give me one." He says and continues licking and sucking at my pussy. Adding another finger until I'm deliciously full of him. "Your pussy is squeezing the fuck out of my fingers." Nate says as his thumb flicks at my clit. He's found out all I need is a little attention on my clit and I shoot off like a rocket. "Let go, Bee. I'll catch you."

With the stiff flicks of his tongue over my clit, my orgasm slams into me. I moan Nate's name as he works me through. My body is a boneless mess and thoroughly sated as I pull him up my body. Some of my release is on his chin and I lick it up, not missing the animalistic growl that comes from Nate.

"Now can you make love to your wife?"

"Gladly." He says and enters me on one thrust and I cry out as he fills me for the first time. Nate stays still as I adjust to his size. The intrusion is a welcome burn and he kisses my shoulders, and my neck, rubbing my leg that's hiked up around his waist as I wait for my body to relax and let him all the way in. "Fuck, you feel like heaven. Are you okay?"

"Yes," I whimper.

He kisses me all over my face, taking my mind off the intrusion. His hips pump shallowly inside of me, loosening me up to take him. "Relax for me baby. You can do it. Let me in."

I take deep breaths and focus on that. I focus on willing my muscles to let him all the way in and Nate slides even deeper when I focus on us.

"That's it baby," he coos and waits until my body fully accepts his. "I always knew we'd fit perfectly."

"Nate, I need you to move." I make my point by wiggling my hips and the moan he lets out against my neck sends shockwaves down my body.

Nate pulls back and pushes my bralette up by the band. He doesn't take it off, but instead he twists it and leaves it bound around my wrists. "Hold onto that, Bee. And don't let go."

My head falls back as Nate begins thrusting in and out of me. He hikes my leg over his shoulder and a whimper falls from my lips. God, he feels so good. Why was he denying me this? We're a perfect fit. Nates lips fall to mine as his hips tunnel in and out of me. Each swipe of his tongue against mine has my toes curling. Each thrust pulls a gasp from my mouth. Each caress of his hands along my body causes me to fall more in love with my husband.

Our positions flip suddenly and I ride Nate as best as I

can with my hands still bound. Each roll of my hips in the new position has my clit brushing against his pelvic bone. My arms bracket his head, making it easy to fuse our lips together as we fly higher and higher to the sun. Nate's thrusts meet mine and I feel my orgasm building up. Our movements get more wild. The sound of skin slapping against skin echoes throughout the room. Our moaning and sighs of ecstasy become our new soundtrack. A layer of sweat covers our bodies the longer we stay entwined with each other.

My breath stalls as my second orgasm slams into me. Nate holds my hips steady as he thrusts into me, chasing his own orgasm. The sound of our release mixing together and my muscles squeezing every drop from him has me gasping into the kiss. My tongue dances with his as I feel him swell and come inside of me. He laxes on his grip on my hips but still moves them to milk him dry. Nate holds me to him and reaches up to untie my bra from around my arms. And when I'm free from the restraint, I kiss him one last time and roll off of him, falling to the side.

"Holy shit," I pant out.

"You–fuck," Nate fails to say and I giggle at that and then sober at the serious look on his face. "I may not have been your first," he says and my heart aches because it was supposed to be him, "but I promise to be your last."

I turn my head to look at him. "You better."

"And we're doing that again every chance we can get."

"Deal." I tell him and get up to go to the bathroom to clean up. Nate joins me after he takes care of business and when my head hits the pillow, exhaustion finally decides to take over.

I HEAR Nate's muffled voice through the bathroom. We're seeing his Mom and sister tomorrow, but tonight is date night. Our first real date night as a married couple and just the thought of this one of many, sends a thrill through my body. The hotel has a few restaurants attached to it and if staying here calms Nate down, I'm not going to argue. I just want the best for him and if this is it, I'm not going to try to change his mind.

I ended up rewashing my hair after this morning's activities, so my hair sits in tamed curls framing my face. I kept my makeup light with a couple swipes of mascara, eyebrow gel, and a dark mauve liquid lipstick. My neck is adorned with gold necklaces tastefully layered and I paired it with some diamond studs. With a spritz of my Jo Malone perfume, I step out of the bathroom and look over my outfit in the floor to ceiling mirror that's right in front of the closet.

The place we're going is somewhat fancy judging by the pictures I saw when I snooped their social media accounts. I survey my outfit in the mirror. Smoothing my hands down the ribbed material of the mini sweater dress I'm wearing, I turn in the mirror and look at the back. The black pantyhose I have under compliment the cream color of the dress. I pull out the thigh high black leather boots I stored in the closet and head to the bed to put them on.

My cheeks heat when I see Nate watching my every move.

"You look beautiful, Bee."

"Thank you."

Nate takes my boots from my hands and kneels on the floor to put them on my feet. His brow is furrowed in concentration, likely hoping to not accidentally pinch my skin when he zips them up.

"I like you in this position," I tease.

He smiles as he stands back up to his full height, keeping his hand on my waist. "I was just thinking the same."

I feel him growing against my hip and I back away because I'm starving. "Nope. I'm starving and you do not want a hangry wife on your hands." I turn away and grab my black small purse from the dresser that's housing some of our smaller items.

"Well, what my wife wants, my wife gets." Nate says and wraps his body around mine and together we walk out the door and to our date.

34

NATE

After eating breakfast at one of the popular spots in the area, we're finally headed to my parents–my mom's–house. I purposefully drive down all of the back roads I can possibly take until there are no more back roads to take and the road to the neighborhood looms right up ahead. Jax has kept our hands linked together the entire drive. Maybe she knew what I was doing and I love her even more for not calling me out on my stalling.

Mom retired last year, so her car and Kayla's are parked in the driveway when I pull up and park on the street. My thumbs tap out a mindless rhythm on the steering wheel. It could be that I'm mimicking my heartbeat. I should see a cardiologist. This isn't normal.

"Natey," Jax says softly from next to me.

I look over at her sitting patiently in the passenger seat and give her a soft smile. "Ready? I ask instead.

She nods and leans over the center console, offering me a kiss that I will never refuse. Her hand comes up and cradles my face. The small touch calms me down just slightly.

"I love you."

"I love you too, Bee. Let's go."

I take the key out of the ignition and meet Jax around at the front of the car with my hand outstretched. She leans into me as we make the walk to the front door which swings open before I can ring the doorbell.

"Hi, LaLa," I greet my sister. Jax drops my hand right as Kayla launches herself at me. I've mostly stuck to FaceTimes to see my family. Every once in a while they'll fly up to see me, but it's been about a year since we were all in the same place. I can admit that I've failed as a son and a brother on more than one account.

"Stop being gone for so long, Nana." Kayla scolds me.

She's about to start her second semester at the local community college, with no clue what she wants to do with her life. And that's fine. This year is all about Kayla exploring her options.

"I'm a terrible brother."

"Yeah you are."

Kayla steps back and I get a good look at her. Maybe I expected tired eyes and a gaunt face, but my sister is healthy. I hope the same can be said for Mom.

"And who is this?" Kayla asks when she looks next to me.

I hold my hand back out to Jax and tug her forward, tucking her under my arm. "This is Jax."

Kayla rears back and holds up her hand. "Wait, *the* Jax?"

"Am I famous?" my wife asks teasingly.

A gust of cold January wind hits us, forcing us to finally cross over the threshold. Nothing like jumping in with both feet. I take Jax's coat and hang it up on the hooks that have been here since college and then place mine on top of hers.

"Famous? No. Legendary? Absolutely." Kayla gleefully boasts while I let loose a groan.

Tentatively we walk deeper into the house. I feel him everywhere. I keep expecting him to be sitting on the couch or stomping down the stairs or hear the popping of the Orbit gum he was always chomping on. But I know I won't because he's gone. It's a sobering realization as the hallway opens up to the kitchen and living room that he's nowhere to be found. And it's strange because these two rooms are the heart of the house and have been since we first moved here decades ago. So for him to no longer be here—it's something I have to come to terms with, while Mom and Kayla have been living in it.

"How legendary are we talking?" Jax asks and my mom turns around at her voice. "And why do you call Nate, *Nana*?"

"Let's just say that when he was on his phone, we knew he was texting you. And when I was younger, I couldn't pronounce anything with a T or an H, so Nana stuck."

"Cute." Jax says and turns her head to look at me, sticking her tongue out when she does.

I give her a soft smile and kiss her on the back of the head before moving around her to go hug my mom.

"Hi, honey." My mom says and wraps her arms around my torso.

It's easy to forget that your parents are fragile. The older you get, unfortunately, the older *they* get. So it's easier to tell in small acts of love like a hug. My cheek rests on top of my mom's head and I let her hug charge me like a battery.

"You don't call. You don't visit. I was starting to think you forgot your way back home."

Although she can't see me, I wince. "I know. I needed a reason to come back."

Marrying Jax helped me realize that I can go home. No

matter how painful the reminder of who I lost. Or what I lost.

"Did I hear something about Jax?"

Kayla sighs, but it's with love. "Nate finally brought her to visit."

I groan towards my sister and Mom laughs as she steps away from me, turning her sights on Jax before moving towards her and taking her in a hug. "My goodness you are stunning."

I turn around in time to see a blush and smile covering Jax's face. "Thank you."

Honestly, I always thought college Jax was beautiful. But that version of her has nothing on what she's bloomed into today. Stunning is a tame word to describe Jax. She's...some days I can never find my words around Jax. Yes, my wife's beauty ties me up in knots. And I think she knows that when she teases me.

"What really brings you two here?" My mom asks with her arm still around Jax.

"It was time. And we have news."

My mom and Kayla look at Jax's stomach before looking at me. "Are...you...?"

"No!" Jax and I say at once. I hold my hand out to Jax and Mom begrudgingly lets her go. "We got married."

"What!?" Kayla yells.

When we hold our hands up they're both in shock. Which to be fair is the face Jax and I made when we woke up in Vegas.

"When?" My mom asks as her face drops.

Jax looks at me and wills me with just her eyes that I'm on my own. Her parents were easier to break the news to.

"Uh, November."

You know when it's snowing? And the falling flakes are

thick enough that it mutes the noises around you. You can finally hear your thoughts in a world that's always too loud. Every time it snows in Cincinnati, which isn't a lot as the weather is sometimes very similar to Virginia Beach's, I feel like that. Like the silence is a comforting source of joy for someone whose life is always hands-on and on the move.

But this moment? When my mom and Kayla are stone-faced and slack-jaw after hearing that Jax and I got married almost two months ago? Yeah, I hate the silence.

"Two months? Nathan Alexander," *ouch*, "I know you did not keep this from me, us, for two months." My mom scolds me and I feel about two feet tall.

"We just saw you at Thanksgiving and nothing." Kayla says and her hands drop on her legs in shock and defeat.

I blow out a breath. "Why don't we sit and I'll explain?"

Jax rubs her nails down my back in a soothing gesture as I wait for the two women I've shut out to agree to taking a seat. Exchanging a look, they move to the living room and we follow, getting settled in the broken-in leather sectional.

"Now, November?" Kayla asks.

"Yes. In Vegas. And it was *after* Thanksgiving for Chance and Sophie's joint bachelor-bachelorette party," I explain and feel like I'm now two feet tall when I see my mom looking more upset with me than I've ever seen.

"Nathan," she sighs exasperatedly and I know she's about to say that a mistake like this can ruin my career.

"Mom, don't. I love you and I have so much respect for you—" I start to plead my case.

"So why are you two still married?"

I feel Jax's body flinch like she was hit and to be fair, my reaction isn't any better. I had hoped my mom would be happy for me. Or at least be a little warm. Not question why Jax and I are still married.

"Because we love each other. And because when we woke up the next morning, we ran through every scenario, including divorce and an annulment. Trust us, that was on the table." I look down at Jax and she looks at me with a small smile that doesn't reach her eyes. "The thought of divorcing Jax made me sick. I was already lost without her. I didn't want to lose her again." I don't miss the watering of her eyes or the slight tremble in her bottom lip.

"Wait. Rewind. How *did* you two come back to each other?" this time it's Kayla who asks. My sister is a romantic and also loves her romance books. So me and Jax are like a romance book couple come to life for her.

"Funny enough, she was at one of our home games. I saw her talking with Chance and her sister and I thought I saw a ghost. Because there was no way the one that got away, the one I pushed away, was at a game that I was playing in."

"Let me guess, love at first sight all over again?"

I snort and Jax laughs, burying her face in my chest. "Not even close. Jax hated me. She can deny it all she wants, but she hated me and how I ended us."

"And you had to grovel." Kayla notes.

"Exactly."

My sister goes on about the books she's read where the exact thing has happened. Of course she said she's never known anyone in real life like where that's happened. But Jax and I are living proof that it can.

When there's a lull in the conversation, I tell them the real reason we're down here. "I also wanted to visit Dad. That's one of the other reasons we came down here."

My admission sobers up the room. It'll take a bit longer to win over Mom and my choice to get married without her there. But like Jax, I still want the big wedding with our family and friends present. We're just not in a rush for that to happen.

"It's good that you want to do that." My mom says and stands up. "Excuse me."

"Mom..." I begin and reach for her as she passes, but she evades my touch.

Jax's body is stiff. And for good reason. She knows the good of my family. How when I would come back to Philadelphia I would have a plethora of stories to tell her. But this version of my mom is not the woman I would tell Jax about. It makes it seem like she's not accepting of Jax and that fear of abandonment and unwantedness is probably rushing forward.

"She's–" Kayla begins, but pauses to find the words.

"How has it been? Really? I don't want some fabricated story to spare my feelings. I want the truth, Kayla."

Kayla's eyes drop and my body tenses because I know whatever she says won't make this any easier. "It's been hard, Nate. She shielded most of her hurt from me when I was younger. But I lost my dad. I lost one of the men I looked up to the most."

I swallow hard, because the implication that Kayla lost me too is not lost on me.

"I could hear her. At night. Sometimes in the morning, too. Our rooms might have been on opposite ends of the house, but her crying still made it through the walls. And it didn't get better once you were drafted, Nate. You were gone, Daddy died, and Mom wouldn't even look at me."

Even I can admit that it's hard to look at Kayla. She looks just like Dad, but with softer, feminine features. But she's still my little sister. And she lost someone during the important years of her life. She didn't have him to watch her go to prom, or graduate high school. He won't be there to walk her down the aisle.

"Kayla, I'm sorry."

Her eyes are glass with tears and she shakes her head. "Don't do that. You had dreams to chase, Nate. And we are so proud of you. But it doesn't ease the sting of you leaving us behind to chase those dreams."

Jax runs a soothing hand up and down my arm. But I can't feel it. My body has gone completely numb and I have no clue the steps to take to thaw. I guess I built them up in my mind. Thinking they were healing just fine without me. When they would visit, we'd laugh and reminisce on old times. But I can see how much of a mask that was.

Kayla stands up and I must wear the confusion on my face. "I have to get to work. When are you two leaving?"

"We'll be here for the week," Jax answers for me because suddenly my mouth is filled with sand.

My sister nods and says something. But I can't hear. It's like I'm underwater and generally not attached to my body. The sound of a door closing finally breaks me out of the haze and I look around seeing it's just Jax and I. Her eyes are red from crying and I hate that she cried at all.

"I'm sorry." I tell her.

"No. Baby don't do that. We knew this was a possibility."

I gently wipe the tears that have pooled under her eyes with my thumbs and pull her into me. "I had no idea it was this bad. If I'd have known..."

"You would have what? Given up a dream to be here for your family? While I commend that, you would have ended up resenting them for it."

"The way my mom resents me?" I spit at Jax and I already feel bad for saying it that way.

"She's sad, Nate. She will always be sad. And people

lash out when they're sad." Jax says it with such conviction. Like she's been the one to last out when sad. The realization that I may have been the cause of that is sobering.

I nod. "I'm gonna go see if she'll talk to me."

"Okay. I'll be right here."

I stand up and wipe my hands off on my jeans. Walking back down the front hallway, I turn right and take the stairs to head to my mom's room. Pictures line the walls. From every stage of my life, my parents' life together, me and Kayla; it's all here. I keep walking until I get to my mom's closed bedroom door and knock lightly.

"Mom?"

Nothing except the sound of the ice maker downstairs dropping ice and the sound of a car with too loud music driving past the house.

"Mom? Will you open the door?" I knock again and wait on my side hoping she'll let me in. But after standing here for ten minutes with her clearly ignoring me, I give up. "We'll be here all week."

I turn around and head back down the stairs. Jax is waiting in the foyer with my coat in her hands. Wordlessly I take it from her and put it on before I'm ushering us out of the house. If my mom is sad, then I'm sad. She's the only parent I have left and she chooses to behave like this. I help Jax in the car and round to the driver's seat. With one destination in mind, I start the car and peel out of the neighborhood.

When we pull up to the cluster of baseball fields, fields I played and grew to love the game, Jax and I get out and brave the cold. This is the one place I can go and not think. Or think until I figure it out.

I help Jax onto the bleachers and take the spot next to

her. The cold metal seeps through my jeans and if I can feel it, I know she can too.

I lean forward, propping my elbows on my knees as I look out over the empty baseball diamond. I blink fast, trying to keep the tears from coming but I fail. The first one falls and I quickly try to wipe it away. But then another falls and I lose the battle completely. Jax takes me into her arms, letting me fall apart as I grieve the man I lost and the mother who refused to acknowledge me mere minutes ago.

35

JAX

I lie awake in the early morning watching Nate sleep. The sun is just starting to peek over the horizon and the sheer curtains over the windows bathe the room in a soft purple hue. In this light my husband is relaxed. This whole trip he's been on edge and I've done what I can to make this trip relaxing. But yesterday was rough and it was the first time I saw the fracture in my Nate.

We have two days left in Virginia and he's taken me everywhere except where he needs to go most. Maybe I can barter some things with him? I can't buy him anything. I mean, I can. But Nate gets mad when I spend my money on him. Doesn't the man know that gift giving is my love language?

I lightly trace his left hand that's resting in between us. For a hard man, he's all smooth lines. The tattoos pop against the white of the sheets and my attention goes there. It seems no matter how many times I look at his body–his tattoos, I continue to find new ones every day. My brows furrow as I look closer at this one that's on the top of his hand.

"I was wondering when you would notice," his groggy voice says, breaking me out of the trance.

I look up and see his eyes barely open as sleep is still trying to claim him. My eyes go back to looking at his hand. Nate loves florals. Or maybe because I loved the gardens so much, he needed to permanently ink them on his skin. The letter 'J' is outlined in an array of flowers and isn't noticeable on a quick look but it travels all the way up his arm. I've never noticed, because I've kept my eyes on him. But this, the ink, looks like it's been well-loved.

"It was my first piece the fall after I was drafted."

"That had to have hurt," I note. I don't have tattoos because having a needle repeatedly poke into me seemed like a not fun time.

"Hurt like a bitch."

"And that explains why you got more." I tease.

"I said it hurt. Didn't say I didn't like the pain."

I lightly snort and sit up, placing my elbow on the pillow and resting my head on my fist. I watch as Nate looks at his tattoos, seemingly going back in time to the place he was at when he first got them.

"Would you ever get more?"

"I think I'm tapped out on space."

"Oh come on. How about a slutty thigh tattoo. That'll make all the girls go crazy."

Nate chuckles and pinches my side. "I don't need all the girls to go crazy. Just my wife."

Butterflies takeoff every time he says that. And based on the smile that blooms across his face when he sees me blush, he knows it too.

I sober my expression because the sooner we do this, the sooner my husband can heal. "Are you ready for today?"

He rolls onto his back and lets out a heaving sigh while

he looks up at the ceiling. "No. But I guess I don't have a choice."

"You always have a choice," I start. "You have a choice to heal and grieve the way I don't think you've allowed yourself to. To feel all the pain that comes with losing a parent. Nathan, you have been on the move for six years. Have you ever stopped?"

"No." The brokenness of that one word, threatens to break me.

"Will you tell me why?"

Nate continues to stare up at the ceiling and I watch in sadness at the hard swallow that moves through his throat. "When I went to campus that day for the game, my dad was fine. He was lucid and we were making jokes before I had to leave for my game."

My body ices all over as he tells me the rest.

"During the game he took a turn for the worse. You know the rest. So I like to stay in the delusion that while I'm playing my dad is still alive. Waiting at home for me to get back to tell him all about it. And when I'm not playing, it's like every feeling I've suppressed rushes forward and suffocates me."

I sit in the weight of his story as I watch tears track down the side of his face. Nathan is starting to break, but I still don't think we've reached the top of that iceberg. In a flash he whips the covers off and heads to the bathroom. I hear the shower turn on not even a minute later. Flopping on my back, I reach for my phone on the nightstand and open up my group chat.

Me: My husband is broody.

Emily: Yeah. But in a hot way.

Me: Eyes on your own man.

Emily: LOL

Sarah: Yes he is.

Kammy: How's the trip?

Me: Cold…in more ways than one.

Me: Girls night when I get back?

Sarah: DUH!

Me: Perfect. I'll invite Sophie, too.

I exit out of my message app and head to socials. I have a DM waiting from Ellie, letting me know she'd be thrilled to be a guest on my podcast. We'd have to do it virtually since she's heavily pregnant. But I don't care. I love what she's done with her platform. Checking my email, I see one from my manager about the possibility of a podcast tour with other hosts. I'm taken aback, because this is not what I imagined for my show. Although I can't deny that it would be a great way to reach a bigger audience. I star the email and place my phone back on the nightstand as Nate walks out of the bathroom with a towel wrapped around his waist. His skin is dewy from the steam in the bathroom and my mouth goes dry as a singular water droplet trails down his torso. A shirt hits me in the face and I pull it down.

"Go shower you fein." Nate says with a laugh.

Rolling my eyes, I finally climb out of bed and stretch. My nipples are at pointed peaks and Nate has the restraint of a saint. Or maybe not as evidenced by the tent starting to form under his towel. I ogle his physique then head to the bathroom. I shake my head and the arousal from my body before brushing my teeth and hopping into the shower.

Nate and I sit in the car at the cemetery. We parked a few minutes ago and have been staring out the front windshield. The sun is shining brightly today with a slight breeze that hopefully won't run us off. We stopped to pick up some flowers and when Nate hesitated on which to buy since his Dad wasn't a flower guy, I picked out a peony and tulip combo from Trader Joe's.

"I think I wanna go out first." Nate says, breaking the silence.

I look over at him, but his focus stays on the cemetery. "Okay. Just come and get me when you want me to join."

Nate nods and takes the flowers I hand out to him. The cold January air rushes in before the door closes, blanketing me in silence again. I watch my broody boy walk to his dads resting spot. His hulking stature is still as a statue as he glances down at the headstone.

"Come on, baby. Just talk," I say from my spot in the passenger seat.

I almost want to dance when his shoulders fall from his ears and he takes the flowers out of the plastic wrap and places them on the ground. A sigh of relief and awe escapes when Nate drops down to the ground. I look away to let him have his moment and I feel like no time at all has passed when in reality it's been about an hour as a soft tap on my window knocks me out of my doom scrolling.

Dropping my phone in the cupholder, I snag the keys and meet Nate outside. He holds his hand out to me and I let him lead me to his dad. After knowing Nate for as long as I have, it's not hard to know that his dad was, and still is, his idol. Just because someone is no longer here, it doesn't take away the impact they left on people.

"Dad, this is Jax," my heart warms and my eyes fill with tears. "Jax, this is my Dad, Chris. Only my mom got to call him Christopher."

"It's very nice to meet you. I hear I'm a legend at your house." Nate groans and I elbow him in the stomach. "It's okay. He was a legend at my parents house too."

Nate's hand goes to my waist as he sits back on the ground and I follow suit.

"That summer before our final year of school, he and Mom joked that they were surprised I didn't come home with a ring on my finger from how much I talked about you."

"You and your crush," I tease him and he leans over to kiss me on the cheek. "But look at us now."

"Dad, Jax is my wife. As I'm sure you already know. You have a daughter-in-law who is kind, funny, stubborn, sometimes frustrating, and so full of love that I still wonder how I got so lucky."

I wipe my tears on the sleeve of my sweatshirt. "I'm not frustrating."

Nate wraps his arm around my shoulders and pulls me to him. "See, Dad? I told you she was funny."

A gust of wind swirls around us and I take that as a sign. "Huh. It seems your Dad does agree that I'm funny as well."

We sit at Chris's grave, talking and joking. The mood is light and I see Nate open more than I ever have before.

"I miss you, Dad. Will you at least let Mom know it's okay for all of us to be happy?"

I rub small circles on Nate's thigh, letting him know that his hurt is valid.

"Ready?" he asks.

"Can I talk to him alone?"

Nate looks at me, like I'm DaVinci...or in his case a fat fastball over home plate. "Yeah, Bee. I'll be at the car."

I watch as Nate gets up and places a kiss on the head stone before walking over to the car. He leans back on the side and watches me with a soft smile.

"I hate that we're meeting like this." I tell Chris and his headstone gets blurry from the tears that have formed. "In college he talked about you a lot. I almost felt like you were Bigfoot: legendary but visible to only him. Turns out, you're still legendary but you're far from invisible. If there are ways for you to send signs to Nate and his mom, I'll take it. I can't stand to watch my husband hurting during a time when he should be happy. He's at the top of his game and we finally have each other back." I drop my chin on my closed fists and read over the writing. "I love your son. So much. Without him it was like I was an incomplete puzzle. I kept looking for those missing pieces that when we found ourselves back in each other's lives, I realized he had them all along. You raised an amazing man and I promise to love him the way he deserves. Thank you."

Standing up, I brush off the dead grass and fallen leaves before looking at Chris's resting place one last time and heading to my husband.

"Are you okay?" Nate asks when I stand in front of him. His hands come up and gently wipe away the stray tears.

"Yeah," I say with more conviction than I feel. "One last stop?"

"Yeah. One last stop."

~

NATE PARKS the car on the street instead of in the driveway

like last time. This time, he's not as nervous. I think he's more pissed than anything.

"Come on. The sooner this is done, the quicker we can get back to the hotel and nap."

I snort and meet him on the outside. My shoes clack on the pavement as we walk up to the front door which swings open again before Nate has a chance to ring the bell.

"Hey." Kayla greets and holds the door open wider for us.

Nate doesn't move to take my coat and I make no effort to take it off. He's a man on a mission and Kayla and I are left to follow in his trail. We stand at the entrance to the kitchen when Nate approaches his mom who's doing everything in her power to ignore him.

"Mom, it's clear you don't understand my reasoning for staying married or why I stayed away for so long. You lost your husband. But I also lost a dad. And I couldn't breathe here. Everywhere I turned, I saw him. And I know it was no better for you or Kayla. But I chased a dream that was placed before me and I get to remember Dad the way I want to. Mom," Nate pauses as he thinks carefully over the words he wants to say. And when he does, they cut, "there is no joy here in this house." Kayla and I flinch when he says that and I don't miss it from his mom either.

I wait with bated breath as Nate stands desperately in front of his mom. Waiting for her to say something or at least acknowledge him.

Kayla lets go of my hand and steps forward. "Mom, I miss Dad. But I miss you more."

She looks up at Kayla and I can see that the years have taken a big hit on her. "I live in this house, Kayla."

"No you don't. You might as well be a ghost just like Dad."

The three of them have a stand-off and it's like watching lions circle each other. Round and around. Waiting for one of them to make the first move.

Nate's mom caves first. Her shoulders and face fall in defeat. And it's like the weight in the room has finally lifted.

"I miss your Dad. Everyday I ache and I don't know how to breathe most days." She says and tears stream down her face.

Nate rounds the kitchen island and takes his mom in his arms. "I know Mom. But we're still here." He holds his arm out for Kayla and I watch with a tearful smile as this family comes back together. He places a kiss on his mom's head and steps back.

"Jax, I'm sorry for my behavior the other day." She tells me.

"It's okay. I know it wasn't personal."

She gives me a smile and I see where Nate gets it from. "I am happy for you two. But, really? Vegas?"

"Drunk or sober, I would've still married her." Nate says and is it possible for *me* to get down on one knee and re-propose?

"You two do plan to have a proper wedding, right?" His mom asks and looks between the two of us.

"Maybe one day," I answer.

We end up staying longer than Nate guessed we would. But when he yawns five times in fifteen minutes, we're told to get some sleep.

And as soon as we get back to our hotel room, we both flop on the bed and nap.

36

NATE

The sound of our glasses clinking together manages to be heard over the low hum of conversation around the room.

"Cheers to two months, Bee."

"Cheers, baby."

We keep our eyes locked on each other as we take a sip of champagne. The bubbles and carbonation dance on my tongue and slide down my throat.

"It's so pretty here." Jax notes as she looks around.

The mood turns sensual here at night. The lights are low with tasteful string lights on the ceiling. The black and white checkered patterned floors complement the dark brown wood tones of the small table we're seated at.

"I heard it's nice here in the summer. It's a bit too cold out for my liking, but they do have fire pits if you wanna go sit outside."

Jax looks down at her dress and then back up at me with a smirk. "You just want me to sit in your lap."

"You know me so well."

"I hope so. Because I have a few things I want to talk to you about."

I tilt my head and look at her questioningly.

"Will you be a guest on my podcast before you head off to training? I can talk to your publicist, but I don't think she would have an issue with it."

Jax and I fall into laughter as we think of Sarah saying no. "Yes. Is this about your patterns you were adamant about not working?"

Her face scrunches and she groans. "I'm eating those words, okay?"

"You are." I say and fiddle with the ring on her finger. "What was the other thing or things?"

"I don't know if I can go back to sleeping alone anymore." She ends with a scrunch in her upturned nose again.

"I thought Sully kept you company?" I tease.

"She does, but she snores. And you don't. So I know who I'd choose to share a bed with."

We've unconsciously drifted closer to each other. "So because I don't snore you want to share a bed? Is that all?"

She nods and a smile teases the corner of her mouth. "That's a bonus. I was also maybe thinking of giving you some closet space? Maybe even a drawer. Three if you're lucky."

I push her hair behind her ear and keep my hand resting on her neck. "Jaclyn Marie, are you asking me to move in with you?"

"Yes. If you want to. We can split time at both our places until we decide where to live as a family."

I yank her closer and fuse my lips to hers, forcing her mouth open and tangling my tongue with hers. I feel her moan more than hear it and slow the kiss down.

"Is that a yes?" she asks with eyes glazed and lipstick slightly mussed.

"That's a hell yes."

Jax leans forward and presses a kiss to my lips before leaning back in her seat. "Good."

"What was the other thing?"

She looks at me puzzled and then her face lights up. "Oh. Were you serious about having another wedding?"

"One-hundred percent."

"I love being on the same page as you." Jax fist bumps me and finishes off her drink.

When the waitress comes back around we ask for two old fashions and sit back.

"What would your ideal house look like?" I ask when our new drinks are placed in front of us.

Jax tells me everything. It's a little different from what she dreamed up in college. But it's natural for our tastes to evolve.

"Are you still decided on kids?" She asks after we finish our drinks and are now waiting for the check.

Blood rushes through my ears and I feel the pulsing like an actual heartbeat. "Yeah. Maybe not the four I talked about. But yes. I still want kids. Do you?"

She nods and a smile teases her lips. "Yeah. I think you'd make a great Dad."

"I know you'd be a great Mom." I tell her and lean over, kissing her on the cheek. "Are you ready to go?"

"Yeah."

I drop a $100 on top of our receipt and help Jax into her jacket. Our hands stay linked as we walk out of the whiskey room and to the valet. We may be right across the street, but Jax is in heels and it's cold. I keep myself wrapped around her and usher her into the car when it pulls up. Navigating the side roads is a bit trickier when it's dark out, but I get us back to the hotel relatively unscathed.

"I'm proud of you," Jax tells me when we're in the elevator. "Today was hard and you got through it."

"I got through it with you." I tell her and wrap my arms around her, resting my hands on her lower back. "I spent so long running from this place because all I could associate it with was losing my dad. And you."

"That's to be expected. Your Dad may be gone. But he lives inside of you. The way you talk about him, I see you. You're becoming the man that I'm sure your father always knew you could be. Plus, you got me back."

The elevator comes to a stop on our floor with a beep and we step out, walking as a pair to the door.

"You always know the right things to say. Are you sure you're not a secret therapist?"

"No." Jax says and dumps her things on the dresser-TV stand combo when we're back in the room. "I just learned a lot from my sister and Emily."

I pull up Spotify and put it on a mix with LEON as the main artist. "Do you see a therapist?" I ask and wrap my arms back around her waist and gently sway us to the music.

Jax wraps her hands around my upper arms, following my lead. "I did for a while. But then I chose talking on my podcast over seeking professional help. Kamryn actually suggested I restart my sessions on our way to Vegas, but I'm not as lost as I was last year."

"I'll talk to one if you talk with one," I offer. "We can even do couples counseling. Not that I think we need it."

"Like a sex therapist? Because I think Riley's Mom is one." Jax teases with a blinding smile.

My eyebrows fly to my hairline and I subtly sway us to the wall by the bathroom that's facing the mirror. "Do you think we need one?"

"I can't say I have a lot to complain about. However, I only have our one time together to go off of. So the jury is out on that."

"Hmm." I hum and pull her closer to me. I don't miss the darkening of her eyes when she feels the hardness of my dick pressing against my zipper. "So if I do something like this we won't need help?" I ask and trail kisses down her neck at the same time my hand travels up the side of her leg, heading towards her heat.

Jax's gulp is audible when I brush my thumb over her panty-covered clit. "I might need more convincing."

I lift my head and rest against her forehead. "You do, do you? Let's see if this can convince you that we're good in that department."

I hook a finger on her underwear and slide a digit through her wet slit and up to her clit. Jax's mouth falls slack as I tease her clit and move back down, sliding a finger inside of her. I swallow her moan with my mouth and drink down her gasps. My tongue follows the movement of my fingers. In and out. Twisting. Light flicks of my tongue against hers matching the shallow pumps of my finger inside her pussy. I add another finger and kiss her harder. Her hands grab at anything she can get her hands on the higher I drive her. I curl my fingers inside of her, rubbing the area that has her going breathless against me. My thumb rubs in tight circles tandem with my fingers curling inside of her. Jax's hand tried to push me away as I feel her squeezing my fingers. I grab her hand and link our fingers, placing them above her head.

"Come on, baby. Come all over my hand."

Her cries of pleasure vibrate in my mouth as she falls off the cliff I drove her to. Ripping my hand out from under her dress, I pick her up and carry her to the bed. She bounces in a flurry of fabric. Jax's face is flushed and her lips are kiss-swollen. I didn't let her ride out the rest of the orgasm so her legs are pressed together from the sensation.

I reach under her dress and tear the fabric off of her and toss the trashed fabric over my shoulder. Her wide eyes meet mine, but her retort is cut off when I drag her to the edge of the bed and kneel, putting her pussy in my face.

"My shoes," Jax weakly says.

"They stay on." I tell her and spread her legs wider. I'll never get over her scent. I pull her closer until her legs fall over my shoulders and fuse my mouth to her opening. Jax's cry of surprise by my tongue spearing her is an ego boost. Not that I need one. Her hands grip onto the tight curls on my head and her hips start moving with my tongue. "Eyes." I demand.

Her honey brown eyes lock on mine and darken when I stiffen my tongue and flick it against her clit. Jax tugs her bottom lip between her teeth when I pull her clit into my mouth. The flush on her cheeks as I re-learn the sounds she makes is the soundtrack of dreams. I add a finger to her opening and Jax's head falls back on a cry. I nibble at her clit and her head flies up. My eyebrows raise in a wordless demand to keep her eyes on me. Adding another finger, I curl and keep the suction on her clit.

"Nate, Nate, Nate," she chants and I know she's close. The point of her heels dig into my back and I wrap my arms around her thighs, pulling her closer.

I moan against her and she cries out as her second

orgasm slams into her. I work her through the wave. Kissing and petting as she slowly comes back down. Her body falls limp and I kiss the inside of her thigh and stand back up. My knees crack as I do and I wince but ignore it. Jax's half-lidded gaze locks on mine and I suck my fingers into my mouth, cleaning off her juices. A light sheen of sweat has formed on her forehead and her chest heaves in heavy exhales.

"Still need convincing?" I ask, voice husky.

Jax whimpers and my cock twitches in my pants. "Yes."

I unhook my belt and unbutton my pants faster than I ever have before. I toe off my shoes and pants and fling off my shirt. I take Jax's hand and pull her up to help her get her dress off. Her hands rest on my waist as I pull the zipper down. The material loosens and Jax pulls her arms out of the arm holes. She's still standing taller than normal with her heels on and her dress puddles to the floor with a light thud and I hold her hand to help her step out of the fabric. I bite down on my bottom lip when I realize she wasn't wearing a bra the whole night and her eyes meet mine in a challenge. Shaking my head, I kneel back down and finally help her out of these death traps she calls heels. They bring her down to her natural height and I pick her up and toss her onto the bed.

I shuck off my boxers and crawl on the bed. Kissing up her body as I go.

"Hi." She says and frames my face between her delicate hands. Jax's leg hooks around my waist as I settle between her legs.

I fist my dick at the base and slide into her on one thrust. Jax moans my name as I settle deep inside of her. "Hi, Bee."

"Come on, Natey. Prove to me that we don't need a sex therapist," Jax taunts.

"Your wish is my command." I silence her with a kiss as my hips begin to move. I tease her with fast pumps of my hips to slow and long strokes. I dip my head down to take one of her nipples between my teeth. The action has her walls contracting around me and I groan against her. I release her with a pop and do the same to the other, relishing in the feel of her pulsing around me. Wanting to get deeper, I move one of her legs over my shoulder and Jax's whimper as I hit a spot inside of her is almost my undoing. I put her other leg over my shoulder and am welcomed with her nails digging into my arms as the sound of skin slapping against skin and our arousal mixing together sounds through the room.

"Fuck, fuck, fuck," Jax cries as I feel the slight shaking in her legs.

Dropping her legs, I flip our positions and lift her up, impaling her on my dick. "Ride me, baby."

Jax sits up and places her hands on my chest for leverage. The change in her as she takes charge of her pleasure is of pure amazement. Her hips move in a hypnotic rhythm and she makes sure she hits all of her spots. My hands fall to her hips as I help her move and meet her thrusts with a lift of my hips. Jax moves her hands from my chest, dropping them and bracketing the side of my head. The new position makes her feel impossibly tighter.

"Fuck, Jax," I groan through clenched teeth. "Tell me you're close."

"Almost. Help me?" she whines.

"What do you need?"

"Everything."

My brows furrow at her vague statement. But I do what feels right. I dip my head and pull a nipple into my mouth. My other hand moves between us and I play with her clit.

Pinching and teasing it, rolling it between my thumb and index finger. I feel her orgasm slamming into her before she says anything. It's in the way her breath catches, like the first big drop on a roller coaster. And then Jax is biting down on the spot between my neck and shoulder as she reaches her climax. Her legs shake around my hips and her cunt squeezes the life out of my cock, pulling my orgasm out of me. My hips pump in and out of her in a sloppy rhythm as I ring out the last of my release.

Jax's bite turns into a kiss. Soothing the area that probably has her mark. My arms come up and wrap around her torso, holding her to me as I let my cock soften inside of her.

"Still need a sex therapist?" I ask after she's thoroughly kissed the spot she chomped down on.

"No. I think we're good in this department," Jax says cockily and panting.

I give her a small slap on the ass and she clenches around me causing me to grunt. Jax laughs and I hold her hips still to lessen the movement. "Just good?"

"Great. Does that work?"

"I'd prefer mind blowing but that also works."

Eventually I carry Jax to the bathroom where we shower together before crawling back into bed. Tomorrow is our last full day here and then my workouts get more intense before heading off to spring training. I had a bunch of anxiety surrounding this trip. I couldn't stop thinking of this place to only be the bad place. The place where my dad died. The place where I made decisions that impacted my future. The place where I ended up losing Jax.

And as I watch my wife sleep, with the moon peeking through a crack in the curtain, I've never been more grateful for baseball. Without it, her and I would've never crossed paths again. I still ask myself how we could have possibly lived in the same city for years and never run into each other. Letting her go all of those years ago was the biggest mistake of my life. One I paid for as I lived a life of solitude. I push back a stray curl and in this moment promise to be the best husband and best friend that she will ever have.

37

JAX

I'm setting up the second camera when Nate posts up against the doorway. Since getting back from Virginia a week ago, he's been working out twice a day. Even roping Mason and Riley in for a few workouts. And after getting our schedules aligned, we're finally sitting down to film my long awaited podcast update.

I've never been nervous to film an episode. That could be because I've never had an actual guest in my studio. Everything has been done virtually and I've been able to hide the knee bouncing I do. Or it could be that Nate is finally seeing me in my element. Either way, my hope is that once I start talking the nerves will fade away.

Taking a final look at the camera, lights, and chair setup I turn to my husband.

"Are you sure you're up for this?" I ask and walk over to him. I slip my hands under his sweatshirt and warm my hands, smiling at the shiver that wracks his body.

"Brat." Nates says and kisses the tip of my nose. "But, yes I'm ready."

"Okay. And then we can take a nap after."

His eyes widen and he nods firmly. "I canceled my second workout too. My body is beat."

"I bet." I stretch onto my tip toes and give him a kiss. "Okay. Take a seat on the left. I've just gotta get the cameras going and turn the lights on, then we can get started."

It takes me no time at all to get everything setup. I make sure the mic is set in the right spot for Nate and then take my seat, placing my blanket over my lap.

I look over and see him smiling at me with awe. "What?"

"I like seeing you like this. In your element."

I smile shyly as I press the button to turn on our mics. "Ready?"

Nate nods and crosses an ankle over his leg; the picture of cool, calm, and collected.

"Welcome back to *Life Not Simplified.* I'm Jax and I have a very special guest with me. But before I get into who is in the studio with me, I want to go back to six months ago when I talked about new patterns. Do you all remember that? It started when I met this girl at the dog park. And before you think you know where this story is headed, I'm going to stop you right there. This isn't a love story between her and I. Although, I should thank her for where this story is going. Had I not met her and had my sister not gotten tickets to this specific baseball game–" I look over at Nate and he winks, "I wouldn't have found him again. I was doubtful of introducing a new pattern into my life. You all know this as I've let you in on my thoughts and how skeptical I was. But after my last relationship, I needed to find a way to incorporate color into my life. And I'm not talking about changing up the clothes I wear or what my house looks like. Because, to be quite narcissistic, I love those two things about my life and I was not looking to change those. I had already spent so long molding myself into a version of who my ex wanted me to be that it took me almost a year to find me, as Jax, me as the person who's able to stand on her own two feet."

I pause to take a sip of water. Nate's gaze is the most reassuring look that I could have ever hoped to have.

"So back to the pattern and how I resisted, but then finally welcomed that change. In college, I had this best friend. I told him everything. Maybe way too much considering we were just friends. One day in our third year, he told me he had a crush on me. Shocking, I know. Who couldn't resist me back then?" Nate's foot reaches out and kicks my foot. "Are you denying this?" I ask him.

"No."

"But I shut him down. I refused to believe that he would ruin our friendship over a silly little crush. Until he told me, and I quote, 'I won't rush you, okay? We can take this as slow as you need to. But just so you know, as soon as my lips touched yours, I became yours. And I hope you became mine?'"

"You remember that?" he asks, and I'm sure people will melt over his voice like I do every single day.

"Of course I do. We said a lot of words to each other in the early days of our relationship, but I remembered those so vividly. Now, you may be asking yourself, if you two were so great together why are we just now finding out about this mystery guy? Well, friends, life is not as simple as it seems. That's why I titled this podcast. If everything was simple, we'd be a lot more boring than white paint. We veered off track. He went one way and I went another. Did I think about him? Every single day."

"That's why I have the tattoos," Nate chimes in.

I huff a soft laugh into the microphone. "Yes. And I

promise we are going to get to that, but first we're gonna take a short break."

I push my mic away from me and obnoxiously stretch. Nate is more reserved as I feel he doesn't want to touch or break anything.

"How long are your breaks?"

"About five minutes. Just enough time to stretch my legs and hips before camping out in my chair again."

"Do you go on vocal rest after?"

"Not usually." I tell him, sitting back down and pulling my mic close to me again. "But today I might." I wink and turn on the intro music. "Welcome back, friends. What were we talking about?"

"My tattoos," Nate speaks up.

"Ugh, not quite." He and I laugh. I'll never get over that sound. Nate's laughs are rare, but around me, I've noticed he lets them out easier. "The burning question for you all is how we got here? How did a simple baseball game over the summer lead us to this spot? First, you have to know that I was angry and hurt. I hold onto my anger and hurt longer than anyone. That's something I should talk to a therapist about. Anyways, I'm going to skip the in-between because it's painful and tell you that we have mutual friends who just want the best for those in their lives. One trip to Las Vegas on a joint bachelor-bachelorette party and we woke up married."

"You're married?" Nate asks.

"I should probably introduce you?" I raise my eyebrows at him questioningly.

"I think your listeners would love to put a name to the voice."

"If you insist. My husband is Nathan Holloway. Yes, that

Nathan Holloway who plays baseball for Cincinnati. I call him, Natey."

"Don't say that on the air," he whines with a smile.

"I'm sorry, it can't be edited out."

He and I fall into laughter again. This is what I've always wanted in a relationship. Laughter. So much laughter that my stomach hurts.

And love. Yeah. A lot of love.

"That's fine," Nate begins as we finally compose ourselves. "What my wife wants, my wife gets."

I hold my flaming cheeks and Nate smiles like the cat who caught the canary. "Yes, he is this romantic all of the time," I say into the microphone. "So, Natey. Tell the people what our second chance has been like."

I SEND off the podcast and video files to my editor and make sure the studio lights are unplugged before turning off the overhead light and heading to the living room. Nate is laying on the couch, the TV playing some highlight reel of past games, and pats the spot in front of him. I greedily squeeze in next to him, wrapping my arm around his waist and settling my head on his shoulder. He's like a furnace most days and it doesn't take long for my body to accept the heat to pull me into a sleep.

"Sophie said she wants to celebrate our getting married," I tell Nate with my eyes closed.

Nate's chest shakes with a suppressed laugh and a snort. "Do you think Sophie just wants an excuse for a party?"

"I didn't think that at first, but now I do." I throw my leg over Nate's and burrow closer into him. "When I said

Sophie wants to throw us a party, I mean she already planned it."

"Of course she did. She probably had Bryce help."

"He was on our group chat. Requested strippers. Naturally I had to decline."

The volume on the TV turns down at the same time Sully's snoring gets louder. I look over my shoulder to see her sprawled on her dog bed and snort-laugh before turning back to Nate.

"Naturally," Nate whispers sarcastically.

"Did you know–" I'm cut off by a yawn, "that..."

"Sleep, Bee." Nate tells me and kisses me on the top of my head.

I WAKE UP AN HOUR LATER. On the couch. Alone. I hear voices coming from my front room and in my sleep-ridden brain, nothing is clicking. I could use so much more sleep with my husband, but the universe apparently has other plans. Stretching from my spot, I slowly sit up, yawning as I do. I get up and quietly pad into the front room.

"Hey," I say slowly when I see Nate with my sister and chosen family. He smiles at me and I walk over to him, sitting in his lap. "Why are you guys here?"

"So, J, when I said we were celebrating you two getting married...I meant tonight." Sophie beams from where she's sitting on the floor.

It's then I noticed that they're all dressed in going out clothes that she's serious.

"But we were going to make dinner," I pout and Nate kisses the side of my head.

"You two are cute," Sarah observes. "But you can also make dinner another night."

I narrow my eyes at my husband's publicist. "Like you wouldn't be upset about your plans being derailed."

Sarah opens her mouth to object when Nate and Riley burst out in laughter.

"Who says I can't eat wherever we're going?" Nate asks as he whispers in my ear.

My body heats all over and the sound of everyone's chuckles hits me in the back of the head. "You're terrible." I tell him and lick and tug his earlobe between my teeth, then turn back to the group. "We're in. Give us like thirty minutes to get ready." I slide off Nate's lap and head for the stairs. "Kam, will you take Sully out?"

"As long as you wear something white!" she shouts from the couch.

Nate and I walk into my bedroom and head for the closet. Making room for his things wasn't as hard as I thought it would be.

"Something white?" I huff as I go through the dresses I have.

"It's a good thing I have clothes over here." Nate says from his side of the closet. I turn my head and see him standing with his hands on his hips as he looks at his selection.

The plush carpet mutes my steps as I walk up behind him and wrap my arms around his waist. The lavender scent from the laundry detergent, mixed with Nate's already intoxicating patchouli scent, does something insane to my hormones.

"What if we just tell them to leave?" I whine.

"You are such a homebody, Bee." Nate laughs and turns in my arms. The motion has my arms resting low on his hips and I look up at him with, what's hopefully, my version of puppy dog eyes. "Don't give me that look. Think of this as a hard launch to the world knowing that we're married."

"Normal people would just change their status on Facebook," I tell him.

His blinding white teeth show in a smile that has me feeling delirious. "Well, we're not normal people."

"Let's go, you two!" Someone yells from downstairs.

I drop my head on Nate's chest and groan. His arms wrap around my shoulders and he drops his lips to the top of my head before he releases me and turns me back to my clothes. I end up settling on a silver mini dress with a strappy back. Thank goodness for my lack of boobs otherwise this dress would show everything. I mean, it still shows a lot, but in a tasteful way. On an impulse shopping day over the summer, I saw these silver heels with a butterfly disguised as the strap that lays over my foot. I never pictured myself wearing them so soon, but the silver lining is that my toenails are painted.

I head into the bedroom and toss the dress on the bed, then head to the bathroom to do something with my hair. It's been in a bun since we filmed the podcast and anyone with curly hair knows that once it's in a bun there is no way to style it correctly. So I settle on a slick back ponytail and style my curls that way. I quickly wash my face and get started on some simple makeup that will last through the night.

When I'm satisfied with my hair and makeup, I head back into my bedroom and find some pasties that will hopefully conceal what the cold will expose. Unzipping my jacket, I place the pasties on and head to the bathroom.

"Baby, will you put lotion on my back?" I ask and turn, giving him said naked back.

"Is what you're wearing going to make me want to gouge out the eyes of every man who looks your way?"

My body is jostled side-to-side as my back is moisturized. "Your possessiveness is very hot. But you must be immune to the looks you get from men and women, so don't start because I have nails."

"I'm aware," Nate says and I hear the smile in his voice. "Okay you're all set."

"Thank you, baby."

He kisses me on the back of the neck and gives me a little push back to the bedroom. Smiling, I drop the jacket from my chest and pull the dress over my body. Once it's on I pull my sweats off and survey how it looks from the mirror in the corner of the room.

"Holy fuck."

"Is that a good, *holy fuck*? Or a bad *holy fuck*?" I ask, hoping I know the answer while I twiddle my fingers in front of me as the insecurity from Trent's snipping words echo in the back of my mind. I know Nate would never make me feel less than for the outfits I choose to wear. But it's hard to break the habit of expecting people to tear you down for the little things.

"That's a holy fuck I can't wait until I can peel this dress off of you," Nate says as he erases the distance between us and hovers his hands above my waist. "After tonight, we are never leaving the house."

"Let's go, you two!" A deeper voice, I'm assuming Bryce, calls from the stairs.

"Is it too soon to move to Alaska?" I ask when I back away and sit on the bed to put on my shoes. I wink at Nate when he sees the shoes I'm putting on.

"Maybe I can reconsider." He says with his bottom lip

pinched between his fingers. The entire time, his eyes stay on where I'm fastening my shoes.

When I stand up I head back into the closet and grab a black peacoat so I can somewhat match him. Walking back into the room, Nate is still standing where I left him. Dressed in black jeans and a grey sweater with loosely tied boots, he's everything.

I take his hands in mine and walk backwards, heading to the stairs. "Come on, baby. The sooner we go out, the sooner we can come home." I let go when we get to the top and do a spin when the girls catcall.

"That's more like it. Come on you two."

I LEAN into Nate's side as we toast to getting married again. We've done this a few times already and every time those around us cheer.

Sarah rounds the table as an upbeat song sends most of us swaying in our spots, and pulls me from Nate. "I promise I will have her back in one piece."

I make a noise of protest when Nate releases me. "One song."

"We'll see about that." Sarah says as she pulls me to the girls.

Our dancing is apparently the cue for everyone else to finally join. The music is turned up to a non-conversation holding level and we move to the beat of the music. Sophie dances her way over to me and takes my hands in hers. Spinning us around until we're a giggling two-some.

"I'm sorry I didn't tell you we got married." I tell her as best as I can over the music.

"It's okay. If Chance and I got married and had no recollection, I wouldn't tell anyone either." Our hands go up as cued by the music. "I'm just glad our meddling worked."

I throw my head back and laugh because it most certainly worked. We go back to dancing and hands land on my waist making my skin prickle. And not in a good way. I step away from whoever had their hands on me and my jaw goes slack.

"Trent." I say, my blood turning ice cold at the sight of my ex for the first time in over a year. I thought I was moved on from him. The way he made me feel. Like every move I made was an attack against him.

"Hi, baby." He says and tries to move closer. I take a step back.

I swallow and look around. The dance floor has gotten even more crowded and the guys are no longer in our sight.

"Come on, Jax. Let's dance like old times." Trent tries again and steps forward.

"No."

His hands wrap around my arm and I try to shake him off, but his grip tightens. "I promise to let you lead."

"Let me go." I tell him again.

"You always loved going until I wore you down." He sneers.

What did I ever see in him? I ask myself that for the last time as he's in front of me. He's skinnier now, his hair is greasy, and he's definitely not wearing the approved attire to get in here. So the question is, how? Although that could be because he's wearing a 'STAFF' shirt. So the question is, how did he get away? And how did he know I was here?

38

NATE

The music gets turned up and soon the girls are swallowed by the crowd. I turn my focus back to the table and see them all with raised eyebrows and barely contained smiles.

"What?" I ask.

"It's weird seeing you smile so much." Chance says and takes a pull of his drink.

My brows furrow and I look at him. "I smile."

"No. You brood. You're broody. Or at least you were until you married Jax. Now you just look like a lost puppy when she's not next to you." Bryce says while he bounces to the music.

Mason, Adam, and Riley all snort at Bryce's comparison of me. Jax and I have done a poor job in integrating ourselves with them and I make a mental note to change that. They're with women that Jax adores and looks up to. By proxy that means the guys should become my friends as well.

"I think they all bring our gooey side out," Riley chimes in from across the table.

"From what I heard, you were already gooey." Mason pipes up and Riley shrugs agreeingly while looking at Mason with stars in his eyes. I can't blame him. Even though Mason retired due to a career-ending injury, he's still a legend in the sports world. Hell, I even look up to him and he's my brother-in-law.

Our attention turns back to the dance floor, which has gotten exceedingly more crowded. I don't know why, but something seems off.

"I'm gonna go dance with my wife." I say and push off from the table.

"Right behind you." I hear.

I weave through dancing couples and dodge grabbing hands. The lights in here are dark enough that whoever you're dancing with won't scare you off. But, unfortunately, also dark enough that anything can happen without you seeing. I keep walking until I see Jax and my body relaxes. Until I see some guy holding onto her arm.

"Shit." Riley says when he comes up behind me.

"Who is that?"

"Her ex."

My steps get more determined. Brushing past everyone to get to my wife, I look over what I can see of him. From his scuffed shoes to the black jeans that have seen better days with the T-shirt that has the club's logo covering the back and 'STAFF' printed on the bottom.

"Let me go." I faintly hear Jax say over the music.

I'm not sure what he says to her but her face goes ghostly white and I see Jax try to break free from his hold.

"Get your hands off of my wife." I say when I reach them. My hands form a fist as I hold them at my side. My first inclination is to hit first, talk second. But his grip on Jax is strong and the last thing I want is to hurt her.

Jax swallows and when he turns, my eyes go to their point of contact and I see red.

"Who the hell are you?" Her ex sneers.

"Her husband. Now get your fucking hands off my wife."

In my anger, I note that the sound in the room has dulled and my body heats from eyes on us. I'm usually a fly under the radar type of guy. But in this instance, I'm not.

"You married him?" Her slime ball ex asks with a sneer.

I step closer, angling my body between them so I'm slightly in front of Jax. "I won't tell you again. Get. Your. Fucking. Hands. Off. My. Wife."

"Do I need to hit you again?" Riley asks as he steps up.

Jax lets out a gasp of pain and I feel her body tense. I look down to see the death grip tighten on her arm.

I smile, but it doesn't reach my eyes. My hand reaches out to her ex's other arm and I squeeze. His eyes meet mine, wide and terrified. "You now have five seconds to let go of my wife or I will not hesitate to lay you out on this floor."

I start my countdown. The crowd around us has their eyes and phones pointed at us. It's a good thing my publicist is here.

"...2."

His grip tightens on Jax and she whimpers.

"...1."

I don't even have a chance to raise a fist before he's sprawled on the floor. Looking over I see Bryce shaking out his hand. Security barrels through the crowd and picks her ex up off the floor and carts him out. I still want to know how he got in.

"What the hell?" I question my teammate.

"He should've taken his hands off your wife when you first told him to." Bryce looks at me and then to Jax all the while flexing his hand. In a breath he pushes through the crowd and Sophie and Chance follow him.

What was that? I ask myself.

"Nate, can we go?" Jax asks from next to me.

I gently place my hands on her shoulder and look her over. Then I take her arm into my hand and note the fingerprints that have already left a mark and I know it'll bruise. We'll ice it when we get home.

"I'm gonna fucking kill him," I murmur.

"Don't." Jax says and steps closer. "I just wanna go home. Or maybe find Bryce?"

I wrap my arm around her shoulders and kiss her on the top of the head. Her arm goes around my waist and I make sure the others are in range and ready to go. We push through the crowd and head to the coat check.

"Hi, I'm Donovan, the manager. I want to express my deepest apologies for what happened. Trent has been let go effective immediately."

"Thank you." I tell him and help Jax get in her coat.

He hands me his card. "If you ever come back, it's on the house."

"Thank you." I tell him again and pocket his card, doubtful that we'll ever come back because if they can hire my wife's ex, then who knows who they'll hire. Are background checks not a thing anymore? I pull out my phone on a whim and see a text from Chance.

> Chance: Turn right and we're at the end of the block.

With my arm wrapped around Jax's shoulder, we head outside and turn to the right. The line to get in is long and I don't miss all of the whispers about seeing us out and about. It's not unusual to see athletes around town. But we do tend to hibernate when it gets closer to getting ready for spring training. And when we're all in season, you won't catch any of us dead out on the town.

"Chance," I call out when we reach the corner.

He untangles himself from Sophie and heads our way. Behind him I can see Bryce shaking out his hand and Sophie trying to talk him down.

"I don't–" Chance begins, but loses his words.

"Can I talk to him?" Jax pipes up. She's not said more than a handful of words since we zoomed out.

"Are you sure?"

Jax nods and pulls herself away from me. I watch them with furrowed brows as she approaches him. Bryce stops pacing, his face relaxes, and whatever Jax says to him has my friend blinking back tears. He tells her something that has her head tilting in what looks like understanding. Everything in me wants to join her. Join them. To also tell him that his actions were justified. When his head drops, my wife steps forward and wraps her small arms around him. Jax has always been a master at comforting people, it's just who she is. They must still be talking in their embrace because I see each of their heads nodding. Her presence and the way she is with her words has people opening up to her. It's what makes Jax so special. It's what makes her, her.

LATER THAT NIGHT, Jax and I are laying in bed. *The OC* is playing on a loop and the light from the TV bathes her in a blue light. After the incident at the club, we all decided that it was time to call it. I haven't wanted to push her for what she talked about with Bryce, but the not knowing is killing me. I've never been a nosy person. But seeing my wife and friend bond in a way I didn't think they would, has me wanting to know everything.

"I know you wanna ask," Jax says. Her fingers have been tracing over my tattoos, focusing mainly on the bees.

"Is Bryce okay?"

She lets out a deep sigh, pausing her tracing before starting up again. "Yes and no. He has a twin sister."

"He does?" I ask completely surprised.

"Bub, how well do you know Bryce?"

I rub my hand up and down her back and mindlessly watch what's happening on the screen. "Apparently not well enough. I've played with the guy for years and as open as he is, he's never opened up."

"Well, how open were you?" Jax turns that around on me and I groan. "Exactly. Baby, even the happiest people can have the darkest memories. They can be the cheerleader, the class clown, the go-to guy, and they can be an All-Star. But you never know what people are hiding behind that. What they're hiding behind the jokes and the smiles. That's Bryce."

I blink and swallow hard. "Was it like that with you?" I don't have to clarify when I meant. Jax knows.

"No. I never made it a secret to those who knew me. My parents saw the aftermath of you. And surprisingly, so did Kamryn. Even in my sister's worst period of fighting with Liam and then losing him, she saw me."

I kiss the top of her head. I've apologized more times than I can count. I've made sure my actions backed up my words so that Jax knew that I was hers, that I'm staying. But no matter how much time passes, the guilt will still be there.

"Bryce's twin sister was in an abusive relationship with his best friend. They were in high school when it started." Jax lets out an aggrieved sigh. "He beats himself up for not helping his sister. For listening to his friend when he mentioned how clumsy she was."

"What?"

"I know. I think that's why he's so lively all the time. He wants that joy. He wants to see the good instead of the bad. So tonight was a trigger for him."

"I've been a terrible friend," I say.

Jax sits up and straddles my lap but not in a way that could lead to more. "Don't do that. Don't beat yourself up for not knowing Bryce's past."

"But if I would've asked–"

"Then what, baby? Would you have tried to change it?"

I look at Jax. Her silhouette is framed by the TV light and she looks like an angel. Not the best thought to have while talking about this. But hey, she's in sleepwear and on my lap.

"No. I guess you're right."

"I know I am." Jax says and slides off my lap. "Maybe now you can just be a better friend to Bryce. He's all alone out here. I won't be opposed to you hanging out with him more."

I tickle her sides. "Thank you for the permission."

"Anytime." She says with a yawn.

"Sleep, Bee." I tell her and kiss her on the lips before turning off the television.

With the room bathed in darkness, Sully in the corner on her bed snoring, my mind runs a marathon. I think back to every instance and interaction with Bryce. He's always been my goofy friend. But then I think back to celebrities who hid behind humor because the darkness was threatening to take over. I don't want that for my friend. We leave for spring training in two weeks and I promise to myself to do what I can to be the best friend that Bryce can have.

39

JAX
MID-FEBRUARY

"They loved it?" I say into the phone.

My manager called to tell me the latest numbers from my episode with Nate. I already reach more listeners than I could have hoped for, but this episode shot me up to number one for the last few weeks. Apparently people love a second chance.

"Jax, they want more episodes with you two."

"I don't know, Ness. The reason Nate and I work is because we have separate hobbies. I don't wanna monetize our marriage."

She sighs and I hear the tapping of her keyboard. "I know, Jax. But they're offering a seven-figure deal. They take over the hosting, the distribution. If you thought your reach was great now, with them it could be astronomical."

"Seven-figures?" I choke out. I make enough already from ads that run on my show, plus my Youtube channel. But this number, this illusive number, is more than I could ever dream of making.

"Yes. I know you're wary of agreeing so fast. These deals take a while, so you have time. I'll email you their proposal and you can look it over. I think this deal would change your life. As your manager, I think this would be great exposure for you. But as your friend, I see why you're wary. But know that I support you either way."

"Thanks, Vanessa. I'll think it over."

"No problem. Bye, Jax."

I hear the silence on the other end signaling she's hung up. My email pings with the email from Vanessa and my heart flies to my throat. I'm not equipped to handle this sort of thing. I started my podcast as a way to get my words out. Did I think I'd reach anyone? Of course not. I thought Kamryn and my parents would be my only listeners. So to think I could reach more than the people in the states, send my heart to my throat. But contracts and the legalities of what this entails is more than I can handle.

> Me: Are you at your office?

> Sarah: I am. Did you need something?

> Me: Maybe.

> Sarah: I'll be here all day.

I tap my finger against my desk. I'd ask Nate, but he's already in Florida for spring training and I don't want to bring this to him just yet. I don't want to distract him. So I make a list. I mark down everything good that would happen if Nate and I started a show together. Then I mark down everything bad that would happen if we started a show together. When I finish, they're both even with the same pros and cons. Groaning, I change out of my lounge clothes to head out and talk to Sarah.

Making the drive into the city, I smile as I see people rushing in at the last minute. One of the pros to being so good at what I do is that I can work from home. But I won't deny that sometimes I get a little envious of people having someplace to be every day. That is until I remember my work commute is so close that all I do is roll out of bed and stumble to my office.

I find a spot in the parking lot at Sarah's office and snag my keys and phone. Walking through the sliding glass doors of the lobby, I contemplate taking the stairs and only have a mild freak-out when I decide to take the elevator. When the doors of the elevator open, I think of Nate and press the button before heading into the corner. I keep my gaze on the top of the car as I'm whisked to the top.

When the doors open, I hurry off casually and head to the reception desk.

"Hi, Tessa. Sarah said I could come by anytime."

"Hi, Jax. Head on back."

"Thanks." I say and wave to her.

On second thought, I think to myself as I walk through the cubicle farm, I'm glad I work from home. Sarah's boss makes this place look inviting but the idea of being chained to a desk like this, where everyone can see what you're doing, is my personal nightmare.

I knock on her closed office door and wait for her response.

"Hey." I say and pop my head in.

"Hi. Come in Mrs. Holloway." She says with raised eyebrows.

I roll my eyes and shut the door before taking a seat. "Very funny."

"I know. But I *love* saying it," she sings. "What's up?"

I tell her about my phone call with Vanessa, the number, the show, and my thoughts.

"Let me see the list." Sarah holds her hand out.

"What makes you think I made a list and then brought it?"

She quirks a brow as her hand stays out between us and I grumble as I pull it out of the back pocket of my jeans. Sarah's smile is smug as she unfolds the note. I tap my index finger on my thigh as I wait for her to finish reading my pro's and con's.

"I see where you're torn. Jax this list is even."

"I know," I whine. "And I can't take this to Kam or Emily because they'd both tell me to follow my heart which does not help me in the slightest. And I figured since you deal with contracts and deals for your clients, my husband included, you could maybe give me some advice."

"Okay. Well, as Nate's publicist I do think this would be a good move for him. But I don't think he needs it. Even before you came back into the picture, he was already very successful and very much resembled a turtle. But I'm with Vanessa on this in that you two were incredible on your show. Then the feminist in me is skeptical. Why now? Why are you getting an offer like this now?"

I huff and sit back in my chair. "That was the first thing that ran through my mind. You know how it is. Having a man by your side makes you an asset."

No matter how many strides a woman makes in this world, she'll always be held to a lower standard than a man. But if that woman makes strides with a man by her side, suddenly everyone wants a piece of the magic. That mindset continues to set women back for the fear of being seen less than their counterparts.

"I'm gonna say no."

Sarah's smile is one of pride. "I was hoping that's what you were going to say. Plus, I think you just found your next episode."

"Thanks, Sarah."

"How is Nate? This is your first time apart since Vegas. But how are you?"

I let out a sigh. "How did Kamryn do this? How do you do it? I miss having him in my bed. We talk a little, but he's so exhausted after each day that he usually falls asleep on the phone after a few minutes."

I try not to think too much about the day Nate left for training. It brought up weird emotions from college and I knew he was thinking the same. But I'm trying to not be too dependent on him being around to make me happy.

"Just remember that he's yours. And that planes fly to Florida almost daily." Sarah says with a laugh that I can't help but join in on.

Later that night, Nate finally has a chance to call me when he wraps up training for the day.

"Hi, Bee." He says into the camera.

"Hi, baby."

"What's wrong?"

My face scrunches that he can read me like this. "Who said anything is wrong?"

Nate gives me a *be serious* look.

I take a sip of my wine and set it on the table next to me. "I was on a call with Vanessa this morning. The numbers came in from the show you were on and they were my highest numbers to date."

"Bee, that's incredible," he praises.

"Yeah, it is." I agree with him.

"But...?"

"You're a hot commodity and always will be. So I'm skeptical if these numbers are because of me or..."

"If it's because of me?"

I wince because, yes. "Yeah. Plus Vanessa told me a

studio was interested in hosting a show with the both of us. But again, why now?"

"Baseball and you are my main focus. Bee, I've never had any interest in hosting a podcast like you do. It has never crossed my mind."

"Do you think it's weird that I'm only being approached because of you?"

His mouth sets in a straight line. "Yeah. Jax, your podcast is great. I thought that when I was trying to figure you out. And if a company couldn't see that before I was on it, then they don't know the talent they're missing out on."

"It's a lot of money though." I tell him.

"I have a lot of money too," he says like it's no big deal.

"Nathan." I scold.

"Jaclyn."

I breathe out through my nose and roll my eyes when I see him smiling on the screen. "I guess I was hesitant about saying no and telling you I was going to turn them down, because I didn't want to hurt your feelings. Because what if you said yes? What if deep down you really wanted to do a show with me? There would be no separation and, I love you, but I would kick you out so fast."

He laughs at my confession. "No hurt feelings here. You're making the right move, Bee. Screw them for not noticing your talent before I came along."

"Thanks, baby." I tell him. "I miss you."

"I miss you too."

PODCAST

"Welcome back to another episode of *Life Not Simplified*. I'm your host, Jax. And today I want to talk about the unfairness of women still being treated less than men in the workplace. Now, I've already sent my refusal to my manager so this won't come as a shock to her. But I was approached by a studio because they tuned into the show with me and my husband. Full transparency, that was my highest rated show to date and the numbers are still climbing.

"Has it always been about the numbers for me? When it comes to reaching new listeners, yes. It is about the numbers. Because every podcast's goal is to continue to reach their listeners and draw in new listeners every week. But as I was on the call with my manager, then talking with my husband's publicist, who's also one of my close friends, and then my husband, I wondered why now. Why was I being approached by a studio once I have a man, who also happens to be my husband and the love of my life, on my show when I have over fifty episodes published with just me and over thirty published with me and guests. So why now? Is it because my husband kills in on the field for six months out of the year? Is it because they want to tap into a new audience with a woman by a man's side? Trust me, that has been done already. But for a studio to undermine me and think my podcast is only worth something because of my husband–well that's a slap in the face for all women who try and succeed on their own, but then choose to bring a man in on a guest spot.

"Nate has never wanted to be on a podcast. He did that one episode because he loves me. And that was our way of getting in front of the media by announcing our marriage to the world. If my podcast does get picked up by a bigger studio, it will be because they love me, Jax, as the host. Not because of who I'm married to or who I'm related to. The title of my podcast is *Life Not Simplified* for a reason. If everything was so simple, then I would have said yes and dragged my husband into something he doesn't want. But life is not simple and it would have ruined who we are as a married couple.

"So to any woman hesitant to start something without a man by your side, I did it when I launched my podcast. I was in charge of my editing and uploading for a very long time until I reached out to someone to take over the editing and uploading. And that was a big step for me. Reaching out for help when I realized I could no longer handle the small tasks on my own. Letting someone help me when I hate asking for help.

"As a host, I know my worth and as much as I love my husband, my worth is not dependent on him. No woman's worth is dependent on a man.

"That's all I have for today's episode of *Life Not Simplified*. If this episode resonated with you, sound off in the comments and maybe you'll find others who are in the same boat."

40

JAX

LATE MARCH

Nate's alarm goes off and I groan into my pillow. I hear the smack of his hand against the alarm clock, yes my husband prefers that over using his phone, meaning that we have about fifteen minutes until the next alarm sounds.

Today is the home opener after the first ten games were on the road and it's like we're hopped up on life. His mom and Kayla flew in last night and are staying at Nate's house. I offered to let them stay here, but they both insisted that Nate's house was perfect. Since visiting there in January, things have vastly shifted. I now talk with Kayla and Nora, Nate's mom, once a week.

Nate snakes his arms around me and pulls me closer. I love my husband more than life. But he's a hot sleeper.

"You're hot," I grumble.

"I know," he says against my neck and I can't ignore his erection pressing against me from behind.

Nate isn't a superstitious guy. So sex is always on the table. I think we're both of the understanding that we're making up for the time we lost.

"You have a big head."

He grinds his hips into me. "I know."

I snort. "Use your words, Natey."

"I wanna fuck you so hard like this." He says and slips my sleep shorts down. "Fill your pussy with my cum." I feel his bare skin against mine and whimper as he pulls my leg over his, opening me up. "And then I want to take it slow until your legs are quivering and every time you walk, your pussy throbs remembering how hard I took you." He says and thrusts inside me on one stroke.

I gasp and my head falls back on his shoulder as he kisses along my jaw. The sound of our arousal and heavy pants as the bed rocks, heightens my need for him.

"Nate." I pant when he holds my leg up and pulses in and out of me with small strokes.

"Every time," he pants. "You feel like heaven every time."

I clench around him and his grip on me tightens. "Harder."

Nate opens me wider as his thrusts become unrelenting. Each slap of his hips against mine pulls a gasp out of me. Each slap of his hips against mine sends my heart rate rocketing. I bite my bottom lip to keep from screaming out. My hands grip at the sheets, claw at him, as he sucks on my neck and hammers into me.

"Are you gonna come on my cock, baby?" Nate grunts out. His arm slides between me and the bed and his fingers find my nipple. Pinching and tugging, urging me to find my release. "Come on Jax. Give me one."

Nate's hand moves to my clit and pinches. My breath is stolen from me when my orgasm slams into me. Over and over. My climax pulls me under, threatening to drown me. Nate drops my leg and rolls me over to my stomach. He kisses along my body and climbs over me with his legs on either side of my waist. My orgasm is still moving through me and he pushes his cock back inside of me.

I moan as the fullness from this position is enough to bring tears to my eyes. Nate ruts into me and hits that spot that has my mouth open in a soundless cry. I can do nothing but lay here and feel everything. My clit rubs against the sheets on every thrust and I clench around him as I feel another orgasm climbing.

"Fuck, Bee." Nate groans as his strokes get more punishing before he stops and turns me so I'm laying on my back and he thrusts back in, burying his face in the crook of my neck and rocking into me. This time it's slow. Our skin glides against each other and he lays kisses on my neck. On every stroke his pubic bone rubs against my clit and I clench around him as my final orgasm rolls over me. Nate grunts before I feel his release fill me. He continues his languid strokes and the sound of our mixed release causes a little tremor to roll through me.

Nate stays buried inside of me and rolls us to the side. My head drops onto his shoulder while his hips continue to move in a lazy motion. I love the feel of him inside of me. Nate lets his cock soften and he continues to kiss up and down my neck.

"I like waking up like this." I tell him when I can finally catch my breath. I curl my hand around his neck and run my fingers in small circular movements.

"Me too." He says and the alarm goes off again making me jump and him grunt. "That's a record."

I mourn the loss of him when he slips out of me to turn the noise off.

"Come shower with me." He tells me and whips the covers off.

"I was gonna wash my hair," I whine.

"That's not going to stop me." Nate says and pulls me towards him and carries me bridal style into the bathroom. He uses his foot to lift the toilet seat and sets me down. We're long past modesty in our marriage and Nate cares about my health just as much as I care about his. Once I'm done taking care of business, I take off my pajama top and join him in the shower.

My mouth pools with saliva as I watch water from both shower heads slide down his dark ochre brown skin that's decorated with tattoos. I'll never get over seeing the art that he's covered himself in. Every day I look at him feels like I'm seeing him for the first time and I get that fluttery feeling in my stomach like it's our first kiss, first touch, and first time. Nate takes care of me in a way I never dreamed a man could.

"Are you excited for the game?" I ask as I wrap my arms around his waist.

Nate turns in my arms and moves me under the stream of water. "Yeah. First home game of the season. What's not to be excited about? Plus I'll have my wife and family in the stands."

I smile as he grabs my shampoo from its spot and begins working the product into my scalp. "You like saying that."

"Love, Bee. I love calling you my wife so much." He says and tips my head back to wash the suds out of my curls. "I like being sweet with you and if my calling you my wife gets that look from you, I'll continue saying it until we're old and gray."

"How do you know we'll be gray?" I tease.

"Hmm," he hums thoughtfully and rings out my hair before putting conditioner in and raking it through with his sure fingers. "Because I know that you would never do anything to ruin your hair. And if that means letting the gray decorate your hair like glitter, then so be it."

"It's weird how well you know me," I say with amazement as he makes sure all of the conditioner is out before pulling it in a clip and stepping back.

His eyebrows quirk up and then relax before he's tapping at his temple. "I have everything stored up here in my Jax library."

"You'll have to tell me what else you have stored in there."

"Never." Nate says and kisses me on the tip of my nose. "Now finish up so we can go eat."

I finish my shower with a smile on my face. And an even bigger one as I watch Nate wash his body. The arms that hold me whenever he can flex with each move of the loofa across his body. Those legs that carry him home to me are strong with muscles that make him desired here and on the field. Every day I fall head over heels in love with my husband for the little things he does. Not for the grand gestures. But the little things. Like washing my hair or picking up a toy for Sully because he decided she needs a new one.

Every day, Nathan Holloway proves why he and I are meant to be.

41

NATE

JUNE

"Excited for tomorrow?" Bryce asks as we're warming up for the game.

We have a series in Philly this week and knowing that we were playing in Jax's hometown, I knew I wanted to kick my plan into overdrive. Chance, Bryce, and I have the third game off and with a lot of convincing from the front office and our general manager, we're able to surprise my wife.

"Definitely. I also have something for you."

"Me?" He asks, confused.

Bryce and I have been hanging out more. I've gotten to know him on a deeper level than him being my goofy teammate that I've been playing with for the last six seasons. He's still goofy, but get him talking about world issues and he will go on a tangent. And don't get him started on romance books.

"Mm hmm. You won't know what it is until tomorrow though."

His face scrunches up under his hat. "Has anyone ever called you a tease?"

"Yeah. My wife when we were in college." I say with a

chuckle as I think back to the day she said that. It was when I was teaching her all the things about intimacy and how to touch me. Geez that feels like a lifetime ago.

Bryce laughs at that. But what he doesn't know is that I'm surprising him with his family tomorrow. It was easy to sneak their numbers. Bryce has a habit of leaving his phone unattended and with no passcode. Which for a guy whose contract is as big as it is, you'd think he would be a little more careful.

"Well, it paid off for you."

I nod with a smile and slap him on the back as we head back into the clubhouse to get ready for the game. When we come back on the field, the crowd is a mix of cheers and boos. Which is common for any away game, but certainly amplified because of how passionate Philly fans are. I look to the right field line and see Jax with her whole extended family. This. Seeing her joy with them in tow is why tomorrow night will be one to remember.

I PULL the rental car into Jax's parent's driveway, a bit reminiscent of college. Except this time I'm not parked on the street or driving a hand me down that sounds like nails on a chalkboard when I turn the key in the ignition and I don't have a duffle with clothes and plans to head home after a week here. I pocket the keys and stroll up the front walk with a bouquet of tulips in my hand and I ring the doorbell.

"Hi, handsome." Jax says when she opens the door. Dressed in a blue eyelet dress and white wedges with strings that tie up her calves with her curls as voluminous as they were all those years ago when I realized my crush on her was stronger than I realized. Her time outside has brought out the light dusting of freckles on her face and the tan lines from her recent trip to Mexico with the girls are still prominent.

"Hi, Bee. These are for you." I tell her when I hold my hand out.

She takes them and sticks her nose in the bouquet. "They're beautiful. Come in."

I cross the threshold and follow her inside. When we came here to tell her parents we got married, it was like walking into a time capsule. Not much in the house changed, but at the same time it felt like everything had changed. Or maybe it was me who changed. The only thing missing is Jersey's nails tapping on the hardwood floors as Jax moves from room to room. The Rawlins never did get another pet after he passed away. Can't say I blame them. He was irreplaceable.

"Are you sad about missing the game?" I ask as I lean on the counter and watch her fill a vase for the flowers.

"It would break my attendance streak and Dad is a little bummed. But since you have the night off, I am not going to complain. Dad on the other hand might have grumbled a little bit."

I smile as I watch her flit around the kitchen and smile even bigger when she comes to stand in front of me.

"Why are you all smiley?"

"No reason." I lie. You would think I'd be nervous for what's about to happen. But Jax and I have been happily married for the better part of a year. I know she said she loves the ring I drunkenly got her, but I want her to wear something that I consciously picked out. It's still the same style as the one she has, just with a few minor adjustments.

"Okay. Are you ready?" She asks.

"Yep." I nod. "But first I need you to put this on." I tell her and pull the blindfold out from my pocket.

Jax quirks an eyebrow at the fabric in my hands. "This isn't some kinky, role play thing you wanna try, is it?"

"No," I say with a laugh. "But it's good to know where your mind is at. Now turn around."

She does as I say and I tie the blindfold around her head, careful not to smoosh her curls.

"Will you grab my purse?" Jax asks as we take steps out of the kitchen.

I tuck it under my arm as we walk towards the foyer. "Got it. Let me open the door for you."

Jax stands patiently as I open the door and I lead her to the car. Once she's safely in the vehicle with her seatbelt secure, I run around to the drivers side and startup. I found one of our old playlists and cue that up before heading to her surprise.

"Nate, what are you up to?"

I reach over and take her hand, linking our fingers together and placing them in her lap. "Don't you worry your cute button nose off."

Jax snorts and rubs her thumb over my hand.

When the opening seconds of Phil Collins begins, Jax gasps. "I haven't listened to this song in ages. I would air drum but I feel that would look suspicious to other drivers."

"Damn, I definitely didn't think about that," I say smugly.

When I turn into the parking lot with the only vehicles belonging to our nearest and dearest, it's taking everything in me not to crash through the gates. I knew I wanted to propose to Jax again since the morning we woke up with rings on our fingers. But we needed time. *She* needed time to accept that I wasn't going anywhere.

And now here we are. Seven months later and I'm proposing to her where one of the biggest decisions of my life was made. And I had Jax by my side.

I park and unbuckle my seatbelt. "Hold on." I tell her.

"Not going anywhere," she jokes.

I chuckle and hop out of the car, jogging around to her side and opening the door. I take her hand and help her out. Together, and carefully, we walk towards the entrance.

"I know this smell," Jax says with a smile in her voice that triggers my own.

"You do. Step up." I tell her and then take off the blindfold when we're on the sidewalk entrance.

"Nate," she sighs out when she sees we're at the Botanical Gardens.

I bought the place out for the late afternoon and into the night. It was tricky, planning something behind Jax's back. But when I went to Sarah and Kamryn with my plan, they were all aboard.

I take her hands in mine and walk backwards. The skirt of her dress ruffles around her legs and at this moment, with a look of awe on her face, Jax is the most beautiful woman I've ever laid my eyes on.

We walk through the gate and her eyes bounce everywhere. Twinkling lights and solar ground lights, begin to create a path for us to where the real surprise is.

"I figured I would bring us somewhere only we know to do this."

"What do you mean?" Jax asks as we get closer to where we need to be.

I fiddle with the ring she's still wearing and when we get to the right spot, where her family can see and where the photographers can get the right shop, I slip it off her finger and put it in my pocket.

"Nate," she scolds and it soon turns into a gasp when I drop to one knee and pull out her new ring.

"Almost ten years ago, you bulldozed into my life. You didn't give me a choice to not be your friend. And for that, I'm so grateful. I feel like I've loved you before I knew what love was. And I feel like I've known you for my whole life. There was never a time after we met where I could imagine my life and you weren't next to me. I know I'm to blame for those years apart, but you have been with me whether you knew it or not. I am so grossly in love with you Jaclyn Marie Rawlins."

I look up at those honey brown eyes that are filled with tears as I pour my heart out to her.

"I know you said you didn't want a new ring. That the one I don't remember picking out was perfect. Well, I'm ignoring that."

Her laugh is watery and she tries to wipe the tears as they fall, but fails.

"I want to do this the right way. So here I am, on one knee, about to ask you a very important question the way I should have all those years ago. Jaclyn Marie Rawlins, my best friend and the absolute love of my life, will you marry me?"

"Yes," she says in a watery response.

I slide on her new ring and instead of looking at the ring, Jax is looking at me. Standing up, I dip her into a kiss and hear the sounds of our loved ones cheering.

"I wanted them to be part of the magic." I tell Jax when we break the kiss and look around to see our friends and families cheering and whistling.

"Holy hell, I love you so much."

42

JAX

THREE YEARS LATER

"Are you sure we have enough space for everyone?" I ask as I look at our dining room with a now very critical and a bit of a self-conscious eye. The large twelve-seater dining table is made up with plate, silverware, a runner, and candles. Moody wallpaper contrasts beautifully with the oakwood dining table and the area rug underneath ties all of the color together.

"Yeah. The room is done to your specification," my husband says from his spot at the counter while he chops up a basket-full of vegetables for tonight's dinner. Nate's right, although I'll never outright tell him that because I love keeping him on his toes. He'd find me standing in the threshold everyday after the room was finished because I loved the way everything turned out.

I HAVE SOMETHING FOR YOU." He told me one night after I finished up my last meeting.

"Oh, yeah? What's that?" I asked distractedly while scrolling through social media. A sheet of what I guessed are blueprints,

covered my phone and it took me a minute to place them before I looked up at Nate. "This–is this..."

"The blueprints and a 3D print for the house you dreamed up when we were in college? Yes, it is." He admits and drops next to me on the couch.

I looked at each room on the paper in awe. He remembered everything. Down to the built-ins and landing from one end of the house to the next. I remembered him telling me he had these drafted up, but seeing them in hardcopy form is still an out-of-body feeling.

"Nathan Alexander, if I wasn't already married to you I would drag you to the courthouse."

"Good to know." He told me and leaned over, kissing me on the cheek.

"So why are you showing me these now?"

Nate threw his arm over the back of the couch and leaned into me. "I want to build a home with you, Bee. A life. A place where we can hear our kids running and laughing upstairs. A place where we can host our families and friends. A place where you and I can grow old and gray together. This house is your dream and you're mine."

I look over at him with tears in my eyes. "I love you."

"I love you too, Bee."

"So do we go practice making babies now?"

"I thought you'd never offer." Nate says and stands up, tossing me over his shoulder and walking to the bedroom. Our joint laughter echoes through his house as he goes down the stairs to the bedroom where he keeps his promise and we practice making babies for the rest of the night.

"Yeah. I do have good taste."

Nate snorts. "Come try this. I need to know if it's missing anything."

I scrutinize the dining room one last time before walking the handful of steps to the kitchen. My wine glass finds a spot at the end of the kitchen island and I slide my hand in the back pocket of Nate's jeans. He holds his hand out with the spoon and I test what he's making.

"Maybe more garlic?"

"You have impeccable taste."

"I know." I say and tap him on the butt.

The sound of forks tapping and scrapping on plates fills the dining space. A lot has changed in these few years, but one thing has remained the same. We've all shown up for each other. We've healed in ways beyond our wildest imaginations. Sure, we've lost a couple of people along the way. But we've gained so much to make up for those losses.

A throat clearing at the end of the table has us all coming up for air from our food.

"I have some news," Kamryn says from the other end of the table and I narrow my eyes at her. She looks at Mason before looking back at the rest of us and I think I know where she's going with this. "I'm pregnant."

"Shut up!" Sarah and Emily say at the same time.

"How far along are you?" Sophie asks.

"Twelve weeks."

"Is that why you've been treating her with kid gloves?" I ask my brother-in-law.

Kamryn and Mason had begun trying to conceive fairly quickly after they got married. I know my sister would never admit to it, but every negative test wore her down. Apart from losing Liam, I had never seen my sister so defeated.

"I told him not to," Kamryn whines.

"Since we're sharing news," Sarah says.

"Not you two too." Bryce groans and his girlfriend gives his neck a squeeze.

"No. We eloped." Riley perks up.

"Why?" Kamryn asks, sounding a little like she's on the verge of tears. Which is highly possible due to the hormones.

Sarah looks at Riley and they share a look. "We didn't want the big wedding. We wanted the two of us and our parents in attendance. Plus, the justice of the peace."

"Well, congratulations!" We all cheer.

I look around the room at my family and chosen family. Years ago I could never picture this. I could never picture being in a room with those I love unconditionally. Where we can come together at least once a month, when schedules allow, and have dinner or lunch together. I sit back in my chair and swing my leg over Nate's thigh. He gives me a wink before joining in conversation with Mason and Adam. This is a good life.

~

Four Years Later

"Daddy!" I hear through my office door and smile at the greeting as three voices greet Nate. Soon after my sister announced she was expecting, Nate made it a goal to start having kids as soon as possible. It took us a while after I had my IUD removed and seeing the negative tests over and over, broke me. I almost told Nate I didn't want to try for kids anymore because it was just another reason that I failed. He held me as I cried. Confused why we weren't pregnant.

. . .

"Hey, Bee. If this is not our time, it's not our time. We'll keep trying." Nate said to me after one of my many breakdowns over a negative test.

"But this is supposed to be the easy part," I cry.

Nate rocks us back and forth on the hard bathroom floor. "Your body needs time to reset."

I REMEMBER the days leading up so vividly. A production company finally approached me for my podcast, because they liked me and what I had been doing with my show. My numbers were better than ever and the guests I had sparked deeper conversations with those who tuned in weekly. But my joy was snuffed that next morning. My period was late again. Later than it had ever been and I was riding on cloud nine. I thought, *finally.* This is it! Because all I wanted since Nate and I got married was to have his babies. But the negative test staring back at me was like it was laughing at me. My husband, my caring and in-tune with my body husband, constantly assured me that it would take time for my body to regulate the hormones after having been on birth control for so long. Deep down I knew that. But when you get so many negatives, it's hard to look for the positive.

Nate took control of everything. I always joked that he should've gotten a degree in women's studies because I learned so much about my body from him that I finally stopped stressing over my set timeline to get pregnant. Well, he worked his magic because on vacation we conceived. Seeing a positive test after so many negatives, I was convinced I was hallucinating. And now we have three beautiful babies. My husband likes me pregnant and he's very close to getting that fourth baby he talked about all those years ago if he keeps this up.

Sully paws at the door, begging to be let free. Her face is lightly coated in sugar-colored fur and her gait isn't as strong as it once was. But every time I'm in my office, she's right by my side. I think she just wants a little slice of quiet from our lively bunch outside.

"Come on, Sully girl. Let's go see Natey." Her tail wags slowly and together we walk down the hallway to where chatter greets us.

"Hi, Miss Sully." I hear Nate greet her.

Leaning on the threshold that leads into the living room, I see our son Samuel with his curly hair, tucked into Nate's side as he holds the bottle for our daughter, Eden. Who doesn't really need anyone to hold her bottle, but Nate has spoiled her. Our three month old, Ivy, is still asleep in her bassinet and won't be up for hours. For a little one, she loves her sleep.

For a while I didn't think this was possible. Before I gave Nate a second chance, I thought my time had run out. But this–my husband, my kids, it all felt like an illusion. This house I live in with a career that fills up every cup I hold out is the most real thing I could have ever wished for. I'm so grateful I let my sister drag me to that baseball game, because if I would have resisted, I would have missed out on my life with Nate.

EPILOGUE

"Every hour?" The flower shop owner questions on the other end of the line.

"Yes, ma'am."

I hear the clacking of keys and I assume it's her putting my order in in-advanced. My wife loves Valentine's Day and I love my wife. Does that love veer on obsession most days? Absolutely. I'm obsessed with her drive, the way she is with our beautiful babies, how she manages her career and keeps the house afloat with the minimal amount of help we ask for, and I'm obsessed with the way she makes time for her friends. I love so many versions of Jax. The wife, the mother, the sister, the friend, and the godmother.

So here I am in January placing an order for a bouquet of roses, tulips, and sunflowers to be delivered to the house every hour. Will she want to strangle me? Yes. But as long as she does it in the bedroom, I won't complain.

"Okay. I can send you the invoice to the email you provided me and you're all set, Mr. Holloway."

"Thank you, Evelyn."

A towel hits me and covers my face when I hang up. "Jax

is going to kill you." Bryce says from his spot at the squat rack.

"Kill me. Fuck me. Makes no difference to me." I say and put my phone in the front pocket of my duffle bag.

Chance snorts from where he's bench pressing. I try to be sympathetic and not rub my marriage in his face. Him and Sophie have been going through a rough patch. If by rough patch, I mean sleeping at mine or Bryce's house more than his own home. I guess when you burn so bright in the beginning, the darkness seems like more of a nightmare.

He's going into his fifteenth season playing and has decided that this will be his last. I can't blame him for walking around with a chip on his shoulder. Losing baseball and possibly his wife? I'd be acting the same way. Although I'm not far behind him. But with baseball, not losing Jax. I did that once and would not survive a second time. We're some of the oldest guys in the league. I now have four kids with the love of my life who are getting more and more active. Putting the school drop-offs and pick-ups, after school activities, and weekend tournaments on her is not us being equals in our marriage.

I told Jax that when I retire, I can't wait to handle everything that she's handled for the last five years. Plus, Samuel has been chomping at the bit to get me to coach his Little League team.

"Are you good, Chance?" I ask before moving onto the final round in our circuit.

He clears his throat and throws on a smirk that Bryce and I know is fake. "Yeah. All good."

Bryce and I share a look before putting our heads down and finishing our workout.

An hour later we clean up and with an extended

goodbye that our wives tease us over, I'm finally on the way home.

When it's the weeks before spring training, with the house empty because the kids are at school, Jax and I have time to ourselves. Most of the time we find ourselves napping. Because with four kids under ten and in activities that keep the calendar busier than mine when I'm in season, Jax needs it. But with the community we have around us, in our friends and family that have decided to make the move up here, the workload lightens when a bat signal is sent out. Usually with a crying emoji or a plain "HELP!" text.

"Jaclyn?" I call out when I come in through the garage.

"Upstairs." I hear distantly and grab a bottle of water from the fridge before taking the stairs two at a time and heading to my wife.

The walls leading upstairs are covered in a mix of family pictures and framed drawings the kids did from school. Jax and I don't quite have the heart to tell any of them that their artwork won't see outside of the house. Shoes are stacked on the stairs ready to be taken upstairs and jackets hang on the posts. It's messy, but it's home.

Turning the corner when I get up the stairs, I see her in all her beauty. Ten years ago I thought she was stunning. Hell, twenty years ago I thought she was the most beautiful girl I had ever seen. And she was. She still is. But after four kids and a decade of dealing with my baseball schedule, she's gotten breathtaking. Her hair is still full and curly, she has smile lines and crinkles at the corners of her eyes from years of laughing at my jokes, and the hips I love to grip onto are fuller than they were back then. Even now, she's still my dream woman.

"Enjoying the view?" She asks as she folds clothes from the pile of laundry on the table without turning around.

"Always." I say and push off the doorframe and saunter towards her. Jax still makes my heart flutter. We still date. We still laugh. We still do everything we did before we had kids, but with a bit of scheduling. I kiss and nibble on her neck and then move to the side. "Have you talked with Sophie?"

Jax's eyes widen and I know she has. "Yeah. I wish I could help them."

"You could if you wanted to. But I don't think them having a baby will help solve their problems."

"That's what I told her. But it hasn't been easy for them." Jax says, sounding defeated for our friends.

The pop of a shirt sounds as I shake it out. "I know, Bee. Hopefully they'll be able to find their way back to each other."

"Is he...?"

"Planning for this to be his last season? Yeah." I nod.

Jax and I finish folding clothes in silence. Once everything is done, we take care of taking them to each kid's room and putting them away because lord knows they won't.

"Hi," Jax says when we're finally back in our room.

"Hi, Bee." I reply and pull her into me.

"I was thinking..."

I snort and start to sway us to no music. Just a song that only we know. "About what?"

"I want us to get married again with the kids watching."

"That'd be three times, Bee." I say with a laugh.

"Well, you know what they say—third times the charm."

I laugh and move us around the room, considering what she said. "Okay. When?"

"Over the summer if possible."

"Okay. Where?" I ask and my eyes travel over the face I've known since I was eighteen, have loved since I was twenty-one and found again when I was twenty-eight. It's been a decade of falling in love with each other every day. Showing our kids that laughter is a soundtrack in our home, that showing affection is par for the course in healthy relationships, and to never go to bed angry because you never know if those final words you speak to someone will be your last.

"Somewhere only we know."

ACKNOWLEDGMENTS

Bleh! I've put off writing the acknowledgments, because that means I'm closing the chapter on my Healing in Cincy series. I remember the day I started writing this series in 2018. I was at work and I had a bunch of downtime between projects. And between work and deciding to try my hand at putting a fictional world together, my romantic life was falling apart.

I love second chances in romance books and like Jax said, there was no way that a second chance was realistic. But for my fictional characters, I make it believable. And if you've ever gotten back together with an ex just for the second go-around to fail, you'll see where I'm coming from. There was a lot of resentment on my end, so I wanted to write about a girl who was wanted–not just by one guy, but by her childhood best friend and got a second chance with one of the guys that lasted beyond the HEA. So that's how The Night We Met was born. And subsequently the rest of my Healing in Cincy series.

Healing was a big part of my character's journeys and the overall theme that while writing this series, I found myself healing as well.

I have to give a massive thank you to my alpha readers. Kalie, you've been with me since before book 1 when you sat next to me on the adirondack chairs at CycleBar and forced a conversation out of me. You've been such an amazing friend and supporter through this entire series. Sammie, I knew I found an all-star alpha reader and friend in you from book 2. You've been the best help for me shaping these books the way they're meant to be. I couldn't have done it without either of you two sending the most unhinged comments for these last few books.

My beta readers! Katty and Hayley! I cannot express how thankful I am for you two. Your eyes and your insight, helped shaped me as a writer. Thank you!

To my cover designer, Kimberly. Big forehead kisses to you. We've come a very long way from the first book design to now. Thank you for bringing my book babies to life and I can't wait to work with you again.

To you, the reader. THANK YOU! If you've been with me from my debut, you have no idea how much it means to me that you stuck around for three more books. This series would not mean a thing if it wasn't for you all reading and telling your friends about this new world from a new author. THANK YOU again!

Thank you to Lemmy and the team at Luna Literary Management for handling the ARCs for these last two releases. You and your team make the ARC process extremely easy and I could not be more grateful for you all.

To Kamryn, Mason, Emily, Adam, Sarah, Riley, Jax, Nate, Liam, and James. The ten characters I got to know and explore for the last few years, thank you! I used to hear that the characters you write become like your family and that's what these characters became: my family. I won't say goodbye to these characters forever because I have other stories to tell and they'll be apart of them in some aspect. But for now, I say goodbye to this group. Bring on The Hayes Brothers!

ALSO BY ELLEESE BLACK

The Night We Met

Make It Without You

Let It Be Me

WHAT'S TO COME?

More cozy city romances with the small town feel

You met them in Make It Without You, well get ready for the Hayes Brothers coming in 2026.

ABOUT THE AUTHOR

Elleese Black is a thirty-something millennial. With a degree in Psychology, she took her love of the subject to dive into fictional characters. She grew up reading romance books with swoon and tears, fortunately, they all end with a happily ever after. When she's not writing or working, she's a cat mom to two zany cats, taking spin classes or doom-scrolling until the wee hours of the night. Elleese loves to hear from her readers. So send her a DM on Instagram (@elleeseblack.author), she'll love it!

Website:
https://www.elleeseblackauthor.com

Sign up for my newsletter: